The invading darkness ⟨...⟩ ⟨...⟩ She gasped and reached out with her hand to steady herself. Her fingertips ran straight into his chest. His hard, naked chest. "Sorry, I . . ."

"No problem."

Latigo flattened her hand beneath his own. She could've pulled her hand away, but pulling away from him was the last thing on her mind. The very last thing.

Bending down to her, he drew her body tightly against his. The perfect blending of hard angles to soft curves. He leaned closer, following his fingers with his lips, kissing her everywhere he touched.

"Latigo, we don't even know each other."

"Right." His breath touched her skin like a warm hand.

"Much less like one another."

"Right."

She tried to speak, but his mouth dipped low again to smother any more protests.

"You taste like peaches, darlin'. Sweet juicy peaches, and it's been a long time between summers."

Once more his lips touched hers. The kiss was searing. Deep. Possessive. Overwhelming sensations engulfed her—and the last of her inhibitions melted into darkness . . .

Gifts of the Heart

Bonnie Jeanne Perry

ZEBRA BOOKS
KENSINGTON PUBLISHING CORP.

ZEBRA BOOKS ARE PUBLISHED BY

Kensington Publishing Corp.
475 Park Avenue South
New York, NY 10016

Zebra and the Z logo Reg. U.S. Pat. & TM Off.

First Printing: February, 1994

Printed in the United States of America

ACKNOWLEDGEMENTS

The author wants to thank some very special people:

PEGGY MOSS FIELDING, who protected the flame. Every writer should have such a dedicated teacher and devoted friend.

DEBBY CAMP, my friend and colleague and so much more.

ANNA EBERHARDT, who cares and shares and always has time to dish.

DONNA JULLIAN, who takes time to be both a friend and an inspiration.

PAT McCANDLESS, SANDIE GRASSINO, BARBARA SCOTT, and CARM UTZ, the goddesses of my Wednesday night critique group. Thanks for the cheering.

DENISE LITTLE, my editor, who believes in and nurtures this child.

For FRANKIE, who has managed to wipe the look of surprise off his face. What an adventure, babe, and to think it's only begun.

To Sam Murray, the man who taught me to love cowboys. Livermore, California, isn't the same without you, big guy. Miss you, miss you, miss you.

BJ

One

"Didn't you use to be Latigo?" a boy's voice piped above the din of the crowd leaving the junior rodeo.

Latigo? That's the man I'm looking for. Maggie Callahan quickened her steps, weaving her way along the row of parked vans and horse trailers behind the grandstands. She stood on tiptoes beside a dusty gray van watching the boy approach a clown. Latigo, her elusive neighbor, dressed like a rodeo clown?

The white paint around Latigo's eyes wrinkled into tiny sunrays. "Yes, I was—once upon a time." He thumbed back the brim of the boy's cowboy hat and grinned down at the freckled face. "Actually, I'm still Latigo."

Latigo looked bigger than she envisioned a rodeo cowboy would be. Taller. And broader through the shoulders, too. Dad said bronc busters were tough, but Latigo didn't look so tough. Of course the red long johns, lapping below his plaid pants, might have something to do with that. On second thought, she decided, the tight-fitting jeans certainly left no doubt as to the gender of the wearer.

"But you don't ride the circuit anymore, do you, Latigo?" The boy's lower lip drooped.

"No, son. I gave up rodeoing a few years back."

"Gee, my pa says you were the bestest ever."

Nothing like hero worship. Soak it up, cowboy. I'm going to burst that bubble. Maybe it won't be that bad, she reconsidered. There's plenty of land around for him and his horses.

Latigo knelt to eye level with the boy. "Well, you thank your pa for the kind words."

"Know what, Latigo?"

"What, son?"

"I'm your new neighbor."

"You are? Bet you're renting the Ferguson place."

"We sure are."

"What's your name, son?"

"Jimmy Lee. Jimmy Lee Thompson." The boy held out his hand for a shake and Latigo obliged.

"You like rodeoing, Jimmy Lee?"

"Yeee-es, sir."

"Well, I've got something here for you." Latigo grabbed the truck's door handle and hoisted himself to his feet. He stretched one shoulder, then the other, leaning to the side.

Maggie winced when she heard the vertebrae in his back pop. He'd had a rodeo injury? Injuries, she corrected. From what she'd heard from the visiting neighbors, Latigo had been injured several times. He pulled his Stetson lower over his eyes. Was he trying to hide the pain from the boy? Too bad she couldn't see his eyes. They'd be a dead giveaway. His eyes couldn't fool her. She knew all about watching someone hurt. She knew that watching someone she loved hurt was far worse than experiencing the pain herself. She studied Latigo trying to see any of the telltale signs, but there were none.

People brushed past. She waited her turn, not wanting to interrupt Latigo and the boy.

Latigo stuffed his other hand into the pocket of his pants. "Here they are." He shook the dust from two folded papers and handed them to Jimmy Lee. "You tell your pa, when the Nationals come here to Tulsa, they're on me."

"Gee thanks, Latigo." Jimmy Lee's eyes sparkled as he pumped Latigo's hand again.

"And tell your pa I said howdy."

"I will. I will."

Latigo flipped Jimmy Lee a hat-brim salute and the boy charged between the grandstands.

One day, Maggie prayed, her daughter, Jenny, would run like that. It had been the singular focus of her life since Jenny's birth. That hope was the reason why she stopped at the rodeo today. The sale of the farm Maggie inherited from her uncle would help clear up most of those unpaid medical bills and maybe even finance a portion of Jenny's next operation. An operation that might mean Jenny could throw away her braces. Maggie forced her thoughts back to the rodeo clown.

Oklahoma's best all-round cowboy really had his moves down pat, she thought, marking Latigo's slouching stance. Taking a quick inventory of his long legs, she bet he had the slow strut so inherent to rodeo riders perfected, too. He turned his back and until he took a step, the injury that had ended Latigo's career five years ago, hadn't been apparent. A group of boisterous teenagers followed after the clown then turned deeper into the parking lot, oblivious to his identity.

She continued at a discreet distance, until he swerved to the left and moved along a row of trailers. A blonde

9

in silver-trimmed leather waved a poster for an autograph, and Latigo stopped for a moment.

So, she's one of the fringe benefits Maggie had only heard about from the neighbors. There'd been New York models, Hollywood starlets, a Miss Oklahoma, quite an assortment over the years. But since he'd quit the rodeo, there'd been no special woman in his life according to the neighbor ladies.

Maggie let her gaze wander from the third button of his bright lavender shirt, up to the square chin. It took a brave man to wear a lavender shirt. A man secure in his masculinity, she thought. That would describe Latigo all right. He had the bigger than life appearance of a John Wayne hero. Latigo was built for Westerns—tall and handsome with an added flourish of a flirt in his bold appraising eyes.

Ms. Spangles batted her lashes in an open invitation and the amusement in his rakish eyes died. Ms. Spangles swivel-hipped away until she reached the grandstand, then she fired one final hip motion his way. Still no reaction from Latigo. His reputation didn't seem quite so tarnished when he ignored the final bump and grind. Perhaps the neighbor lady who had told her about Latigo might've been right after all.

"Are we ready to move out, Tommy Joe?" Latigo hollered to the white-haired cowboy standing alongside a lavender van.

Lavender was Latigo's favorite color, all right. Maggie studied the large lettering painted on the lavender siding. *Latigo Ranch, Broken Arrow, Oklahoma. Breaking and training. Specialty: Cutting and roping. Trainer/Owner Wade Latigo.* So, that's his first name. Everyone she'd met called him Latigo. She continued reading the lettering on the van, *I sell the best and ride the rest.* Modesty wasn't his strong suit, she thought.

"How about a beer?" Latigo continued, mopping his forehead with the back of his sleeve.

Tommy Joe lifted the cooler lid. "Got one right here, only take me a minute to pry it loose from this six-pack."

"I'll start working off this paint." Latigo faced the van and the hanging mirror glinting in the sunlight.

"How'd it feel, being out there again without pulling leather?" Tommy Joe asked.

"I got aches in new places." Latigo rubbed his right thigh. "My chute-busting days are over."

The obvious regret in his voice caught Maggie off guard. Surely there were other things more important in his life now than bronc riding? There had to be.

"I'm too old." Latigo one-handed the can of beer Tommy Joe tossed him. "Hell, it's been too long between broken bones and prize money." He chugalugged the beer and belched.

Typically male, Maggie mused, shaking her head. The sound made her think of sitting around the kitchen table. Her father would take a can of beer from the refrigerator and lean against the sink, downing the brew. She'd heard him do exactly the same thing on too many an occasion to be offended.

"I'll be sore as hell tomorrow." Latigo yanked a fist of tissue and swiped at the paint on his face. "Pass me that jar of cream, TJ. So help me—if you *ever* volunteer me for another rodeo half-time show—I'll nail your hide to the barn."

"There are fringe benefits, though, boss. That little gal with the sparkles, kinda took a shine to you." Tommy Joe poked his head around the van door and gave Latigo a toothless grin. "Them longhandles do show off your purty legs."

Maggie's shoulders shook with silent laughter when she heard the word *purty*. She'd come to enjoy the Oklahoma speech pattern. In California, most people sounded the same. In Broken Arrow, the speech patterns varied as much as the unpredictable weather.

"Stick it, TJ." Latigo rifled the empty beer can against the van door as Tommy Joe ducked back inside.

Maggie moved in closer, then stopped. She'd never done business with a clown before. What are you waiting for? It's your land. Walk straight up to him and get it over with.

"Mr. Latigo?" Maggie asked, stepping up behind him.

"Yeah?"

"I'm Maggie Callahan."

"Ma'am?" He slapped at the grease paint while appraising her from head to toe in the mirror hanging from the side of the van.

You've got busy eyes, Latigo. She made the most of the opportunity and stepped closer to get a better look herself. His eyes were the color of gun metal. Hard. Cold. And, she decided, twice as deadly. He made another pass with the facial tissue and targeted her breasts in the mirror. With the calculated appraisal of a cattle buyer, his gaze slipped lazily over her waist and hips before he crowded the reflection in the mirror so he could take in her legs.

"You missed one." Always a toucher, Maggie reached out to direct his hand, then thought better of it. They were neighbors, but hardly friends. He might take the gesture as being too personal. She had no intention of getting personal with any man. Not since she'd broken

12

her engagement. A man wasn't even on her top ten list. She had more important things to do.

Oh, nuts. Why should she let what'd happened in the past determine what she did? She had so little control. Grab hold of your life had become her motto. Go on, I dare you, her head challenged. She took Latigo's hand and guided it to the white smudge of paint that blended with the hair at his temple. His hand was warm, his forearm smattered with dark hair.

"There." She let go of his hand. "That got it."

He continued wiping away the paint, revealing an expressive full mouth above an out-thrusted stubborn chin.

She took a deep breath steeling herself for the worst. A trace of his after-shave hung bravely in the horse-scented air. Smells like lemon, she guessed, a fresh sun-ripened California lemon. California she knew, but until eight days ago, the only cowboy she'd seen was on a movie screen. How was she going to broach the subject without coming off as a pushy outsider? This spur-of-the-moment meeting was a mistake, she thought. A major mistake. And the luncheon with the real-estate broker had gone beautifully. Why hadn't she quit while she was ahead? The inherited farm would be on multi-list as soon as she finished painting the bedrooms.

"Lady, if you want something, spill it." Latigo snapped the suspenders from his shoulders, letting them dangle along his lean hips. "It's been a long day."

He looked tired up close, she thought, especially around the eyes. Older, too. Middle thirties, she estimated. Oh, he appeared utterly approachable from a distance, but Maggie knew better. Nothing about Latigo's rodeo-hardened body suggested the gentleness he'd shown the boy, Jimmy Lee. And yet, the squint lines around his eyes proved he did smile—once in a while. But the only trace of a smile she could see lay smudged on the tissue he wadded in his fist.

"It's about your horses," she said.

"Which ones?"

"The ones grazing on the Callahan property."

"They're spoken for." He curried his sun-tipped brown hair with the impatient fingers of a man always on the move.

"Oh, I don't want to buy any horses. I'm Mike Callahan's niece."

Latigo blinked at her reflection in the hanging mirror. "Mike left *you* the place?"

"That's right. And I've plans for that land."

"I just bet you have." He whirled about to face her and his shoulder clipped the hanging mirror, sending it crashing to the pavement. Oblivious to the broken mirror, he stalked toward her, favoring the right leg. He stopped suddenly, legs wide apart, and when he took another step, his gait was considerably shorter as if he'd become self-conscious about his limp. A pang of regret hit her like a punch in the solar plexus. It wasn't fair for a grown man to look so vulnerable.

"I thought Mike Callahan had more smarts than to leave his place to a . . ."

Cancel the bit about comparing Latigo to a bigger-than-life Western hero like John Wayne. All this man had was an inflated ego. One she would take delight in deflating. In the name of women everywhere, she filled in the vacant silence, "A woman?"

He stopped short of her open-toe sandals and towered over her. "Don't put words in my mouth. I was going to say, I thought your uncle had better sense than to leave

14

his place to a city relative." He eyed her sandals. A smirk rode his mouth. "Where you from?"

"San Francisco."

"Another Californian." The mockery in his tone was reflected in his eyes.

"Bingo." It was her turn to smirk.

"Screwed up your own state, huh, prune-picker? So now you're out here trying to do the same to us poor, ignorant Okies." He planted both hands on his hips and pushed his face closer to hers. "Well, listen good. Mike Callahan and I had an agreement and it doesn't suit me to move those horses right now."

"This agreement, was it in writing?"

"We shook hands. That's better than any signed paper, ma'am." He looked back at TJ and passed a cocky wink between them.

"The name's Maggie. Maggie Callahan."

He swung around and faced her again. "Well, Maggie Callahan, you picked a bad time and place to talk business." He dismissed her with a cursory glance.

She wasn't a woman to be put off so quickly. She had a purpose for being here and she wasn't leaving until she was good and ready. She scoured his face with a scathing look, but didn't put a dent in his arrogance. He's tougher than she figured. The calluses she'd seen on his hands went deep. Probably clear to his heart.

"I decided to stop when I saw your van. Lavender is difficult to miss," she muttered.

"It's not lavender. It's purple. Only pansies and city cowboys wear lavender. Besides, it wasn't the color of my van that attracted you. You want me off your land, and you couldn't resist doing the hatchet job yourself. Why?"

He mocked her with a blast of forced laughter. "You've got 210 acres of grass. You can afford to let my horses chew."

"I'm leasing that property to Five Star, and they insist I remove all livestock before putting in the road."

"Five Star? That means horizontal drilling, I suppose?" He shook his head. "The oil boom is over, lady."

"Five Star seems to think otherwise." That news seemed to tighten his jaw. Good.

"They were paying thirty-five dollars an acre for drilling leases. What did they offer you?"

"That's my business."

His jaw muscles tightened again. "So, now we have it. You're after money. Cold hard cash. Without regard for anything else. Did you think I couldn't figure that out myself?"

"Move your horses and stay out of my affairs, and you and I will get along fine." Better get out of here fast. You have to live in this town for three more weeks. And you want to sell the farm. Be practical. Don't make waves. Not here. Not now. She started to walk away, but his strong hand on her arm stopped her cold.

"Let me go." The calluses burrowed deeper into her skin, the fingers unbearably hot. The touch calculated. Impersonal.

"Don't swing your backside at me, lady. I've seen that move hundreds of times, and I'm not impressed."

She yanked her arm away. "How I walk is *my* business." With a quick toss of her head, she flipped her strawberry-blond hair over her shoulder and faced him. He was asking for a fight. Almost forcing one. Why? Was he testing what he'd heard about California girls? Well, she wasn't one of those beach babes. She was from

16

Northern California. The weather was harsher. The low-lying fog denser. The tides stronger. The storms rougher. She could handle a storm—even one he might decide to kick up.

"Not bad." He gave her a quick once-over. "Hell, you're no bigger than a minute."

"What's that got to do with you moving those horses?"

The devilish glint in his eye zeroed in on her breasts. "I figured if you had ten minutes or so, we might work us up a compromise."

"Ten minutes?" She gave his clown costume a hasty reappraisal. He was coming on to her like she was a rodeo groupie. You want to talk sexy? *You* got sexy. "Well, Okie, where I'm from ten minutes is a back-seat quickie."

The pupils of his eyes dilated. She'd struck a nerve. And it suddenly occurred to her, that if she'd been a man, he might have punched her silly.

"Darlin', I guaran-damn-tee ya, it'd be the best ten minutes of *your* life."

There was that Oklahoma ease again. She almost laughed aloud herself when she heard TJ's lusty chuckle from inside the van. Touché, she thought. She deserved that comeback and her admiration for Latigo jumped a notch. So he had a quick mind. So what? Sew buttons, that's what. She was here on business. Dollars-and-cents business.

"Let's not waste any more time, Latigo. My letter about removing your horses from my pasture was explicit."

"Letter? Come on, you can do better than that."

"Registered letter, Mr. Latigo?" Latigo's lips straightened into a thin line and she knew she'd won her point.

"Shit," Tommy Joe said and stuck his head outside of the van window and gave Latigo a sheepish look. "Latigo? I plum forgot about them chicken scratches."

"Any discussion between us is pointless," Maggie continued without missing a beat. She'd had little or no control of her life since Jenny's birth, but she meant to exercise complete control when it came to the farm. She'd made a start with the real-estate agent. Getting Latigo's horses off her land was number two on her list. "When you locate the letter, contact my attorney. *Her* name is on the envelope."

Latigo's jaw dropped open. His baggy trousers sagged.

"Careful, Latigo," she called over her shoulder, "you're losing your pants."

He fisted the gaping waistband, mouthing a cuss word anyone could read from two blocks away.

Where had the morning gone? Maggie wondered the next day. She glanced at her watch before squinting out the kitchen window. The late-afternoon sun glistened on the wind-stunted trees. She'd never seen so much land. So much space. Pivoting, she tossed the paint rag into the sink. She'd done enough for one day. Time for a break.

"Think I'll take a ride, Dad," she hollered toward the living room.

"You do that," her father answered. "I'll stretch out on the couch."

"Jenny won't be up from her nap for an hour or so."

"I can look after my granddaughter. You go ahead. And try not to worry," her father cautioned. "Things will work out. The doctor swears they can fix Jenny's hip this time."

Please, God, let Dad be right. But how long would the doctor wait to be paid? Maggie wondered, remembering the stack of unpaid bills she'd left behind in San Francisco. At least, she didn't have to face them each time she opened the desk drawer. "If only that insurance company hadn't folded."

"The newspapers listed three more companies that went belly up today," Dad said. "That new insurance policy you signed will help with Jenny's doctor bills."

Dad always looked on the bright side since his heart attack two years ago. An illness that'd made them appreciate every day and the love they had for one another. They'd always been close, never more than now. To Maggie, her father was her best friend as well as her father. To her daughter, Jenny, he took the empty place as the Daddy the little girl had never known. They were a family—a family of the 1990s.

"You're right, Dad." But that policy doesn't cover any treatment involving Jenny's legs or hips. Maggie kept the added thought to herself.

Pre-existing condition—that's what the insurance agent called it. Jenny's malformed hips certainly qualified as a pre-existing condition. Since their new insurance agent had quoted the infamous words, Maggie's life had slipped into a running battle to stay even with the medical bills—bills their new insurance policy failed to cover.

Three years ago, Maggie took a second mortgage on Callahan's Wine and Spirit Shoppe, the shop she and her father owned. She'd been backed into a corner financially like a lot of folks. She'd pinched every penny until the proverbial copper buffalo hollered. Pinching pennies was a way of life. Now with the second mortgage payment, her monthly bills had become a juggling act. She had no choice if she wanted to catch up on Jenny's hospital bill. The money from the second mortgage had helped for a while. It'd eased Dad's worries. With his heart, Dad didn't need any added stress. But he hated feeling like an invalid. She had to be careful to be honest with him about their finances. To make him feel a part of what was going on in their lives—up to a point.

"We're really up against it this time, Dad."

"I still believe that's why your uncle left you this place."

How many times had she heard Dad say that? Too many. What they needed to do was get this farm on the real-estate market as quickly as possible. She stopped short of thinking of how deflated the sales in rural farms were now. She meant to keep a positive attitude. Most people knew the interest rates were certain to climb higher. It was still a buyer's market. Perhaps someone would make a decent offer for the farm.

Dad raised a questioning eyebrow. "Your uncle knew *you* wouldn't accept a loan. You'd turned him down often enough."

"It seems Uncle Mike is getting his way after all." Thanks, Uncle Mike, Maggie prayed as the back screen door wagged behind her. How about putting in a good word for us with the main Man upstairs? From the looks of things, we're going to need it.

She stepped onto the porch. How fast could she get the farm fixed up and sold? Jenny needed at least one more operation on her hip. How much would this surgery cost? No matter. Whatever the cost, Maggie knew that she'd sell everything she had so Jenny would walk and run like the other five-year-olds.

If need be, she'd sell Callahan's Wine and Spirit Shoppe too. She had no sentimental attachment to it. Practical Maggie couldn't afford the luxury of sentiment except where Jenny was concerned. Her whole world revolved around Jenny. Everything else, including the San Francisco shop, was business plain and simple. Simple. That was the perfect word to describe her lifestyle. Their doll-size apartment above the store meant that Jenny could play in the fenced yard out back, and they could have their picnic lunch every afternoon. The time Maggie spent with Jenny more than made up for the tiny apartment. She and Jenny shared one bedroom, while Dad had the other. They were cramped for privacy sometimes, but happy. Now if only Jenny could . . .

Flattening her palms inside the back pockets of her jeans, Maggie shifted her gaze to the house. It needed work to be sure, a new roof for starters. Why, in California a thirties bungalow like this would cost . . . her mind wandered. California. Prune-picker. Latigo's words bore through her with the precision of an Oklahoma drilling bit.

Meeting Latigo at the junior rodeo had been a mistake. The idea of moving those horses had set him off. Him being dressed like a clown hadn't helped matters either. She shook her head. What choice did she have? None. Zero. The oil leases with Five Star stipulated full access to the land, and she meant to see they got it. In less desperate times, she'd have let Latigo's horses graze. Now she had to focus completely on Jenny and getting the oil-lease money necessary to pay those doctor bills.

No matter. In exactly twenty-four days she'd be back

21

in San Francisco. The porch stairs creaked, and she made a mental note to add fixing them to her growing list of repairs. Dad insisted they could save money if he did the carpentry, and this time, she fully intended to let him have his way. Dad loved recounting stories about the summers he'd spent on this farm. She chuckled, remembering his boast about how good he was with a nail and hammer. She'd noticed the lightness in her father's step since they'd arrived in Oklahoma. They'd avoided any mention of his heart attack. Letting him make the farm look as it had when he was a boy was the least she could do since they were selling the place. There was no question about selling. She'd sell the place off acre by acre, if need be.

Taking a deep breath, Maggie deliberately focused her attention on the wind-spun clouds. Smells like rain. Good, that will keep the hills green. According to the real-estate broker, the greener the hills, the greener the dollar price paid for the farm. Green. Green. Her favorite color.

Minutes later, she sat behind the steering wheel of the borrowed pickup truck rattling over the back road behind the house. The Nighthorses, one of the neighbors who'd known her father when he was a boy, insisted they use their old truck. Nice people the Nighthorses. Come to think of it, every one of their Oklahoma neighbors was friendly. On second thought, there was one neighbor who—

She gripped the steering wheel tighter, keeping the tires in the rutty grooves. Yesterday's confrontation about the south pasture would be settled when she signed those oil leases. Then Five Star could deal with Latigo, she thought smugly.

She turned the truck off the road and cut the engine. As soon as her feet hit ground, she slammed the door and stood quietly for a moment.

Beyond the creek, a boulder-studded rise rounded away into a pocket of green grass. Maggie shivered when the rush of air hit her. The grass shivered, too, but the wind felt good—the freedom even better. Getting used to Oklahoma would be surprisingly easy. Getting along with a neighbor like Latigo might be a horse of a different color. *Horse?* Oklahoma meant horses. She shivered again, not that she was cold. The mere thought of being near horses did that to her. She hadn't been near one since her seventh birthday. Since that horse stepped on her, severing the tip of her second toe. The accident hadn't been life threatening. Like most seven-year-olds, she'd gotten the hang of walking without a limp in a matter of weeks. She wouldn't let the pain stop her. She didn't want to be different than the other kids. Maggie wanted the same thing for her Jenny. She meant to see that Jenny had her chance.

She flexed her foot inside her Reeboks. Horses were king in Oklahoma. Well, this might be quarter-horse country to many folks, but she wasn't one of them. Latigo had to move his horses and that was that. It was her land now. Hers for a while anyway.

She looked up. Clouds huddled in the corner of the late afternoon sky. That's odd, she'd never seen a green sky before. And where were the cardinals and wild canaries that'd been here yesterday? Suddenly, the wind went deathly still and the hair on the back of her neck stood on end.

"Maggie?" a man bellowed. "Maggie Callahan?"

A clopping sound came from the far side of the creek.

She turned as a spotted horse shot from the pecan trees, the rider low, his yellow duster flapping against the saddle.

Something about the spread of the broad shoulders triggered a frown. "Latigo." He rode like a cowboy out of the past, wild and reckless, certain he could tame any horse. Any wind. Any time he chose. Her mind jerked to attention. She narrowed her eyes. She knew why he was here. He thought he could tame her, too. He'd better think again. She wasn't one of his prized quarter horses. She knuckled her hands on her hips as the horse splashed across the creek. He'd called her a California prune-picker the first time they'd met. She'd been called that before, it was a common enough term. But she'd never heard it spit out with the implication that she was stupid.

She arched a brow, welcoming a chance to tell him what she thought of him. Looking for me, cowboy? Come on. She'd show him a thing or two about prune-pickers.

Two

"Don't just stand there," he shouted, covering the distance between them at a rattling clip. He reined in hard and the horse's front hooves left the ground. Latigo hit the dirt on a dead run, his limp hardly noticeable. Beneath the pulled-low hat brim, his face reddened and shone with sweat. Catching her arm, he yanked, half-dragged her toward his horse. "Come on."

She sucked in her breath sharply when the horse pawed the ground. Panic twisted inside her. "Let me go."

"I'd like nothing better, but I promised your father I'd locate you."

Anxiety diluted her fear. "Is Dad sick?"

"Callahan is fine." He shouldered by her, towing her along behind him like a wayward mare.

"I can take care of myself."

"Oh?" He hitched his chin toward the far horizon.

The sky darkened. But so what, she thought, masking her fear of the horse. "I've seen summer storms before, we have them in California, you know." She must've sounded convincing because he let go of her arm.

"You got a rude awakening coming, lady.

"Dollar," he hollered to the horse.

The animal's nostrils flared and it trotted to Latigo's side. The thought of getting close to this wide-eyed animal terrified her. With the utmost control, she slowly backed away. The horse waited patiently as Latigo stripped the saddle from its back and dropped it on the ground. Squatting, he made a pad with his hands. "Step up."

"Me?" Was he crazy? Did he actually expect her to ride that animal? The tip of her severed toe throbbed inside her shoe as if reminding her of what a horse had done to her foot. Her stomach flip flopped.

Latigo thumbed his hat to the back of his head and gave her a paralyzing look. "I said, step up into my hands."

She set her chin as stubbornly as his. There's no way she would get any closer to that snarling animal. There was also no way her pride would let her tell Latigo why. Her childhood fear of horses would seem laughable to an Oklahoma cowboy. She had no intention of making a fool of herself. She already knew his low opinion of Californians. She wouldn't give him any more reasons to bad-mouth her home state.

"Maggie, I said, step up into my hands."

"No."

Circling slowly, he maneuvered her between himself and the horse. "Stay away from me." Her voice sounded perfectly even, but she'd never been good at a bluff, and a quick glance at Latigo's face told Maggie that she needed more practice if she wanted to out-bluff *this* cowboy.

"I'll toss you over Dollar's rump like a sack of taters,

if need be." He twanged the last word, "taters," with an exaggerated drawl.

She knew an idle threat when she heard one. Well, he was trying to bluff the wrong lady. She meant to go back to the farm the way she came—in a borrowed truck. She started to say so, but the look on his face stopped her cold. He was bluffing, wasn't he? That grab-her-hair and drag-her-across the ground approach went out with the cavemen. This was the 1990s. "Get real, Latigo."

"This is as real as it gets, lady." Demonic delight fired his eyes. He was serious. Dead serious about tossing her up on his horse. Dead serious!

"You wouldn't?" she asked, haltingly.

"Try me."

"Latigo?"

He walked his hands around her waist and in one easy motion, lifted her off the ground. Hadn't he read *Cosmo?* This kind of thing went out when women got the vote. It just wasn't done. Men didn't pick women up and carry them off. Her white leather Reeboks hung in midair. She'd have kicked her feet, but didn't want to appear more juvenile than she already did. Actually, she felt helpless and she hated the feeling.

"Put me down. You . . . you caveman." She squirmed in midair, her feet still dangling like those of a rag doll.

"You're an original. I'll give you that. I've been called many things, but never prehistoric. So you think I'm crude and brutal, especially toward women."

"Well, aren't you?"

"A real Neanderthal, huh?" He challenged her with a cocky, off-center grin.

"In spades."

"Have it your way." With calculated skill, he lowered

her in front of him, his eyes momentarily hidden by the brim of his hat. When they finally came face to face, they were so close he was a blur. A tanned blend of leather and muscles. At this moment in time, she could care less about what he looked like. He was letting her go. That's all she cared about. All she wanted—for the moment. Once she was safely on the ground, she was out of here. Gone. She dropped her bunched fists to his shoulders as gravity swung her against his chest.

The collision was instantaneous and joltingly intimate. Her belt buckle clicked against the pearlized snaps on his shirt like the tick of a clock. One o'clock. Two o'clock. Her breasts lifted and stalled, completely out-muscled by his broad chest. For a moment, she forgot everything except the primal harmony of their bodies. Heat flamed up from her toes and burned straight toward her face. His body tensed as his cold blue eyes leveled into hers, his face as brightly colored as hers must be.

Suddenly, he released her. Her knees buckled when her feet slammed into the ground. He steadied her for a moment with one hand on her waist. Then, he clamped a fist into Dollar's mane and swung up onto the horse.

"Good-bye." She stomped toward the truck with Dollar trotting alongside. Fear dictated flight, but pride over-ruled. She'd never give Latigo the satisfaction of seeing her run. Her breath came in ragged jerks as he swung the horse closer and closer. When the animal's snorting breath blasted her shoulder something inside her snapped, and she veered to the left, running full tilt.

The horse and rider caught up to her. One more step and she felt herself being hauled up by the back of her jeans. He dumped her in front of him, her fanny unceremoniously pointing skyward.

"Latigo." She hissed a curse at him and kicked wildly. He grunted in pain when her knee clobbered his thigh. He rewarded her efforts with a hard slap, a slap that burned clear through to her panties. Neanderthal? He was pre-Neanderthal.

"Kick again and I'll shine your britches good. What's with you?"

"I don't like being manhandled. Besides, it's only a rainstorm."

"There's storms and then there's storms, city gal."

What was he talking about? She looked up. The sky looked different, darker than when she'd left the farm. "Why is the sky so green?"

"Green means trouble with a capital T. It also means we're riding horseback. I can't leave you here. And there's no way I'd let you get into that truck. A pickup is the last place you should be with a twister—"

A quick blast of wind muffled his words. "A what?"

"Never mind. Hang on."

Before she could ask him to fill in the rest of the word, the stallion's strides lengthened. The ground blurred and bile bubbled in her throat. She was going to vomit. Desperately, she clutched at Latigo's leg, but the slippery smooth jeans made holding on impossible.

"Whoa. Have you finally gotten some sense?" Latigo jammed his fingers into her belt and hoisted her onto his left thigh. "Give up?"

"Never." She teetered precariously between his thigh and Dollar's shoulder as lunch settled back into her stomach.

"Have it your way." He relaxed his leg. Afraid to touch the horse, she faltered sideways and flung her arm around Latigo's waist. The duster he wore felt damp and pliable.

The man inside—hard and unyielding. Without a give-away gesture, he wedged his right hand behind her knee and flipped her leg over Dollar's neck.

Her body went rigid. "I can't touch . . . the horse." She swallowed her fear like a bitter pill.

"Don't talk crazy. Dollar won't hurt you. If we had more time, wrestling might be fun," he teased.

Fun? He actually enjoyed this. Oh, how she wanted to rake her nails over his smug face. She lifted her defiant chin, stifling the urge.

"Dollar." The horse lunged forward, sending her crashing backward into Latigo's body. She clutched at his thigh trying to pull herself forward.

"Relax," he murmured.

For a second she stopped clawing at his thigh. She had to admit the fuzzy warmth of Dollar's hide felt better *under* her fanny. Perhaps if she pretended he was a painted horse on the merry-go-round in Golden Gate Park. Closing her eyes, Maggie could almost hear the oom-pa-pa of calliope music. Almost feel the seductive movement of the wooden horse.

Latigo's chest expanded, his breathing labored.

She forced her eyes open. Clumps of mud flew from the hooves of the galloping horse. This animal was real. And so was the belt buckle that sawed up and down intimately against her. It would take more than a fantasy about a merry-go-round to distance herself from Wade Latigo. She shifted her hips as far away from him as possible, which wasn't much.

"Quit squirming. We're almost there."

The farm. Safety. Thank God, she thought, only three more hills. The flat, spread-out rise of earth covered with thick green grass and the grove of native pecan trees.

She took hope. Yes, yes, there's the river birch. And the two smaller hills. The creek and then—

Abruptly, he reined in, and she flattened against him like his well-worn yellow duster.

"Why are we stopping?" she asked.

"Were you born stupid or do you work at it?" His eyes scanned the horizon. "You city folks are all alike when it comes to survival."

Survival? He made a storm sound like a life and death situation. She could read him like a book. All he wanted was control. That's all this show of force was—a blatant power play. There was something else—a hidden agenda. He also wanted to get even with her after their disastrous first meeting at the rodeo. No way, Jose! She wasn't fooled for a moment. "Don't be melodramatic, Latigo. I've seen all of the John Ford Westerns. Nice try. But no sale."

"This isn't a Hollywood set. This is real life, lady. Where were you raised anyway? Even a wild mustang turns his rump into a storm." He wheeled the horse around, and they bolted off in the opposite direction.

Before she could reply, thunder rolled overhead. She jumped, and Latigo's arms cinched her tightly against him. Every muscle of her body quivered with fear. They cleared the ridge, and Dollar galloped toward a white clapboard house. Thank God! Civilization at last. Somebody is bound to be home, she thought. And she could get off this horse.

Latigo reined in behind the house and slid to the ground, dragging her with him. He stripped the bridle from Dollar's neck. "You're on your own, boy."

Lightning smoked along the grass, snaking between the blades like a sizzling rattler. She jumped back. The snake slithered away as reason dictated flight. Her feet needed no other encouragement. In a futile attempt to reach the safety of the house, she bolted up the hill and into the pecan grove.

"Don't be a fool, Maggie."

She kept on running. The wind whipped the tree limbs like lariats. Swirling bits of dust and leaves stung her eyes shut. She turned her head this way and that, trying to see. By the time she felt his hand on her arm, she'd lost all sense of direction.

"During lightning, *nobody* runs into the trees," he bellowed.

Terror fired her movements, making her arms fly above her head like the tangled strings on a puppet. "We can make it to the house. We've got to."

"Not through these trees, we don't. We've got to get clear. These trees are like lightning rods. They attract the lightning. Now, get!" His fingers dug into her upper arms as another ring of lightning flashed around them. Branches snapped like kindling. "Do you hear me?"

"Yes, but—"

"No buts. Move!"

Something cracked above her head. She wasn't certain if it was a tree about to crash down on them or only the thunder. Either way, she knew the sound of trouble. She knew she'd been a fool. She'd let her fear of horses overrule good judgment. What a fool she'd been. She should've listened to Latigo. "Latigo, I'm—"

"Look out." He lifted her from her feet and shoved her away from him.

Tree limbs smashed against her. The ground came up to meet her. Everything blurred green. She landed hard, the first jarring impact unhinging her knees before dark-

32

ness swamped her. Reason failed. When she lifted her head, particles of dirt coated her throat even after she masked her mouth with her shirt collar. She tried to blink. She tried a second time. Nothing about her reflexes seemed to work. Every movement had to be forced, thought out. She tried to blink again. She couldn't see a thing. Were her eyes closed or was she buried alive?

"Latigo?"

No answer.

She rubbed her eyes, straining to see through the green blur. A larger tree had fallen and tented the smaller ones like a log cabin over her. Chips of shattered wood littered the grass. She batted away the broken branches, but her eyes still refused to focus. Only the distant glow of something yellow seemed real.

His duster.

Slowly she crawled toward it. A hard-knuckled fist punched through the twisted tree limbs. At least he was moving. The thought made her tear at the tree limbs, pulling away the leaves. Wanting to get to him. She pried branches loose, tossing them away until she saw him. Her hands froze, bits of pecan leaves smashed between her clenched fingers.

He'd been moving a moment ago. At least, his arm had been. But now? Nothing. Her lungs stalled. Was he alive?

He lay sprawled on his back, his body angled downhill. Beads of sweat dotted his face, shining the goose egg on his forehead a bright purple where a part of a tree must've hit him. The goose egg was bad enough. But it was the fear she saw in his eyes that startled her. Made her shrink back momentarily. A man like Latigo never showed fear. It wasn't in his nature to wave his emotions like a red flag.

"Are you all right?" Frantically, she ripped at the branches still covering him. A scream rose in her throat when she saw the quarter section of tree trunk resting crossways on his thigh.

"O-oooh." His moan sounded weak and far away. "My leg, it's caught." He thrashed about like an angry bull knocking wood chips right and left.

"Don't move." He fell back at her command. She worked her fingers lower over his thigh, before slipping her hand to the other side of the log. Thank God, his kneecap felt intact.

"Stop pawing me." He muscled himself onto an elbow and tried to jerk his leg free.

"That'll never work. Unless you're planning on ripping your knee out of its socket." Her gaze darted toward the house. "I'll get help."

He grabbed her shirt front and rocked her forward until she was staring down into his face.

"Forget it. I told you, there's no help up to the house. Edwards took relatives to Hot Springs."

"You mean we're alone?"

"You got it. Looks like I'm stuck with you."

"Thanks for the vote of confidence."

"Confidence? If you had your way, you'd be laying out there in a smashed truck." He ran his fingers through his sweaty hair. "What did I do to deserve you? And this?" He pointed to the downed tree trunk stretched across his leg.

His words stung, firing her Callahan temper. Obviously, he didn't want her help. How could she blame

34

him? They might've outrun the storm if she'd gone with him quietly—quietly had never been her style.

Her first instinct was to let him try and pull himself free all by himself. She couldn't do that, not even to a Neanderthal. "Guess you're just lucky."

"Some luck." He gulped a deep breath, fanned his fingers across his thigh and jerked on his leg again. His face reddened. The veins in his neck stood out like rawhide.

"For God's sake, stop." She tore at his fingers, trying to break the hold he had on his thigh, but she lost her grip and her hand skidded to his belt. His body tensed.

He glared at her. "Feel anything you like?"

"No, not especially." She detested his off-color remarks. He enjoyed embarrassing her. She steeled herself for the other insults that would inevitably follow, but his attention shifted to the sky.

"You've still got time," he muttered. "There's a clear patch, see?" He motioned to their left, to the small patch of blue sky. "Damn, but you're one lucky woman."

"All of the sudden I'm lucky?"

"Yeah. The storm has moved off toward the road. Good thing you didn't take that truck home. You'd have been driving straight into the middle of it."

He lifted his eyes to the sky again, and his expression tightened. "But from the looks of the sky, it'll be back. And soon. You've got to get out of here. Edwards has a cellar up there, behind the house. It'll be the safest place. Go on. You can find the door. Look for the metal bolt. It's there in the grass. You can make it."

"But you're pinned."

"Brilliant deduction."

She chalked the remark up to pain and mentally de-

35

clared a truce. This was no time for a show of Irish temper.

He grabbed her wrist and drew her down to him. His eyes looked as dark and dangerous as the Oklahoma skyline. "Go on, Maggie. There's no call for you to stick around. Find that cellar while there's time."

"I ran before. I . . ." The rest of the words got caught in her dry throat.

A banging sound came from the top of the hill. She squinted toward the barn and the banging sound. The wind whipped a large pitchfork against the weathered siding, and an idea shot into her mind. She squeezed his hand.

"Smart lady." Latigo nodded and tilted his head to one side so she couldn't see his face. "Now get gone."

She darted toward the barn, ignoring the directions he'd given for finding the cellar. A gust of wind drove her sideways. She stumbled, almost falling. Crouching low at the waist, she righted herself and kept going. Latigo actually believed she'd desert him. Well, she hadn't given him any reason to think otherwise. Letting the thunder frighten her into the trees had been stupid, but she'd never seen lightning coming straight down to the ground before. As a rule, California lightning went across the sky. It never hit the ground around a person.

Running like she had tried to do made her look like a contemptible coward. That's what any sane person would think, especially a straightforward Oklahoma cowboy who'd only been trying to get her to safety.

What a jerk she'd been. She bent lower, fighting to get to the barn. Well, she may've looked like a first-class coward, but she wasn't. She wasn't foolish enough to play a plucky heroine either. But she'd never leave another human being when they were in trouble. Trouble she'd caused him.

Regardless of why she'd run, it was her fault he was trapped under that tree. Guilt drove her on. She could taste the dirt in the air. Feel the grit on her tongue. On her face. In her eyes.

She reached the barn and, bracing her back between the barn and pitchfork, twisted the prongs from the dirt. This was exactly the tool she needed to help work Latigo free. Dragging the heavy pitchfork behind her, she started back down the hill. The wind howled around her, swirling dirt up into her eyes. Blindly, she let the driving wind at her back push her along. The pitchfork bounced along behind her like a rickety old wagon. When she heard the snapping tree branches she stopped, protecting her eyes with one hand. She could barely make out the fallen trees.

His yellow duster blew by before she saw him. He'd managed to clear away a pile of branches. Something shiny caught the light. She froze when she saw the Rambo-style knife in his hand.

Three

"Latigo, wait."

"What the hell?" he shouted. "I told you to get."

Maggie watched his surprise boil over into anger. Then he saw the pitchfork and the blistering anger vanished. With a quick swipe of her hand, she snatched the knife from him.

"Give me back that knife. You're going to cut somebody, and the way my luck's been running since I met you, it'll be me."

Before she could answer, he yanked the knife back and hacked off a branch flapping in his face.

She ignored his angry scowl. "Try and forget how much you dislike me and listen. If we raise the log with this pitchfork, we might be able to slide your leg out."

"We? Lift?" His eyes narrowed. He glanced at the tree. Then, he rotated his upper body to one side and stabbed the knife into the dirt beside his pinned leg. "It might work."

"From your mouth to God's ears," she prayed, grabbing a flat stub of wood. "Here, wedge this between your legs in case the tree shifts."

"You expect this twig to protect my . . ." He cleared his throat. "Never mind." He settled the piece of wood snugly against his groin.

"Hurry. I don't like the look of the sky."

Afraid to look up, she stomped the pitchfork into place along the edge of the trunk. With her shoulder under the widest part of the pitchfork's handle, she shuffled forward on her knees. The fork bent toward the tree trunk. Pain tore down her back as the blades angled tighter against the fallen tree. But the agony was worth it—the log moved, raising slightly from his thigh.

"Damn." His breath hissed through clenched teeth as he powered the broken tree trunk away.

"It's lifting," she cheered.

He took a deep breath and relaxed his hold. Suddenly, the tree rolled back toward his groin. "Lifting? Hell, it's smashing my thigh."

She let the pitchfork flop free and scrambled to the down side of the hill. The log inched toward Latigo's belt. She reached back across him and yanked the pitchfork free and with one swift stroke sunk the blades between his legs.

"God almighty," he hollered. "Are you trying to castrate me?"

"How else was I supposed to stop it? Shut up and push."

He pushed.

So did she.

The log teeter-tottered on his thigh.

Air exploded from his lungs. "Stop. It's tearing me all to hell. Not again. Not my leg."

She was afraid to stop. Afraid to keep pulling for fear of doing more harm to his leg.

He swore, and she shoved the tree one last time before they both yanked on the pitchfork again.

Gravity took over. The full weight of the log shifted. Latigo kicked at the tree with his free foot. The trunk lifted slightly giving him enough time to drag his leg from beneath it.

"Are you all right?" she asked.

He sat up, rubbing his leg. His thigh muscle quivered, and even the press of his hand failed to stop the tremors. "What do you think?"

That was a stupid question, she thought. Stupid. "I'm sorry."

"It's a bit late for apologies."

She might've been angry except for the pain she saw in his eyes. Pain she'd caused by running into the trees. She wanted to forget their disastrous first meeting and their argument over her oil leases. For now, she simply wanted to get to the safety of the house and do something, anything, to ease his pain.

"Hurry." He looked back over his shoulder.

She froze, tracking his gaze.

The sky darkened suddenly. Clouds rotated near the horizon, then swept higher like a whirling top set free from its string.

"What is that?"

"A Tulsey twister, ma'am."

She recognized the reference to Tulsey, the word most native Tulsan's used for their beloved Tulsey Town. She also recognized the meaning of the dreaded word twister. "A tornado?" Her insides churned. She'd only seen tornados on the six o'clock news. The San Francisco news. First hand, the funnel cloud with its whipping tail looked more frightening than anything she'd ever seen.

"Come on." He rose up on all fours, and half crawling, dragged her along with him toward the knoll of the hill. "There's an old fruit cellar. It's here. It's gotta be."

"But we can still make the house."

"That frame house will explode if the tornado hits."

"Explode?"

"Like a Fourth-of-July firecracker. Find that cellar. It's our only chance now."

In the distance, a low roar, reminiscent of a freight train, rode the wind. Flying debris stung her eyes shut. Blindly, she combed the grass with her fingers, feeling for any sign of the cellar door. Her hand struck rough wood. Flakes of old paint struck against her palm. "The door. It's here."

Clawing at the bits of dirt and grass, they dug out the edge of the doorframe.

"Get clear, Maggie. This door's coming at you."

She heard the clang of metal as he unhooked the padlock from the swivel latch and threw back the door. She crawled on the ground to the edge of the black hole. She could barely make out the stairs leading to the cellar.

"Can you make the steps?"

"Are you kidding?" He shoved her in front of him.

The stairs were narrow, closed in on both sides by cement-block walls. Moving ahead of him, she felt her way along, reaching for the beams of light from the air shafts. Even with the air shafts, the air inside smelled stale with humidity. Thickly spun webs stuck to her cheek. Spiders. Her skin crawled. She hated spiders. But she batted away the webs without uttering a sound.

"Damn."

She knew from his curse that his boot heel had hit the first step. She knew the pain he must be feeling right about now. Pain he wouldn't want her to notice. With great effort, she did what she knew he wanted her to do—she kept on moving down the stairs.

He stumbled by her and slumped to the floor, facing the stairs. Her eyes gradually adjusted to the dim light until the door behind her blew open.

"The door," he hollered.

"I'll get it." She reclimbed the steps. The wind banged the door shut. Her knees shook and she stopped, momentarily blinded by the darkness.

They were trapped.

Gathering herself, she controlled her panic, feeling along the inside of the door for the slide and slammed it into place. Still shaking, she backed down the stairs keeping her hand in constant contact with the wall for support. The uneven blocks of cement protruded sharply against her spine. She kept moving, one step at a time.

"Where are you?" She blessed the round plates of light coming from the air shafts and looked around. The cellar resembled a long narrow closet. Weathered wood lined the ceiling and one wall. A drape of flowered chintz hung beside a sagging row of shelves crowded with rows of canning jars. She huddled by the shelf using it for support.

"Over here, Maggie."

She looked in the direction of his voice to where the light puddled in the far corner. Latigo lay almost flat on the ground, a boot heel braced against the bottom step.

The cellar vibrated, and jars rattled. The timber overhead creaked.

"Latigo!" Sand and clumps of dirt pelted her shoulders. She tumbled to her knees and threw herself across him, bracketing his head with her arms.

42

Rocks slammed down the vertical air shafts and were sucked out of the cellar when the door blew off. Like a magnet, the wind tore at her. She felt herself sliding away. Latigo criss-crossed his arms around her.

"I've got you." He rose up slightly, drawing her lower. Lower. Lower still, until it was he who sheltered her.

"This time, I can't run," she whispered.

"I wish you could, darlin'. But there's no place left to go."

Closing her eyes, she went limp. Jenny? And Dad with his bad heart? "Please God, keep Jenny and Dad safe. Don't let the tornado . . ." The rest of the prayer died on her lips as the freight-train sound rattled closer.

"Here it comes." Latigo shifted his body, throwing his left hip over her.

The cellar shook. Ceiling timbers creaked. The freight train roared overhead. His mouth moved against her temple, but the terrifying noise muffled his words. She shivered, and he hugged her tighter. All around them glass popped against the cement floor, and the unmistakable aroma of peaches coated the air.

Then silence. A silence more threatening than the howling winds.

Minutes passed.

"Are you all right?" he asked, lifting up on one elbow.

"I think so. You?" The light from the air shafts splintered between them like the ghostly picket from a shattered fence. His face shone with sweat. The goose egg, where the tree had struck his forehead, already showed signs of swelling. Yet he gave no sign of hurting anywhere, although she knew he must be aching all over.

"But your head?" she continued. "Your leg?"

"No need to pull such a long face." He fingered the

43

red bump on his forehead. "This? It's nothing. My leg is fine. No broken bones. No blood. See?" His palm grazed his thigh, flipping open the tear in his jeans. "I've taken harder licks in the rodeo. This leg mended long before the doctors could take it off."

Because of a rodeo injury, the doctors wanted to amputate his leg? He not only kept his leg, but he managed to joke about it. Maybe he was a Western hero afterall. She shook her head, utterly amazed at what she was learning about this Oklahoma cowboy.

Favoring his right leg, Latigo got to his feet and hoisted her up along with him. The cellar walls spun in a gray blur. She reeled dizzily, leaning her forehead into his chest.

"Light-headed?" he asked.

"A bit." For a moment she managed to shake off the dizziness.

"A Tulsa twister will do that."

Not wanting to appear wimpy, she straightened up. "Let's go." She picked her way through the broken canning jars littering the cement floor. The smell of peaches filled her nostrils. She'd forgotten how good home canning smelled. "Smells much better in here now."

"Porter peaches. Oklahoma's finest." He limped up the stairs. "I'll have to thank Edwards for the use of his cellar."

Halfway up the stairs, she froze. It was too dark. Light should've been streaming in through the doorless cellar, but it wasn't. Her eyes widened in disbelief. A pointy, zigzag of broken tree limbs blocked their escape.

"We've a slight problem," he said, his voice guarded.

"We're . . ." She caught herself before uttering the fateful word *trapped*. Panic clutched at her insides. They

44

were alone. Trapped and with no hope of help. No one knew where they were. Not even Dad. It might be hours, days even, before they were located.

What about her truck? Someone would see it. Hope paled when she recalled Latigo telling her about the pickup. Her truck, the only clue to what direction she'd taken, could've been blown miles from here. Even Latigo's horse was gone. The cellar walls closed in around her. The blur of gray dizziness whizzed around her. Her chest heaved. She couldn't catch her breath. Smothering humidity surrounded her.

For an instant she thought she'd pass out. Slumping against the cellar wall, she tore the collar of her blouse open wider. She needed air. Fresh air. She clutched at the chintz material hanging next to the canning shelves, fighting the urge to run up the stairs and claw at the blocked opening. She wanted out. No matter what kind of storm might rage outside—she wanted out. And now! She fought the urge to flee, fighting it to a standstill. Seeing how Latigo reacted to their plight gave her the ability to reach down inside of herself and grab hold of her own courage. If he could do it. So could she. So *would* she.

"Damn," he muttered, working a twisted scrap of wood loose before tossing it to the far side of the stairs. "This looks like part of a barn, probably Edwards. See if you can find a longer piece of wood, shelving maybe, to use as a shovel."

Still fighting panic, she stood rooted to the spot. She wanted to help, but the only parts of her moving were her blinking eyelids.

He threw a second length of wood beside the other. "This cellar isn't much bigger than a closet. But if we

45

stack everything on the right side of the stairs we should have enough room. Are you having any luck finding that long piece of wood?"

Maggie stared into the musty blackness. "Not yet." She meant to move, but her feet refused to budge.

"This ought to work." He grabbed a piece of broken shelving and started digging. "Well? Do you want to get out of here or not?"

She clenched her teeth together and counted to ten. Did it never occur to him that some people might not be as brave as he was? The man had the sensitivity of a large rock. Never mind, she'd show him what she was made of. She might be from the city, but she could be tough if need be. Straightening, she bullied her feet into moving. "Being stuck here with you is *not* my idea of a fun evening."

"Neither one of us has any choice. So get busy."

"Stop ordering me around. I'm not one of your ranch hands."

"If you were, I wouldn't have to tell you twice."

"Here." He brushed by her. "I'll get what I need. Just clear out of my way. "

"All right, Mr. Latigo. Go right ahead."

He jabbed with a piece of wood at the debris blocking the door. Hunks of wood dropped onto the stairs. Dirt hammered down upon his strapping shoulders. He backed away, coughing at the cloud of dust.

Well, that ought to show him. She crossed her arms over her chest smugly. "Still want to dig us out alone?"

He turned around. His face streaked with sweat and dirt. Their eyes connected and held for several seconds before he laughed. His unrestrained laughter bounced off the cellar walls filling the small space to overflowing. "What do you think?"

Life had taught her one thing for certain. There were a handful of people impossible to dislike for more than a minute, and, at this moment, Wade Latigo was one of them. She chuckled. "I think you could use help."

"For once, ma'am, you're absolutely right."

The accented *ma'am* sounded more Southern than usual. She liked the tribute and the slight nod he gave her when he'd said it. If they avoided the subject of her oil leases perhaps they could be friends—at least for the time being. Any man who dressed like a clown for a bunch of kids at a junior rodeo couldn't be all bad.

"You mean it's possible this prune-picker might be right?"

"Strange as it seems, I think that's what I said."

"That's quite an admission. I hope it's the first of many." She kicked the broken pieces of wood and dirt out of the way and climbed the stairs, taking the step above the one he stood on. The level evened up the height difference. She liked being on equal footing with him. She liked looking him straight in the eye. From the way he smiled, she guessed he liked it too.

"I've been wrong plenty of times," he confessed, suddenly avoiding any further eye contact.

"But how many times have you admitted it?"

"A few."

"Too few, I'll wager." She tugged at a small bit of wood over her head and dodged the bits and pieces of dirt that fell around her.

"Nice move." He wiped his hands on the sides of his jeans and looked her straight in the face. "We'll get out of here."

"I know."

He reached over and squeezed her hand. His palm was gritty, but warm. She was grateful for the contact. Grateful for the unspoken truce.

"TJ knows I'm out here. He and the boys will be beatin' the bushes looking for any sign of me."

"But for tonight?"

He squeezed her hand harder. "We'll bunk here."

Here? The two of them? She glanced down at the slab of cement flooring. There'd barely be enough room for him to stretch out his long legs. With the two of them sleeping here, it'd be tight. They'd have to sleep like a pair of spoons. Never mind. If you're lucky, she reminded herself, you'll only be here a few hours.

"That air shaft light won't last much longer," he added casually. "See if there's a flashlight somewhere."

It was more of a suggestion than an order this time. "I'd better get at this floor while I'm at it." She wadded up some newspaper from the bottom shelf below the canned peaches and brushed away pieces of the broken canning jars.

"Good thinking." The smile he gave her meant more than anything else he might've said.

Moments later, she found the antique lantern stuffed behind a stack of *Oklahoma Today* magazines. "Look at this." She shook it, listening for the shift of kerosene inside. There was barely any sound. "I'm afraid it's almost empty."

"We'll make do."

"Of course we will," she added. He gave her a funny look. Did she have dirt on her face? She brushed her hand across her cheek. She found a small patch of caked mud on her chin and whisked it away with the back of her hand. Otherwise, everything on her face felt normal. She dismissed his scrutiny and concentrated her attention on clearing away the last of the broken glass. The juice from the peaches made the floor sticky. Using bunches of rumpled newspaper, she managed to clear out a small space in the corner. The meager daylight was fading fast when she pitched in, helping him with the last of the protruding tree trunks that hung low over the stairs.

"You're making headway," she said, yanking on the long tree branch he'd pulled halfway down the steps.

"We're making headway."

Even after he corrected her, he kept his head down. She had the distinct feeling he was smiling. "Three more steps and we can reach the opening."

"Careful there, Maggie. It could cave in."

His words were prophetic. Rubble crashed about them in a cloud of dust. He bent over her, guiding her back down the stairs.

"Well, that's one way to do it." She coughed, fanning the air.

They stood facing one another. For Latigo, it was the first time he'd gotten a close peek at her since the storm. She looked different than when they'd met after the rodeo. Gone were the silk dress and those crazy open-toed shoes. She looked smaller without her high heels. Younger. Prettier too, he thought, even with the smudges of dirt on her forehead and cheeks. Without thinking, he brushed the bits of grass from her hair. His touch took her by surprise, and she jumped.

"I can get it. Thanks."

He left the remaining leaf tangled in the wisp of hair over her ear. "Suit yourself." He jerked his shirttail out of his jeans and pretended to shake out more of the dirt sticking to his back.

Actually, he watched her. She bent from the waist, head down, and shook out her hair. Most of the women he knew, especially the short ones, wore their hair short, too. Not her. With a flick of her wrist, she twisted the strands and anchored them with a pin atop her head. Too bad, he thought. He liked her better with her hair down. He liked the way it bunched into big loose curls on her shoulders. He unhitched his belt buckle to get at the last bit of scratchy dirt, and her eyes widened.

"What are you doing?"

He did a double take. "I'm not taking off my pants, if that's what you think." He shifted to an exaggerated drawl, "A cowboy kicks off his boots *before* his britches, ma'am. As you can see, I'm still wearing mine."

A pearly pink singed her cheeks. "Right."

He'd been right. She had thought he was going to drop his pants. She had been watching too many Westerns. Probably those spaghetti Westerns. Laughing, he ran his thumb around his middle between the elastic on his undershorts and his skin, pitching out what remained of the dirt particles. "Find anything resembling water?"

"Only the canned peaches."

He scanned her from hip to toe. Oh, he'd taken in her legs the first time he'd seen her at the rodeo. *Come on, cowboy,* he admitted, *you looked at her so closely that day, you could pick her out of any crowd.* Okay. Okay. We may not agree about those oil leases, but that doesn't mean I can't appreciate a good-lookin' lady.

Rotating his shoulders, he jammed one arm down his back trying to loosen the dirt stuck to his sweaty skin. It felt like a herd of red ants had set up a feeding farm alongside his backbone. He unsnapped the front of his shirt while he jerked it from his britches.

This time, she didn't bat an eye. Instead, she took a jar of peaches from the shelf and tried to turn the lid. Without so much as a howdy-do, she banged the jar on the shelf and gave it a twist. The lid snapped open. The scent of cinnamon and peaches met him head on.

"Drink?" she asked.

"You first." He watched her intently. From the way she'd opened the jar, she was accustomed to taking care of herself. Every move she made reminded him of that. She was stubborn, too. Stubbornness in a horse he could handle. But with a woman, this woman in particular, now that would be a challenge. She took a long drink. The peaches shifted in the jar, and a trickle of juice ran down her chin, settling into a pool at the pulse point of her throat. It stayed there glistening like a liquid pearl.

"It's wet, but I can't say the juice does much for my thirst." She hooked a peach with her finger and plopped it onto the upside down lid before handing him the jar. "Your turn."

He set the jar to his mouth and took a big drink. She was right. The peach juice was sweet. It didn't do much to quench his thirst.

"Hope you've got matches." She fiddled with the kerosene lamp, lifting the cracked chimney to check the wick.

He slapped his front jean pocket, feeling for a book of matches. "Right here."

"The electricity will probably be out in town." Her eyes locked on an invisible spot off in space. He knew she was thinking about her family.

"Probably," he replied, watching her thoughts drift.

51

"The farmhouse will be dark. There're candles in the kitchen cupboard, but Dad won't remember where they are." She stopped fiddling with the lantern. "She's afraid of the dark so I always turn on the night-light for *her*. Now, with the storm . . . it'll be dark." She looked right through him. "I can stand anything, even being cooped up here. If only . . ."

The sudden shift in her mood brought him up short. "If only?"

"If only I knew that *they're* safe."

"Your dad and daughter, right?" The high-pitched wail of a siren startled them both. For an instant, he thought she was going to jump into his arms. No such luck.

"I've got to get back to them." Instead, she moved toward the steps before he hooked her elbow.

"Hold on. That siren is the all clear. The storm is over, and for tonight neither of us is going anywhere." Turning her away from the stairs, he tipped her face up to his. Her eyes, big and round, were swimming with unshed tears. "Nothing I can say will keep you from worrying about your people, but I want you to think on this."

"What?" Her voice shook, the tone unsure.

A sense of helplessness spread over him. Slowly, gently, he put his arms around her. She came willingly, as if more than anyone in the world she needed *him*. He was crazy to hold her like this, but it would be cruel to turn away now. He'd hold her. He'd hold for as long as she needed it. As long as she needed him. Even if it took all night.

Four

Latigo kept on holding her. Kept on talking. Kept trying to ignore how good she felt up against him. How damned good. "That old house you inherited has been standing for years. It'll take more than a Tulsa blow to budge it. Besides, there's the fraidy hole."

The side of her cheek stayed flat to his chest. He could feel the outline of her face, the shape, the tip of her nose. "Fraidy, as in afraid?"

"Right. The fruit cellar. It's like this one, only bigger. You must've seen it."

"I'd forgotten." Her tone brightened, but she stayed nestled in his arms as if she felt safe for the first time since the tornado hit.

"Dad started cleaning it out yesterday."

"See? Your dad's probably sitting there right now bouncing your daughter on his knee." Why was it so important for him to reassure her? They'd only met yesterday. Ever since then, she'd been nothing but trouble. Yet, how could he resist? The way she looked at him made him want to protect her. To play hero. Hero? Him? Where the hell had that notion come from? What kind of an effect was this city gal having on him anyway?

"Do you really think they're okay?"

"Absolutely. I've been in that cellar plenty of times as a kid. Your uncle was my neighbor. My friend. There's a refrigerator there, and light. They all work off a generator."

"I'd forgotten." He felt her jaw work as she spoke. He liked feeling the motion almost as much as listening to her.

"Thanks, Latigo."

"For what?"

"For making me feel better."

"You're a bright lady. You would've remembered your cellar and come to the same conclusion without any help from me." He stepped away from her so he could see her face. She was still worried. He could tell by the frown. But they shared a smile anyway. He knew the hours until dawn would prove the longest of her life. Talking would distract her, keep her mind off worrying about her family.

That's what she needed—to be distracted. But how? They had nothing in common, and he wasn't much on talking about himself. What else could he do? He had to try, but where would he start? Against his better judgment, he took her hand in his. It was small, but strong. Like her.

"What's her name? Your daughter's, I mean."

"Jenny."

"Nice." Her face glowed when she spoke the child's name. Good. The questions had worked. So keep asking. Keep her talking. "How old is Jenny?"

"Five." Her smile broadened, her eyes sparkling with

54

pride. "She starts kindergarten in San Francisco this fall."

"Bet she can hardly wait." The light from the air shafts was only a sliver now. He wanted to hold off using the kerosene, but he figured it'd make the time pass quicker for her if they had light. Get to it, cowboy, before she's standing here in total darkness. Reluctantly he let go of her hand and dug the book of matches from his front pocket.

When she saw the matchbook she reached for the lantern. "We registered Jenny for kindergarten earlier this year." Maggie raised the chimney on the lantern and swung the lamp his way.

"My first day at school was a disaster," he boasted.

"You ran home, right?"

She had him pegged. "How'd you know?"

"A lucky guess."

"My schooling wasn't a total loss. I showed promise in kindergarten, mostly in crayons and Lincoln logs," he said.

"How were you in sandbox?"

"Great. Got an A-plus in digging." He flipped open the matches with his thumb. "All I wanted to do was ride my horse."

"But your mother sent you straight back to kindergarten."

Didn't he wish. "I never knew my folks. A rodeo rider by the name of Jonathan Wade raised me. He's the one who took me back to school."

That sad look shot back into her eyes. "I'm sorry, Latigo."

"Don't be. Jonathan Wade was mighty good to me."

"I'm sure he was, but every child deserves at least one parent."

"Nice notion, but life doesn't always work out that way. At the time, the county orphanage bulged with kids with no place to go. Not much call for a skinny half-breed who wasn't sure which tribe he belonged to. With the help of a local padre, Jonathan got himself a son of sorts." He stuck a finger into his chest. "He never got around to adopting me though. Guess he didn't want to stir up the courts by drawing attention to us since there was no real mother on the property. By the time the judge got wise to the situation, I was eighteen and big as a bear." To bring the smile back to her lips, he leaned closer and growled, "And I was twice as ornery as any old bear."

She smiled. "I bet."

Funny thing though, her voice sounded wistful and faraway. When he saw the sadness still in her eyes, he realized mentioning he was an orphan had been a mistake. "Hey, buck up. How many kids do you know who get to pick their own name?"

From the brightening sparkle in her eyes, she'd be smiling soon. It couldn't be soon enough to suit him.

"That's where you got the Wade part of your name, from Jonathan's last name?"

"Right. Only I reversed it, is all." He ripped a match from the book. Mentally, he tallied the number of matches remaining. Four. Only four. "I got the idea for my last name from the latigo strap on a saddle."

"You did?"

Why had he told her that? She knew nothing about horses or saddles. And from the way she acted around Dollar, she had no intention of learning. Besides, he never talked about himself much, especially to women. But he had to admit, she seemed genuinely interested. *So, what's holding you back? Keep on talking, cowboy. It'll stop her from fretting about that little girl of hers. Her Jenny.* "Most folks around these parts have heard the story about how I picked my own name. Jonathan used to brag on it." He felt inside his pockets for another matchbook.

There was none.

"I'll show you a saddle latigo one day soon if you like," he said.

"I'm not much on horses."

"I noticed. You hurt Dollar's feelings. He's big and brawny, but as gentle as a pup—if he cottons to you."

"Dollar didn't like me at all."

"You never gave him much of a chance." *Never gave me much of a chance either.* On second thought, part of the blame was his, too. He'd come off awfully tough when he first met her. He'd been tired. Lord knows, his leg had been killing him after the day at the rodeo. Chasing after her on horseback today hadn't helped polish his image either. And flipping her up in front of him and galloping off with her—

Yikers! No wonder she'd called him a Neanderthal. Looking at the events from her side, it surprised him that she hadn't taken a swing at him. Most women would have. Not her. Why was she so different from most of the women he'd met over the years?

Because she's not a fan of yours, stupid. She's from Frisco. She's probably never seen a rodeo in her life. Too bad. She might've enjoyed seeing him bust out of a chute, seeing him burn leather like he had in his prime. Lord knows, he'd like to hear his name called over the loud speaker. He'd like to hear the crowd roar as he showed off his flamboyant bronc-riding style. He'd like to be riding the circuit again and not just for her. For him. He missed those rodeo days. He missed the adrenaline rush when he nodded and the chute gate swung open. He missed hearing the buzzer and knowing he'd be number one. He took a deep breath. Those days were long gone.

He struck the match he'd been holding and lit the bent lantern wick. A wick that reminded him of how bent he was since the last time he'd been thrown by that Brahma. The bull had won that day. And all of the days since then. But he was standing. Still riding. Still walking. He'd beaten the odds. "There. That's better." Feeling that he'd come out on top regardless of his limp, he stashed the matchbook safely in his shirt pocket.

The amber glow from the lamp did crazy things with the color of her hair. He watched the strawberry blond deepen to rich mahogany. That expensive wood only used in quality furniture. Those high-dollar pieces. Yes, sir. The woman was a looker. A definite keeper. She'd make any man's head turn clean around for a second look.

His mouth went bone dry. Lord almighty! What had he gotten himself into? He knew temptation when he saw it. He'd given in to it on more occasions than he cared to recall. He grabbed the open jar of peaches she held out to him and took a hefty gulp. Sticky juice raced down his chin. He wiped his mouth with the corner of his sleeve and took another swallow. Looking back at her, his throat felt drier than before.

Latigo eyed the narrow space on the floor next to the wall. Between the broken canning jars and the wood he'd stacked on the stairs, there wasn't much room for two people. The way his thoughts were flying, he was in a heap of trouble. Woman trouble. Maggie Callahan trouble.

To keep her from worrying about her family, he'd distracted her. Now, he needed a distraction quick, one that would keep him thinking of her *only* as a neighbor. Neighbor, his mind repeated. Woman, his body hollered. W-O-M-A-N!

Okay brain. You're the one with the big idea about distractions. Get to working! Come up with something quick!

Nothing half as distracting as her came to mind.

"Damn," he cursed under his breath while he flexed his leg. He tried to concentrate on other parts of his body—those south of his belt buckle. Way south.

His injured right leg for instance. It was fine. A bit bruised maybe, but nothing he hadn't felt before. He looked in her direction again and shook his head. Wasn't it his luck to have drawn as his companion for the night the tempting half-pint who was selling the grass right out from under his horses? And after the way she'd handled herself since they'd found themselves trapped inside this cellar—he'd come to look at her differently. Admit it, cowboy. All right. All right. As ridiculous as it might sound, she was quickly earning his grudging respect.

Why couldn't she have stayed at home today? Better still, why hadn't she stayed in Frisco and let that lawyer of hers handle the farm she'd inherited from her uncle? Frisco is where she and her open toe shoes and silk dress belonged. Not at the junior rodeo where he'd first set eyes on her.

His eyes settled upon her narrow waist and the smooth flare of her hips. Rounded hips. Not the hips of a skinny model. Womanly hips. Full and soft. The kind of hips a man liked snuggled up next to him. Like the neck on a maverick bronc, his manhood thickened.

Luckily, she failed to notice the way he'd looked at her. Luck hell, in all of his born days, he'd never counted on luck in his life. No foundling half-breed would. He wasn't about to start. He yanked his shirttail over his fly.

Since that first meeting after the rodeo the timing between them had been all wrong. Him being decked out like a clown hadn't helped any. He rubbed his aching thigh. See what playing hero had gotten him? Let that be a lesson to you.

"Is it bad?" Her voice swelled with motherly concern.

Mothering was the last thing on his mind. He shifted his weight from one leg to the other, relieving the strain on his fly. Thank the lord for his long shirttail. It covered the bulge in his jeans.

"Just getting the kinks out." He gave his leg muscle a last rub. "Nothing fatal." Neither was the arousal knotting inside his britches.

She stepped closer, brushing his hand with hers. "I'm sorry about your leg."

"Forget it." Her hand lay motionless on his forearm. Part of him wanted her to stop touching him, the other part—the part about to bust a button on his pants, was having the time of its life. Kicking up its heels like a wayward bronc.

"How can I, Latigo? If it hadn't been for me running into that grove of trees—"

"Lightning can do that to anyone. I bet you've never seen lightning come straight down to the ground before, have you?" Couldn't resist playing the hero again, could you?

She shook her head and busied herself taking down

the curtain hanging to one side of the shelves. He was sorry she'd pulled her hand away. He missed the warmth. The softness. The feeling that she really cared about how he felt.

"Tell me something." Her voice dropped to a whisper, "Why did you come looking for me today?"

"We're neighbors." He flexed his toes inside his right boot. The movement had nothing to do with his sore leg. He was stalling. *Truth time again, cowboy. Fess up.* "I figured on mending a few fences so I swung by your place."

The material in her hand went still. "Mending fences?"

"Our first meeting didn't go too well. Couldn't have you thinkin' badly of our Oklahoma hospitality. Your father told me you'd gone for a ride. He'd seen the tornado watch on TV. I could see how worried he was about you. So, I told him I'd find you and bring you back in one piece. Locating you wasn't hard once I spotted the truck."

"Is this an apology?" she teased good-naturedly.

"Can you stand two in one day?"

"Only if you take my apology in exchange. Deal?"

"Deal." He extended his hand, then thought better of it. Whew, that was a close call. They had a long night ahead of them, and there'd been enough touching.

"You got it." She examined the width of cloth in front of the canning shelves and pulled it free. "It's no blanket, but it'll do." She spread the material on the floor and covered it with the last of the newspapers.

"Are you always this practical, Maggie?"

"Always. Girl Scouts get their training early. I had the thickest stack of pine needles under my sleeping bag at camp."

Well, what'a you know? She'd actually slept on the ground before. *"You* went camping?"

"Surprised?"

"Yeah, a bit." He squatted beside her and helped her smooth out the newspapers. He tried to picture her selling Girl Scout cookies, but it didn't work. He was long past thinking of her as a girl. Any kind of a girl. All he could think about was untying her hair and spreading it out on the pillow in his king-sized bed. Hold it. That kind of thinking can get you into trouble. Big trouble. "You want the wall side or the stairs?"

"Whatever." She took another jar of peaches from the shelf.

"I'll take the stairs, in case we get another blow."

Another blow? Maggie tried to shake off the cold chill of fear creeping along her spine. She hadn't considered the possibility of another tornado. She forced herself to ignore his reference to a second storm. Ignoring the broad chest rippling at her from beneath Latigo's open shirt was another matter. Since Jenny's birth, Maggie had intentionally avoided any entanglements of the heart. There'd been men, of course. Two to be exact; both of the relationships casual. That was the way she wanted it. That was the way she still wanted it.

She relaxed. In this day and age, she'd have to know a man for a long time before she tumbled into bed with him. She'd decided that, when she'd split with Jenny's father. It was a decision she'd managed to stick to. Single parenting took all of her time and energy. Inheriting her uncle's farm had changed things. Would the sale of the farm and upcoming deal with Five Star Oil mean that her finances were on the upswing?

Oh, to be solvent, she sighed, wondering what it would

feel like. Solvent? No way, Jose. There were too many of Jenny's unpaid doctor bills to ever consider being solvent.

"Hungry?" he asked.

"A pint of apricot yogurt fades fast after dark."

"What happened to a real breakfast with bacon and eggs?"

"I'm not much on meat." She opened the jar she'd been holding. The subtle flavor of fresh-picked fruit coated the air, making her wish she'd had a portion of that tuna sandwich she'd fixed for her dad.

"Peach?" she asked, in a feeble attempt to distract her gnawing stomach.

"You first."

She took a sip of juice before a peach half floated into her mouth. The fruit tasted cooler than she expected. She dug into another peach. Juice spilled down her chin like honey water. She blocked it with her thumb and licked the last trace of sweetness from her hand.

"Want one?" she asked.

"Sure."

She speared another piece of fruit with her index finger and took it from the jar. Juice dribbled down her arm. He was staring at her again. She forgot about his dark eyes, about the hunger she saw there. The hunger had nothing to do with peaches. The only thing she could think about was his hand when he guided the peach to his mouth. Juice trickled along the back of her hand and beneath his palm. Beyond that she lost track of its journey. How could she think of anything but his mouth coming nearer the peach? She felt the side of his face against her hand. The scratchy stubble on his chin glided through juice stirring the sweet flavor until every breath she took was laced with peaches.

He took a bite. Then another. The second taste was more a nibble than a bite. No teeth. Only the coaxing caress of lips and tongue was as erotic as if he'd kissed the most intimate part of her femininity. The message, as subtle as foreplay, ignited feelings that she'd denied herself for years. Emotions so strong she'd almost believed she'd never feel them again. Never feel so alive. So much in need of his touch. She thought herself beyond those sort of primitive yearnings. She'd been wrong.

Suddenly, the lamplight dimmed, then went out.

The invading darkness startled her. She gasped and reached out with her hand to steady herself. Her fingertips ran straight into his chest. His hard, naked chest. She clutched at his open shirt, trying to break all contact with his skin. A futile effort. "Sorry. I . . ."

"No problem."

He flattened her hand beneath his own. She could feel his shirt pocket and the elevated shape of the matchbook hidden safely inside. She could've pulled her hand away. Pulling away from him was the last thing on her mind. The very last thing. She knew if she were smart, she'd take her hand from beneath his. What had smart to do with what she felt right now? What emotion was she feeling anyway? She hadn't a clue. With a burning certainty, she knew she liked the way his naked skin felt on hers. She needed the intimate contact.

He made no move to press her for anything other than the touching of their hands. For her part—she went along. The longer her hand stayed nailed to his chest the clearer she felt the quick-paced rhythm of his heart. It beat faster than her own, but not by much.

The welcome darkness spread around them like a thick black quilt, making her more aware of him. Of his smooth skin. Of his heat.

"That's it for the kerosene." Bending down to her, he drew her body tightly against his. The perfect blending of hard angles to soft curves left her breathless. Like any two survivors, they clung together. Each bound to the other as if their existence depended upon their never letting go.

"Maggie?"

No man had ever said her name in quite that way. The rasped word was both a question and a plea. She knew what he was asking. Even in the darkness, she felt his body taut with arousal. Under ordinary circumstances their being together, let alone intimate, would be unthinkable. But these circumstances were long past ordinary.

"You don't need these, darlin'." As if he'd been waiting a lifetime, he ravaged her hair removing the pins as he found them. His fingers sifted through the strands until they fell in heavy heaps upon her shoulders.

"That's better. Your hair is too beautiful to keep roped and tied." He knotted his fists in her hair drawing her head back. He touched her face like a blind man memorizing the arch of her eyebrows, her temples, every curve of her cheeks, the shape of her mouth. He leaned closer, following his fingers with his lips, kissing her everywhere he touched. He made love to her face with his hands and his kiss, until his lips found the most sensitive spot—the tender skin on her neck below her earlobe.

Goose bumps covered her arms, then raced over her shoulders to the spots still wet with the imprint of his mouth. His kisses were slow and deliberate, as if even in the darkness his lips knew exactly where they were headed.

Her mouth, open and waiting, knew, too. In a moment there'd be no turning back for either of them.

"Latigo, we don't even know each other."

"Right." His breath puffed inside her blouse like a warm hand.

"Much less like one another."

"Right."

"We have nothing in common."

"Right again."

"I'm still selling those oil leases to Five Star."

"Ri-i-ight."

She tried to answer, but the golden scent of peaches smothered any refusal. Whether it was a combination of longing or lust didn't matter to her. Not anymore. The darkness only intensified her nocturnal feelings. She'd never made love with a man unencumbered by feelings of deep affection. Men did it all the time. They were different. The chief outstanding difference between male and female pressed full and hard against her. Her moist response was immediate.

What would it be like to let herself go? She buried her face against his chest, and the smell of leather mingled with a lusty scent of male heat. It tangled with a need. A need, so ferociously hungry and too long denied, waged a battle inside her. As if he could read her body's response, his hand drifted down her spine nudging her closer to his bruising hardness.

"You taste like peaches, darlin'. Sweet juicy peaches, and it's been a long time between summers." His lips ground against hers, rubbing hers apart. The kiss searing. Deep. Possessive.

66

Sensations, that her mind fought, engulfed her. And to her chagrin, her traitorous body rejoiced almost from the first. Without consciously willing it, her parted lips sought the burning brand of his kiss. She stroked his mouth with her tongue, learning its shape, as the last of her inhibitions melted into the darkness. No one would know what went on between them. They were consenting adults trapped by their emotions. Their needs. How could she resist?

Was thirty minutes of wonderful, out of the months of loneliness, too much to ask? Her heart went mute, but her body spoke again. Dare she reach out to this man? This stranger? She hesitated, listening to the sweet messages singing through her. The passionate song was as familiar as the peach-scented night. *Lord, help me,* she prayed.

She waited trying to check her emotions, but the lure of the forbidden proved too powerful. She kissed him back, tasting the sun-ripened peaches again and again. Tempted by the promise of summertime, she deepened the kiss until the golden taste meant only one thing—Latigo. She was lost, lost in the wonderfully wet contact.

Suddenly his deeply drawn kisses stopped. Her mouth felt cold and needy. Their breathing collided in quick shallow bursts. She shook all over when he stepped away.

"If you want me to stop, Maggie, tell me *now!*"

For once in her life, every practical reason why she should say no to Wade Latigo failed. All of her life, she'd put her daughter and father first. Now, Maggie knew only one thing. She wanted Latigo. She needed him. Needed him . . . now.

Five

Stop touching him.

Maggie's fingertips froze on Latigo's chest while her practical mind tried coaxing her body to its senses. The momentary pause was all the excuse her body needed. Her greedy hands palmed the naked skin inside his open shirt. His stomach was flat and tight as a drum.

It'd been a long time since she wanted to touch a man. He seemed to sense this right away. She felt him holding back. Checking himself. Waiting for her to set the pace. She found herself trusting her instincts about him more and more. Kissing him again increased that trust.

"Touch me anywhere. Everywhere." He took her hands and kissed the tips of each finger, encouraging them to explore. "Put your mark on me. Here." He guided her hand down the center of his body. "And here."

She learned the shape and feel of him, every rodeo scar and well-strung muscle. Like a blind woman, she reveled in the pattern of hair along the middle of his body. Guided by touch, she found his chest muscles solid beneath taut skin. And his shoulders. So wide. So strong . . . so . . . she pushed his open shirt down his arms and felt him shake it off. Her palms traveled around his narrow waist clear to his spine.

He stood motionless, but there was no mistaking the quick intake of air when her hands moved back to his stomach. Her fingers fanned out touching each rib. His breathing quickened. She fought to catch her own breath, but the steamy air, heavy with the heat, only stalled in her throat. Lungs cried for relief.

"Maggie. Darlin'."

The rest of the accolade was muffled against her ear. His heated breath rattled her, and she paused for an instant trying to understand what emotions shook her. It's too late for thinking. Much too late.

He kissed his way across her cheek, talking, praising the taste and feel of her skin. His lips mated with hers until there was only his mouth and the taste of summer peaches. Peaches everywhere. First on his mouth and tongue, then on hers.

The moon above the blocked opening shifted, casting slanted shadows over the planes of his rugged face. His cheeks, broad and wet with sweat, shone like quicksilver. How could she resist touching him? Her fingertips painted away the smooth silver until she felt the scratchy growth of his beard.

"Sorry. I'm a bit rough." His kiss sent shivers rocketing through her. An emotional tornado whirled inside her, driving her mouth and body straight to him. She wasn't afraid, as she'd been in the trees when the tornado hit. She faced the swirling current trapped between them, wanting more than anything to set free the pent-up passion she'd suppressed since Jenny's birth. Oh, she'd learned how to be practical, to stretch pennies, but she'd never learned how to handle the lonely nights. Tonight she wasn't alone. Latigo was here. Reach for what you need, her passion cried.

His hands rested upon her hips for a moment, then traced the waistband of her jeans around to the front. She started to unbutton them, but the pressure of his palm stopped her.

"Let me." Struggling with the tiny button, he swore under his breath before she felt the drag of her jeans along her hips. His lips found the corner of her mouth, kissing their way to the plump center.

He pulled away, and the sound of leather boots crashed to the floor. "These belt loops were never wide enough." His metal belt buckle clanged onto the cement floor before his jeans hit the floor between them, and he kicked them away.

"Lean into me, Maggie. Let me feel your skin against mine."

Hard bones, harder muscles pressed against her. Naked legs met her own, the hair-covered skin a sharp contrast. He made quick work of her blouse. His fingers found her lacy bra. He moaned his approval, cupping his hands to the shape of her breasts before he unsnapped the front closure. She leaned forward into the darkness, filling his hands with her naked softness.

"You're beautiful, Maggie. I wish there were more light. I want to see you." His lips seared a path over her collarbone. "Your skin's fired like a branding iron." He lifted her hand to his chest.

The thud of his heart banged beneath her palm. A whimper locked in her throat and for an instant she was adrift in the darkness.

"Light or no light, I'm going to see you with my hands, darlin'. Touch you and taste you all over."

She shuddered.

His breath mingled with hers, possessing her as intimately as his deep kisses. "Come closer."

She did, and each time she inched nearer he kissed her, whispering tender blessings. While his mouth wandered over her sensitive skin, he spoke again, reminding her of how sweet she tasted. How much he wanted her. No man had ever spoken his desires so candidly. The words in themselves were as erotic as his touch.

She leaned back serving up the ache in her breasts to his hungry hands. His trailing kisses circled the fullness of her breasts, coaxing the nipples tighter. An invisible connection sizzled directly from her breast to the center of her femininity.

His right hand roamed her spine, stroking each vertebra, and in one quick sweep he whisked off her panties. Crumpling the bit of lacy white in his hand like a baseball, he tossed the panties into the darkness.

A rush of unbreathed air eased between them.

He stood motionless while the tornado inside her whirled.

"We're down to the wire, darlin'."

Nothing in the world could keep her from him. She opened her arms, chanting his name in a celebration of life, of being a woman desired.

Muttering promises that the swollen part of him pledged to keep, he lowered her to the floor until she felt the slippery texture of the newspapers against her back. The female in her reacted to the utter maleness pressed against her thigh.

Shamelessly naked they re-explored each other's secrets.

Where her skin burned, his burned hotter.

Where he was hard, she was soft.

Where she was damp, he was stiff and silky.

They did it all by feel. First, as he'd promised, with his hand, then more closely with his mouth. He took her higher and higher. Touching. Tasting until she lay panting beneath him.

He rolled off of her, feeling in the darkness for something. "My pants are here somewhere. Got 'em." He rummaged in his pocket. She heard something tear before the moonlight brightened on a flash of foil. It didn't matter to her that he kept protection handy. She was glad he'd thought of her. Glad he wanted her.

On his knees, he paused above her like a moon-struck cloud.

"Don't tease, Latigo."

"This is no tease, darlin'."

The cloud descended. Hot, hard fullness probed between her thighs. In one swift stroke he planted himself solidly inside her.

She gasped.

They clung together, neither of them moving for an instant. Then they plunged headlong toward climax and the sweet shattering that lay before them in the darkness. Then there was nothing but the feel of their bodies lying face-to-face on the cement floor. She rose up.

"I'm too heavy." He rolled to one side taking her with him.

The pressure of his arms tightened about her. Angled bone and work-hardened muscle dug into feminine places that, until moments ago, had been untouched.

Reality returned. Her breath stalled. Good, God. Her previous prayer hadn't altered what had happened. What made her think that another appeal, after the fact, would change anything now? She flattened her palms against his naked chest trying to get some distance between them. "Let me go."

"I would if I thought that's what you wanted. Unless I'm badly mistaken, you're a woman who likes to be held after."

He'd read her perfectly. She wanted—no, needed—to be held. He accommodated her and tucked her tighter against him. She didn't protest. It was too late, even for regrets.

He kissed her forehead dragging his lips along her temple in a soothing caress.

Half asleep, she blessed the darkness, thankful that he couldn't see any of the emotions she was trying to sort out.

He brought his trademark midnight rasp down to a whisper, "Neither of us is going anywhere until tomorrow. We'll wait for morning and then start digging." He stroked her temple sending the throbbing beginning of a headache into oblivion before he kissed her. "Holding you is so easy, darlin'. So nice. Let me."

She did.

"Don't think." He brushed the hair from her eyes. "Sleep, darlin'."

She did that, too.

The wet open-mouthed kiss against her temple drifted into Maggie's hazy dream. Dreams, that's all she had. The shoulder she'd braced against the pitchfork ached. Sleeping on a cement floor hadn't helped any. But the rest of her felt better than it had in years.

She swallowed. Her mouth was dry. Her lips felt swollen. Probably from all that kissing. Kissing? She froze, suddenly wide awake when her hand struck something satiny hard and scaldingly hot.

Oh, no. It couldn't be. Her eyelids sprung open. It was too dark to see anything clearly. She moved her fingers slightly, then slammed her eyes shut.

She tried to concentrate on the exact position of her body not her hand. Primitive urgings wanted to concentrate on something else. The practical side took charge. She was on her side, one leg angled over a thickly-muscled thigh, Latigo's thigh. His breathing was regular. Thank goodness he's asleep. Careful. Move your hand slowly. No jerky movements. If you're careful you can move your hand away before he notices it. Please, God. I've never asked you for much. Please don't let him wake up. Relying on touch, she guided her thumb across the crescent of wiry hair surrounding his arousal and toward his hip.

He moaned and shifted, nudging her hand deeper into the springy hair. Before she could move again, his hand covered hers, settling her thumb and fingers snugly around his pillared manhood.

She held her breath. Be calm. *You can move your hand in a moment. He'll settle down.* She rephrased her last thought. *Most of him would settle down.* Unfortunately, his manhood showed no inclination toward settling anywhere. Her eyelids shut tighter.

Without lifting his hand from hers, he kissed her temple. "Tell me what you need. It'll be my pleasure to oblige."

Sensations, too many to count, sparked through her. Her lips quivered with unexpected passion. But no words came.

"Morning, darlin'."

Her eyes opened wide. "I thought—"

"A man would have to be dead not to feel you touching him. And as you discovered, I'm very much alive."

There was no mistaking the boyish mischief dusting his voice. The devil had been awake the entire time. Embarrassment outraced her repressed desires.

She jerked her hand away. "You devil."

"I never pretended to be anything else."

"How could you—"

"Your hand was there first. I only made it a mite more comfortable." He rose up on one arm. She could feel his gaze moving across her skin. "Playing coy isn't your style."

For an instant the scent of warm peaches took her back in time. She imagined his mouth on her wrist, felt his tongue tasting away the juicy sweetness. Their breath crashed together before their cheeks touched.

"How long has it been, Maggie?"

"None of your business."

"That long?"

She'd bet ten acres of oil leases that he'd arched a brow when he asked that question.

"I'm not talking getting laid. How long since a man burned down your barn?"

She kept her cool. What else could she do with her spine flat against the cellar wall? "And how long has it been for you, Latigo?"

His jaw muscle worked against hers. "I'm selective. Some might say I'm picky. I haven't brought you anything that you have to worry about, if that's what you're asking." His lips nuzzled her earlobe. Electric shocks sizzled up and down her neck.

"My fire's stoked. But you already know that."

She thumped the heels of her hands against his chest. The slight separation would give her time to think. No thoughts came. She pressed her arms against the sides of her chest, arching her back to take advantage of the cramped space. Too late, she realized she'd served her breasts to him like a pagan offering.

His fingers stroked her nipples to pouty peaks. "Oh, I miscalculated. Thirty minutes of loving you will never be enough."

"Latigo, I never—"

He silenced her with a lingering kiss. "You're embarrassed about what happened between us."

"No I'm not."

"You can lie to me, but lying to yourself is something else."

"I'm not one of those rodeo Ms. Sparkles."

"You mean the gal at the rodeo?" He traced her jaw with his finger before tilting her head up to his. "You're nothing like her, Maggie. That's why what happened is so special."

"Special? If you think—"

"Don't think." His hand drifted below her waist to the triangle of red-gold curls. "Admit it. You're burning too." His finger delved into the honeycomb, stroking the tight kernel, first on one side then on the other.

She shuddered, lifting her hips in a marked cadence with his touch. Her mind went blank as she wrapped her legs around his wrist keeping his hand exactly where she wanted it to be.

"Feel good?"

Yes. Yes, her body cried. There was only his hand and the sensations she no longer bothered to hide.

"Tell me you're on the pill."

Beneath his deeply-drawn kiss, she shook her head.

"Somehow I figured that."

"I haven't been with anyone in a long time."

"I'm glad." His hands went still. "Trust me. I'll be careful. We'll take it slow. Real slow. We've got all the time in the world." His day-old beard rubbed her cheek, and she felt him smile.

She smiled back, grateful for the chance to catch her breath.

"You smell of peaches, darlin'. Fresh, juicy peaches."

"It's the juice from the broken fruit jars. Didn't you feel the sticky floor?"

Chuckling, he kissed her soundly. "No. I was on top, remember?"

"Yes," she dropped her voice, "I remember."

His arms went around her reverently as if he'd found something he'd lost long ago. He buried his face in her hair, crowning her head with kisses.

"I want it to be good for you." He slipped between her open thighs, palming her with his hand. Her legs went limp while he worked his magic. She bucked against his hand, eager for the fullness of him.

"Say my name."

"Latigo."

"No, my first name."

"Wade."

A bruising thrust taunted her hips before he took what she freely offered. She met him more than halfway, repeating his name.

He thrust deeper. "Say it again."

"Wa-aade."

Heat seeped up like seeking fingers setting her aflame.

She reveled in the fire and, heeding his words, she made no effort to save her barn.

"Anybody down there?" a man's voice called from outside the cellar.

Maggie stirred in Latigo's arms reluctant to move. Beams from flashlights poked through the debris covering the cellar opening.

Blinking, she felt Latigo sit up.

"TJ, is that you?"

The beams of light wavered along the cellar walls.

"You betcha," TJ hollered. "He's over here, fellas."

Holding the chintz material around her, Maggie shot to her knees. The cellar went dark. She rummaged along the cement floor for any sign of her clothes. All she found was one tennis shoe. The sound of other men's voices came from outside. Panic struck. Latigo stood above her. She heard him stepping into his jeans.

"Latigo? My clothes."

"Here, take my shirt. I'll feel around for your jeans. For God's sake watch out for the glass under the shelving."

Letting go of the chintz she'd wrapped around her, she slipped an arm into his oversized shirt. Thank goodness it hung to her thighs affording her some covering.

"Got that city gal down there with you?" TJ asked.

"Yes, Maggie's here," Latigo yelled, getting down on all fours beside her. His voice dropped, "Find anything?"

"My panties must be here somewhere."

"Forget your underwear. Find those jeans," Latigo muttered under his breath.

"I knew it," TJ called. "Shake a leg, fellas. They've

been holed up long enough. Latigo, we're goin' to stick a rope down to you. Wrap it around the wood on the other side and shove it back to me. We're bringing one of the trucks up so we'll be hauling away real soon."

"Gotcha" Latigo answered. Then to Maggie, "Here's your britches. And this." He cleared his throat.

Maggie reached toward his voice and grabbed her jeans and the bra dangling from his other hand. Where were her panties?

"Can you see the rope?" TJ called.

"Yeah." Latigo stood between her and the stairs, shielding her from the light.

There was no sign of her shirt. No sign of panties either.

Six

Where were those panties? The men above would be breaking through to the cellar any minute now. And she'd be standing here—naked. The way news spread in Broken Arrow the whole town would hear about her and Latigo spending the night together before the end of the week. Spending the night together? If the men saw her naked, they'd know she and Latigo hadn't spent the night sleeping.

Shaking her head in frustration, Maggie stepped naked into her jeans and crammed the bra into her back pocket.

"I got the rope," Latigo hollered back to TJ. Still shielding her from the flashlights, Latigo turned his head slightly. "You decent?"

She knotted his shirt around her waist. "I am now."

He started up the stairs yanking more of the rope as TJ had instructed. "Here it comes, TJ." He reached behind him for the end of the rope and shoved it back through a beam of light to the outside.

"Give it a pull, fellas," TJ yelled.

She heard the roar of an engine. Bits of wood and dirt fell around her.

"Maggie, watch out." Latigo came down the stairs, keeping himself between her and the opening. "We could have a cave-in." Panic swelled inside her. She clutched at his arm. "You mean we might be buried down here?"

"Easy. Don't go all crazy on me *now.*"

"Sorry." She slumped against the back wall. The cement blocks were irregular against her spine, the damp cold a welcome relief from the confined humidity. Latigo braced his arms against the wall on either side of her. His bare chest brushed her breasts reminding her of how good his naked skin felt.

"You don't have anything to prove, not to me, Maggie. You've got more grit on deposit than any woman I know."

The outright praise startled her. She wished the flashlights would return so she might see his face. The strobes of light did return after the opening was cleared, but by then all she could think about was getting out of the cellar.

Bright circles haloed around them so she could see the muscled, raw shape of him. Neither of them moved.

"Holding you feels so good, darlin'." She nestled her head against his naked chest listening to the reassuring beat of his heart.

"Hey, you two," TJ called from above, "get a move on."

"Ready?" Latigo asked.

He stepped aside. Blinded momentarily, she stumbled. He caught her arm and held her against his side.

"Cut those damn lights," Latigo hollered.

The cellar went dark except for one beam of light.

"Latigo?" she asked when he released her.

"In a minute."

She did a double take. He took a step and winced.

81

She looked up the stairs toward TJ, then turned suddenly and caught Latigo rubbing his thigh. That fallen log had bruised his already-injured leg. A night sleeping on a cement floor hadn't helped either. Neither had their other activities.

"Are you all right?"

He gave her a surprised look. "What'a you think?"

"I think your leg is killing you."

"Forget it." His knuckles brushed the swell of her breasts as he matched the two remaining buttons with their holes. "You missed some."

What she saw in his eyes was pure agony. "I'm the reason you're hurt. How can I forget?" *Anything,* her heart asked.

He settled one shoulder against the wall, watching her. "Think you're pretty smart, don't you?" he asked.

She lifted her chin. "Go on, you've been wanting to take a poke at me ever since we met. This may be your last chance."

He fisted his hand. "Don't tempt me."

She cringed before she heard the tease in his voice. She looked straight at him. "Well? Take your best shot."

His fist blew by her jaw. "I warned you." He curled his fingers around the back of her neck. Liquid lightning jolted through her. She shivered. Her neck had always been one of her most erotic zones. He reminded her of that with a quick kiss. "We'd best go."

"Give me a minute." She stopped on the bottom step, sat down and slipped on a tennis shoe.

"Here's the other one, catch." He tossed her the mate and she put it on.

"Maybe we should get a doctor to look at you."

He plopped down beside her and pulled on his boots. "What makes you such an expert on pain?"

She'd been right on. His clipped words were a dead giveaway. His leg was killing him. Of course, he'd never admit it. Not him. She tied her shoelaces. *Watching someone else's pain could be far worse than experiencing it.* When they got back to her place he'd find out what she knew about hurting.

"An expert on pain? Me? What could I possibly know about it?" she said smugly.

"Exactly. Get on up those steps," he said, letting humor slip back into his tone. "It's time we got some daylight."

He was covering up, but she'd never let him know that she knew. Instead, she held out her hand to him, but he shook his head.

"I can do it."

His refusal to accept any help hit her with the force of a punch. She sucked in a quick gulp of air. If he heard her reaction he gave no sign of it. Instead he picked up a piece of wood, and held it half-hidden beside his hurting leg. Did he think she didn't see it? She shook her head. Pride. Stupid male pride. She thought again. He was different from the other men she'd known. A genuine throwback to the time when cowboys and Indians rode the flat Oklahoma spaces. Good Lord, if he didn't look like a hero right out of a John Ford Western. She smiled to herself, making sure that her gaze avoided any connection with his ailing leg or the piece of wood he used like a cane.

"Ready?" she asked.

He leaned harder on the wood. "Yes." Limping slightly, he took the stairs one at a time. Halfway up the stairs, she paused giving him time to catch up.

"Keep moving." He hung back leaning on the wood until she cleared the cellar entrance.

Fresh air hit her face. Taking a deep breath, she welcomed it. The air was heavy after the rain. She tasted a trace of red dust on her tongue. Closing her eyes, she took a deeper breath letting the misty breeze wash her cheeks. "Thank you, Lord," she murmured before opening her eyes.

The night made a last turn toward dawn, and the morning sun floated higher along the horizon. The hills and gentle slope of land were eerie in the half-light. The Edwards's house stood alone, the barn and pecan trees had been plucked like wildflowers from the ground.

Latigo stood beside her. His fingertips brushed hers. They'd made it. She grabbed his hand, needing to feel the constant press of his skin upon hers. Part of her rejoiced in the passion they'd shared. The other half of her knew that it would never happen again. She'd see to that. A strange feeling of loss swept over her. His kisses brought her to life like no man's had. If things had been different. Things? she asked. It was more than things she was thinking about. It was them. If there were ever two people with absolutely nothing in common, it was them. There was no use thinking of might-have-beens.

Besides, she'd be leaving in a matter of weeks. She must concentrate on those oil leases, getting the farm ready for sale and seeing that he moved his horses out of her pasture. She had no time for anything else. That stack of unpaid medical bills dictated the course she had to follow. She and Latigo might be neighbors, but they'd always be on opposite sides of an issue.

"Well, will you look at that?" TJ motioned toward the

lone pitchfork, stuck in the ground. "Wonder how that got there?"

She turned and looked up at Latigo. She heard his makeshift cane hit the ground. He bracketed her face with his hands, letting his palms surround the curve of her cheeks. "Pitchforks can be dangerous. Mighty dangerous except in the right hands."

Men scurried around them, some of them slapping Latigo's back. One of them draped a jacket over Latigo's shoulders, then nodded to her politely. Latigo thanked the cowboy, calling him by name, but never took his eyes from her face.

"No woman should look so good in the morning." His smile was as slow and easy as his words. Straightforward without pretense, his tone caught her off guard. She never knew what he'd come up with next. He had more facets than a Rubik's cube. And to think that she'd once thought this cowboy would be simple to figure out.

Someone turned on a truck's headlights and they were suddenly bathed like a golden wedding band in a circle of light. He looked tired. His bloodshot eyes testified to that. She sighed and let her shoulders slump. They both were exhausted. When they should've been sleeping they'd been otherwise occupied. She refused to be more specific about the activity they'd been engaging in. Her practical side suggested she think about *that* later.

He tipped his head in the direction of the closest truck. "Shall we?"

Her thoughts flew home. "TJ, did you go by my house?"

"Yes, ma'am. No need to fret. It's standing straight as always, and your pa and little girl are fine."

85

Walking toward the truck, Maggie said another silent prayer.

"They're mighty anxious about you though," TJ continued. "I promised your pa I'd get you home pronto." Then to the men clearing away the last of the debris from the cellar's opening. "That's all we can do here. I'll stop by Nighthorse's place."

"And the Nighthorses' house?" Maggie asked about her other neighbor.

"Same as yours, still standing." TJ slid behind the truck's steering wheel. "Bet you two could use a drink." He reached behind the bench seat and pulled out an army-style canteen. "Whiskey'll have to wait till later, boss."

Latigo opened the truck door and Maggie stepped up into the cab. TJ unscrewed the cap, wiped the lid with his hand, and passed the canteen to her. The cap swinging by a chain banged against her hand. She glanced up at Latigo.

"You drink first." Latigo paused, distracted by the pile of wood being hauled alongside of the truck. She tracked his gaze, focusing her attention on a branch and the lacy bit of white fluttering in the breeze.

My panties. Maggie tightened her grip on the canteen. Good Lord, don't let anyone see them. God must've been listening because the cowboys, looking straight ahead, kept pulling on the rope wrapped around the branches.

"I see them." Latigo moved from the cab and fell into step behind the men. He grabbed the wisp of lace and stuffed it into his jeans pocket. Without a word, he sauntered back to the truck and slid onto the seat beside her.

Thank you, she mouthed silently. He only smiled. From his casual expression, no one would ever guess

86

what he just saved her from. Finally relaxed, she took two big gulps of water. She never knew how good a mouthful of spring water could taste. She took another drink and handed Latigo the canteen.

Latigo reached across her and flipped on the air conditioner. A blast of hot air hit her square in the face, followed quickly by a cooler flow. Maggie tilted her head to one side and let the cooler air hit her neck. "That feels so-ooo wonderful."

"Bet biscuits and a swirl of country gravy would set real good about now." TJ started the engine and headed the truck downhill.

Right on cue, her stomach growled.

"Guess I called that right," TJ chuckled before all three of them laughed.

"I've never had biscuits and gravy for breakfast," she said.

"I knew there was a good reason I never hankered to see Frisco. You'll have to drop by for a dip of my cream gravy." TJ double pumped the clutch and shifted on the fly. The truck responded instantly.

"You cook?" she asked.

"Some might say otherwise," TJ kidded, stomping the clutch again. "Right, boss?"

"Not around me, they don't." Latigo took another drink and passed the canteen back to her. Maggie gulped down more water, letting it drip freely over her chin and down her neck. Oh, to soak in a tub and wash off some of the grit she felt caking her skin. She handed Latigo the canteen. He screwed on the cap and let the jug fall to the floor between his legs.

"Find anything to eat in that cellar?" TJ asked.

"Only Mrs. Edwards's canned peaches," Latigo answered. "We made out fine."

She bit her lip. In spite of drinking the water, her mouth still tasted of peaches and . . . and his kisses. She concentrated on the road ahead, trying to ignore what the taste of peaches brought to her mind.

The sun steamed the wet blades of grass an eye-taking yellow. She'd never seen a more breathtaking sunrise or a more welcome one. Back home, the city buildings blocked out most of the San Francisco sky. Here the flat of the land allowed the sun to spread out far and wide like a path of wild honey.

About a half mile down the road she saw the borrowed truck she'd been driving. It was sitting upside down in a fenced patch of ground. She managed to stifle the gasp. Replacing a truck wasn't one of her priorities. Well, it was now.

"Glad you weren't driving that rig, Miss Maggie. Don't you worry none. The boys will set it right," TJ said. "We're mighty lucky. The twister never set down, just stirred things up a bit with her tail. A female is apt to do that sometimes." TJ cleared his throat. "Pardon me, Miss Maggie. I misspoke myself."

Not wanting him to think she was offended, she let TJ see her smile. "That's all right. I'm grateful that's the only wiggle she made."

"Appears there were a heap of things blowing and going," Latigo added, straight faced. "How's the stock?" he asked, leaning forward.

TJ shook his head. "Scattered some, but we'll start rounding 'em up now that we've located you, boss."

"And Dollar?" Latigo asked, sliding his left arm along the rim of the bench seat. Heat from his naked skin seeped through the chambray shirtsleeve, melting down her upper arm and gathering in her elbow.

"Dollar trotted home to fill his belly," TJ said. "By the by, we found your saddle in that chewed-up pasture over there, figured you were holed up somewhere close to the Edwards place."

"I can always count on you, old rooster." Retrieving the canteen from between his legs, Latigo unscrewed the cap and took a long gulp.

"Went by Nighthorse's farm," TJ continued. "He lost his barn." TJ glanced back over his shoulder. "And from the looks of that stack of wood the men hauled away, it appears that you two were sleeping under most of it last night." TJ threw back his head and laughed heartily. "Ole Edwards may meet his barn on the road back from Arkansas."

"Trucks and barns can be replaced. It's the land that matters. It'll still be here long after Maggie and I are nothing but red dust," Latigo said.

"What makes you think I'll be around that long?" she asked.

He started to answer her, but one of the tires jumped a rut throwing the truck sharply to the left. Maggie grabbed Latigo's leg to keep from sliding into TJ. Latigo snapped his legs together trapping her hand between his thighs.

"The thought came to me, kind of sudden like." His powerful legs squeezed tighter before he relaxed them, freeing her hand. His palm cupped her shoulder keeping her snugly against him. "The best things happen that way sometimes."

He took such delight in the double-entendre. Oil leases or no oil leases, how could she resist laughing? No way.

She relaxed a moment before other thoughts filled her head. "TJ, when did you see Dad?"

"Went by last night after the dust cleared and again this morning, Miss Maggie," TJ said. "Your pa said Latigo took off looking for you. Your phone lines are dead, but you got lights and electricity. Nighthorse lost his barn, but his phone works. Long as I live, I'll never be able to figure these twisters."

"Nighthorse can't afford to rebuild that barn," Latigo said, staring out the truck's window.

"Guess we'll kick up a little barn raising, boss." TJ looked at Latigo.

"Sounds fine." Latigo smiled.

"I'll just check into that. Miss Maggie, you ever been to a barn raising?" TJ asked.

"No."

"We'll be expecting you to fry up something special. Bet you're a good cook, coming from Frisco and all," TJ added.

She hadn't the heart to tell him that since Dad's heart attack, frying wasn't a method in anything she cooked anymore. "I can hold my own."

Latigo pulled her closer, whispering, "I'll vouch for that."

He did more than hold his own, she thought shamelessly. Although her sexual experiences were limited to fewer than the fingers on one hand. She smiled to herself. When it came to lovemaking, for once in her practical life Maggie Callahan had had the very best—Wade Latigo.

TJ stared straight ahead. "Almost there, Miss Maggie."

She leaned closer to the dashboard. "Faster, TJ. Faster."

"Hit it, TJ. The lady's in a powerful hurry." Latigo pulled her back. "Keep your nose away from the windshield. This road is tore up. There's no telling where we might land." His arm tightened around her shoulders.

They rode the rest of the mile in silence. When the truck started over the last hill before home, she leaned forward again. The truck faltered. TJ shifted into low and jammed the gas pedal to the floor. The truck lurched and crested the rise.

She strained her eyes, barely able to make out the pitch of the green shingled roof. "It's there. The house, it's there."

TJ aimed the truck straight ahead and over a grassy pasture, cutting the distance in half. "Sure enough, just like I left her."

The white siding of the thirties bungalow came into view. It was the prettiest thing Maggie had ever seen. "Latigo." Her voice cracked. "Nothing ever shines as bright as the lights of home."

"Nothing but your smile," Latigo said.

Tears clouded her eyes when he pulled her tenderly against his side. It was a place as familiar as this morning's kisses. A safe harbor far from any storm. She felt warm. Most of all she felt safe, as safe as she'd felt with him in the cellar.

"Let 'em go, darlin'," Latigo said. "You've earned it."

She sat upright. "I won't cry. I've got to see Jenny and Dad first."

The truck swept up behind the house.

"Well, get ready because we're here." Latigo opened the truck's door and stepped out. She jumped to the ground beside him. She wanted desperately to run up the stairs and see for herself that everyone she loved in the world was safe.

"Go. Don't wait on me." Latigo clenched his teeth.

"Nothing doing. We're going to walk into that house together. There's somebody I want you to meet."

Seven

The screen door banged behind them, and they stumbled from the porch into the kitchen. Maggie blinked at the ceiling light reflecting off the newly-painted white walls. As she expected, Latigo hung back, nervously dusting off his boots on the back of his pant legs.

"Is that my Maggie?" her father called, the relief unmistakable. "We're in the living room."

Her gaze darted from Latigo toward the door. With a lift of his chin, he urged her to go. Before Maggie could move, her father came around the corner of the refrigerator. Only a head taller than she, he worked his bandy legs twice as fast as most men to cover half the ground.

Her father paused, a grin on his ruddy face. "I knew if anyone could find you, Latigo would." In two choppy strides Dad was beside her, smothering her in a huge bear hug. He stepped away and stared down into her face. "You okay?"

She nodded, fighting with all her might to hold back the tears.

"How can I ever thank you, Latigo?" her father said. Maggie heard the slap of a handshake before she turned and watched the two men pumping each other's arms. With a wave of his hand, her father motioned behind her.

"And," Dad continued, "look who's been waiting for her mommy."

Maggie's breath faltered in her throat while she watched her daughter shuffle forward, her strawberry-blond curls swinging in sync with the braces supporting each of her legs.

From behind her, Maggie heard the sharp intake of Latigo's breath. When she'd first heard him mention pain she knew he never suspected how well she knew it, too. As with him, pain was her constant companion. Only, Maggie shared the second-hand pain with the most precious person in her life.

"Jenny." Kneeling, Maggie showered the heart-shaped face with kisses, whispering, "Grandpa took good care of you like I knew he would."

"We hid in the fraidy hole," Jenny bragged. "Grandpa promised me rainbow sherbet 'cause I didn't cry, not even once."

Hugging her daughter, Maggie let the tears come. "I guess I won't get any sherbet." She took a strand of Jenny's hair and inhaled the smell of sunshine before kissing it. "And rainbow is my favorite, too."

"You can have some, Mommy. But, you'll have to wash your hands first," Jenny scolded, imitating Maggie with a wagging finger. "And you'll have to wash, too, mister. If you want sherbet. That's a Callahan rule." Jenny held up her hands, flexing the tiny fingers so Maggie could see the chipped pink nail polish. "See? All clean."

Latigo nodded, looking unsure and hesitant, as Maggie

had never seen him before. How well Maggie knew the feeling. Seeing a child in braces did that to people.

"What's your name, mister?" Jenny asked.

"I'm sorry, Latigo." Maggie got to her feet and took Jenny's hand. "This is Jenny Callahan, my daughter."

Latigo's eyes looked shiny. If Maggie didn't know better she'd have thought a sudden wash of tears had overtaken him, too. *Cowboys cry? Don't kid yourself. He may be a sucker for a child, but cry? No way.*

Maggie shook her head, her attention dead set on his pale face. Finally he understood why she needed the money those oil leases would bring. Perhaps now he had some inkling about the pain she felt every time she watched Jenny struggle for each step.

Latigo plowed his fingers through his hair. "Glad to make your acquaintance, Jenny. Your mother told me about you." He glanced quickly at Maggie. "But she left a few things out." Then almost a whisper, "Appears I owe you another apology."

She'd been awaiting Latigo's reaction when he came face to face with the reason why she needed the money those oil leases would bring. She'd looked forward to it almost as much as getting out of that cellar. So why was the moment so bittersweet?

Jenny tugged on Maggie's jeans. "What's an *apawogy,* Mommy?"

Latigo leveled his eyes back to Maggie. "It's saying you're sorry when you've misjudged somebody." He stooped and in one quick motion scooped Jenny up into his arms. "It's saying that *I'm* sorry for what I said."

Maggie blinked twice, reeling from the unexpected admission.

Jenny leaned back and the shifting weight threw Latigo

95

momentarily off balance. He grabbed for the kitchen counter. Pain stabbed at her heart. He could've reached for her. She'd offered to help him before. After all they'd been through why couldn't he accept her help?

"We almost fell down, didn't we, Mister Latigo?" Jenny asked.

"Yes, I guess we did."

"I fall lots." Jenny patted Latigo's cheek. "It's not so bad."

"Isn't it?" His voice cracked.

"No, 'cause I got Mommy." Jenny's moist pat smudged the dirt on Latigo's cheek. "I'm lucky. Mommy showed me how to get up all by myself, so I can try again."

"You are lucky, Jenny." Latigo hauled Maggie against his side, leaning on her slightly. She felt as if she'd finally stepped into the sunlight after being trapped below ground for a long, long time. In her heart, she knew the trapped feeling had nothing to do with any cellar. Welcoming the pain in her shoulder, she swung her arm around his waist.

"Pretty soon," Jenny babbled, "the doctor said I could maybe walk, like the other kids do."

"Then we'll have to make certain that the doctor keeps that promise." Latigo cleared his throat. "In the meantime, you're not going to hold this storm against Oklahoma, are you?"

"Nope." Jenny touched his cheek again seemingly fascinated by his two-day beard.

"Ever thought about being a cowgirl?"

"You mean like riding a for-real horse?" Jenny's hand flattened against Latigo's beard.

"When you ride you can move as fast as anybody." Latigo hitched Jenny higher against his chest.

96

The statement hit Maggie straight in the heart. No wonder he kept riding. It was the one place he could be the equal of any man.

The joy faded from Jenny's face. "Mommy doesn't like horses. One hurt her toe."

Latigo flinched. "What?"

Maggie tucked her left foot safely behind her right one. "It happened a long time ago. A horse stepped back and cut off part of my toe." His gaze locked on her face, but she avoided looking at him. "It was my fault. As you might've guessed, I wore sandals that day. The horse stepped back and cut off part of a toe. My second toe, left foot to be exact."

"So that's why you fought me when I pulled you up onto old Dollar? You're full of secrets, aren't you?"

Maggie shrugged, knowing he was still reeling from the sight of Jenny's braces.

"Well, Jenny, I've got just the horse for you and . . ." Latigo eyed Maggie slyly.

"Is the animal toothless and lame?" Maggie asked.

"Not quite, but he sure likes strutting for the ladies. What do you think, Mommy? If the doctor says it's okay, I'm sure I can rig something up so Jenny can ride safely." He arched a brow. "You might even step up onto him yourself."

"You know how I feel about horses."

"Do I, or is there anything else that you've neglected to tell me?"

"No, that's the whole story."

"Good." He squeezed Maggie closer. "Now what do you say, Mommy? Are you going to let Jenny be a real Oklahoma cowgirl?" He whispered in Maggie's ear, "Or are you going to saddle Jenny with *your* fear?"

Maggie's spine straightened. She'd always prided herself on Jenny's courage feeling it was somehow an extension of her own way of dealing with life's unfairness.

"Could I Mommy?"

"I don't know, Jenny. Mr. Latigo has a place of his own and—"

"Plee-eez. Can I, Mommy? Can I?"

"We'll see."

"Let's vote on it?" Jenny asked, looking over Latigo's shoulder at her grandfather. "Right, Grandpa?"

"That has been the custom, Maggie," her father said.

Maggie could see she'd be outvoted. "I know when I'm beaten. If it's not too much trouble for Mr. Latigo, I guess we can give it a try after we check with the doctor."

"Hurrah! Did you hear that Grandpa? I'm going to learn to ride a horse."

"I heard, young lady," her grandfather said.

"Thank you, Mr. Latigo." A nod was all Maggie could muster when Jenny planted a wet kiss on Latigo's smile-swollen cheek.

"You're welcome, Jenny. As long as we're going to be riding together maybe your mother will let you call me Latigo." His gaze wandered back to Maggie.

"I think that'll be fine," Maggie conceded.

He set Jenny down, holding onto her until she was steady on her feet. "Think I'd better be on the lookout for TJ. He should be back from Nighthorses' about now."

"You and TJ have been exceptionally kind to us," her father said, slapping Latigo on the shoulder. "Come by soon."

"I'd ask you to stay and eat, but you must be anxious to get home," Maggie said. Somewhere off in the distance she heard her dad and Jenny arguing the benefits of scrambled eggs versus poached.

"I'll hold you to that invite." Latigo feigned a salute. "Your Jenny makes friends quickly," he added as Maggie walked him toward the back door.

"We could be friends, too," Maggie said.

Leaning down to her he guided her through the open door and onto the screened porch. "We're long past friends or have you forgotten last night?"

"No, I haven't forgotten, but I'd hoped maybe *we* could try."

"Making love isn't something I take lightly."

"I don't expect hearts and flowers."

He dug a boot heel into a crack in the wooden flooring of the screened porch. "Meaning what exactly?"

She watched his temper rise a notch. "We didn't make love, Latigo. We had sex."

He jerked his boot back flicking off bits of gray paint.

"You want me to say everything between us has changed, but I won't." She picked at the loose button on her shirt—his shirt. She had her priorities: Jenny came first; getting the farm fixed up and ready for a fast sale came second. She quickly added repairing Nighthorse's damaged truck to the list. Four weeks, max, that's all the time she had. "Last night was a one-time thing."

He grabbed her suddenly, yanking her closer. "Let's get something straight." His hand relaxed, stroking the wrinkled crease in the cotton shirt. She made no move to stop him from touching her even when he slipped his hand beneath the upturned collar and massaged her neck, kneading the tight cords until her eyes closed and her head fell back.

"Look at me, Maggie."

99

She snapped to attention. Her head erect. Her eyes wide. "I'm not some blonde who follows the rodeo."

"Thought we already covered that ground. You and that rodeo blonde TJ nicknamed Ms. Sparkles, have nothing in common."

Neither do we, she thought. "I won't be another Ms. Sparkles, Latigo. I'd rather go back to feeling nothing."

"You, not feel?" His thumb traced the line of her jaw as casually as if he'd done it a hundred times before.

"Don't you dare make light of this." She batted his hand away and stepped in front of him.

"Why not? You are."

"Wrong. I'm trying to be realistic. Adult. What happened, happened. Each of us has our own reasons why."

He started to speak, but she covered his mouth with her hand. His lips opened wider and he spoke her name before she felt the unmistakable stroke of his tongue trace the lifeline on her palm.

Her eyes drifted shut allowing her emotions to race free like a wild Oklahoma wind. In her mind she was in his arms again feeling the slippery friction of their damp bodies while they made love. All right, she admitted, they'd made love. If it had been just once, it might've been called sex, but the second time? The second time had definitely been lovemaking. Her head buzzed with a dizziness that had nothing to do with hunger. She snatched her hand away from his mouth and held onto the screen door for support. "I asked for that."

"Did you?" Any sign of anger had long since vanished, and for an instant she saw herself mirrored in his eyes. Eyes that looked younger suddenly. He leaned closer. Her heart did a funny double skip making her breath come in ragged jerks. He was going to kiss her. Until this moment, she'd only imagined how he looked when they kissed. The darkness of the cellar had robbed her of that vision. Now blessed by the morning light, she could see him: See the way he angled his head; See the gun-metal gray eyes deepen to black. Was it only passion, or was it another emotion she saw there?

Before she could answer, his face, inches from hers, blurred. She closed her eyes and waited. He took her head between his palms and she felt the wet heat as he centered a single kiss on her forehead. It hadn't been the kiss she'd expected, but oddly enough, she wasn't disappointed. They'd never agree about the oil leases or much else, but at least he didn't hate her.

He stepped away, but his hand stayed possessively on her waist. "Admit you're embarrassed by your responses when we kiss." So that's why he kissed her forehead instead of her mouth. He was testing her like a teacher does a prized pupil. "I've never done that kind of thing with a . . . a stranger."

"There's no right and wrong when it comes to feelings. You set me back on my heels when you frenched me back—"

"I did not."

"Does it matter who did what first now, darlin'? We shared more than a cellar. A heap more." He smiled down at her, warming her like noontime sunshine, and it was barely daylight. "When you're throwed at the rodeo they call it hitting iron bars and concrete. We hit iron and concrete."

That aptly described the breathlessness she felt right now. She stayed in his arms feeling as if they'd been apart for a long time. She wished she could reach up to stroke his hair, feel its texture, and let it curl about her fingers like it curled about his collar. The intimacy of the sudden urge shocked her almost as much as when he pulled away. All thought of touching him died in the chill outside his arms.

"We got plenty to talk about." His hand gripped her elbow. She knew he regretted talking so freely about feelings. He didn't share that part of himself easily; neither did she. Yes, they'd shared more than physical intimacy last night. They'd held one another, first in fear, then in spontaneous rejoicing that they were alive. More alive, she suspected, than either one of them had ever felt.

"Talk?" Before she could think of why he was being so candid with her now, he looped his arm around her, resting the heel of his hand upon her shoulder. She winced as she had when she'd braced her shoulder against the pitchfork, biting back the pain that shot up her arm to the spot beneath his hand.

He frowned down at her before jerking his hand away. "What is it? I hardly touched you."

Her eyes met his, then hers skittered away in the opposite direction. He slanted over her and ran his fingertip gently along her collarbone.

She stiffened. Don't let him see the pain. His hand dipped over her back, grazing her shoulder. The bruised shoulder protested, but she stared through the pain, willing herself to get lost once more in the ever-changing shade of his smoky gray eyes.

"At first I thought you flinched because you didn't want me to touch you, but it's something else, isn't it?"

"No." Her curt answer came quickly, too quickly. He didn't believe her for a minute.

"You're hurt. Here." He tested the movement of her shoulder with a gentle nudge.

She flinched again.

His hand froze in midair. "Maggie, when did you do this?"

"I suppose it was the falling tree."

"Like hell, it was."

She watched him rethinking what'd happened when the lightning frightened her, and she'd run into the trees. She felt like a foolish coward all over again.

"You should've told me." He touched her shoulder once more, and she nipped her tongue with her teeth to keep from crying out. All she could do was shake her head.

"It's swollen. So swollen. I can feel the heat through this shirt." He dropped his head, replacing his hand with the moist heat of his mouth. "And you're such a tiny thing." His breath puffed through the cottony weave spreading out like a hundred fleeting kisses against her naked skin. Only the silky curtain of her hair kept their cheeks from touching when he raised his face to hers.

"We should let a doctor get a look at this." His fingertip scored the shirt yoke, the touch barely perceptible. The gesture was so unconsciously pure, it sent her emotions spinning off in every direction.

"My shoulder is stiff. That's all." She rotated her arm to prove her point.

"Really?" He pulled the unbuttoned collar of her shirt wider revealing her shoulder. "Good lord, darlin'. You got a bruise here the size of a pancake. Why in hell didn't you say something?"

His touch was gentle, soothing away most of the ache. "It happened when you braced your shoulder against that pitchfork to keep it from busting my leg."

No use lying any longer when he could see the truth for himself, she reasoned.

He closed his eyes and rocked back on his heels. "I should've figured you'd hurt yourself."

"Wait. Quit blaming yourself." She blushed freely before sharing the guarded secret. "To tell you the truth, I didn't feel the pain until this morning."

Surprise mellowed his frown into a wry smile. "Me either. Guess we were both distracted."

Their eyes met and held.

"I'm not kidding myself, darlin'. Another time, another place, you wouldn't give this cowboy a second look."

No? You could be wrong, Latigo. "I bet a city woman has never been your type either?"

"You got that nailed." He chuckled. "And you've never made love with a man you hardly knew, have you?"

Did he have to keep bringing that up? She started to answer, but a shake of his head silenced her.

"If I had any question about what kind of a woman you are Maggie Callahan, seeing you here with Jenny put them all to rest. Right about now, I figure you're breaking out in a bad case of the guilts."

"Guilt? Maybe. But if you're waiting for me to say everything has changed, you've got a long wait. What happened last night in the cellar was a one-time thing."

"A two-time thing, as I recall."

Heat rose to her cheeks, and she snapped the loose button from the front of the shirt she wore and stuffed it into the pocket. She'd sew it on tomorrow. And the days in between when she saw him again? What would she do then? Her practical side kicked into gear. Four weeks. Four weeks. Four weeks. That's how long she'd be in Oklahoma. She had plenty to keep her busy, and if he did stop by she'd see to it that they were never alone again. Yes, that ought to do it, no use testing her resistance further.

A random thought escaped her lips, "I keep remembering that blonde at the rodeo and I feel cheap and . . ."

"You can put more tangles in a man's rope faster than any woman I've ever met." He fisted one hand, then flexed the fingers open.

She jutted her chin his way, trying to cover her feelings.

He fisted his hand again. Her stomach cringed, but she looked him straight in the eye. Before she knew it, his hands were in her hair, his fingers idly shifting the long strands back from her cheeks. The pads of his fingertips stroked her temples, until he tilted her face up to his.

"You make me laugh, too. Not many women can do that." The corners of his eyes crinkled when he smiled. Here was a man completely comfortable in his skin, and a borrowed jacket with the sleeves four inches too short.

As if he'd read her thoughts, his grin widened.

God help her, she was a pushover for that lopsided grin.

"You even make the pain in my leg go away."

She hoped he'd kiss her, one last time. It wouldn't change the way things were going to end, but the headlights from the approaching truck killed any chance of a kiss.

"This ain't my first time at the rodeo, darlin'. I learned the difference between having sex and making love a long time ago."

"So did I."

"Wrong, darlin'. You're dead wrong." He glanced at the approaching truck. "There isn't much time. TJ will be here in a minute. I'm going to ask you a question. Do us both a favor and think real hard before you answer it." He never blinked once when he asked, "Is forgetting all that you want from me, Maggie?"

What else could she say without complicating both of their lives? Having sex with Latigo, a man she hardly knew, destroyed any chance for a normal friendship. There was no changing that. Her uncle's will made them neighbors until the farm was sold. Beyond that, they had no future together. Another time, another place, who knows? No, they were too different. Besides, what man in his right mind would consider starting a relationship with a single mother with a handicapped daughter? Relationship? What gave her the idea that he was talking about a relationship? He wanted to get her into his bed. That's all. She met his stare boldly. "Yes. I want you to forget what happened."

He kicked the screen door open and started down the stairs to the truck. Before he got to the bottom step, he hollered back, "Fine. You want me to forget what happened? You got it, lady."

Eight

Would Maggie show?

Latigo glanced over at Nighthorse's north pasture where most of the folks who'd come for the barn raising had parked. It had been four days since he'd stormed off her porch riled at being rejected like a chute-crazy bronc. He was crazy all right. He could admit that now. He'd been turned down by women before. What man hadn't? He pulled his hat lower until the leather band lining the inside crunched against his eyebrows. It galled him to admit, he'd never been turned down *after* he'd made love to a woman.

Day before yesterday, TJ delivered that borrowed truck to Maggie's father. The tornado had added more dents to the truck's hood, but the engine ran fine.

Latigo had purposely kept himself too busy working with Blue, the horse he felt would be perfect for Jenny's first ride. After all, he had promised Jenny. Maggie was too caring a mother to let the harsh words they'd exchanged prevent Jenny from learning how to ride. Besides, he reasoned, the promise was made to the daughter, *not* the mother. If Maggie objected, he knew Jenny would point that out. So when TJ mentioned that the truck was ready to be driven over to the Callahans', Latigo had the perfect excuse—he was getting the saddle rigging set up for Jenny's riding lesson. TJ gave him a questioning look and said he would take the truck over to the Callahans' himself.

Actually, the carefully crafted plan had worked out better than even he figured, Latigo thought smugly. When TJ delivered the truck, he told Maggie about the barn raising. Her father promised that they'd be here. What else could she do? Nighthorse had lent them the truck, and it was his barn they were rebuilding.

So, cowboy, if the plan worked so well, where is she?

Everybody else that lived in Broken Arrow was here. The Tulsa suburb had plenty to celebrate. The tornado caused only minor damage except for flattening Edwards's and Nighthorse's barns. They'd rebuild those barns. That everyone agreed upon. On oil drilling, the community split 70/30 with Latigo's opinion carrying the short end. Most folks prayed for another oil boom. A boom he hoped never materialized.

The picnic tables were set end to end in a giant rectangle under the pecan trees, leaving a wide open space in the middle for the fiddle players. There'd be country music come sundown—the type of music he was certain wasn't Maggie's style. He wondered if she knew that a barn raising was an all-day affair? No matter. There'd be plenty of time to relax later for those who cared to stay. By then he was certain she'd be long gone. If she ever stopped by at all.

His gaze searched the far horizon. The land always survived somehow. He focused on the black silhouette of a deserted oil rig. His jaw clenched. Those damn

108

drillers, he'd like to run all of them out of town, out of Oklahoma. All except Maggie, that is. Now that he understood why she needed the money made all the difference. There were other ways to make money off the land: leasing pasture land for grazing; leasing for crops. He'd managed to do it himself, but now the land values were at an all-time low. Her land wasn't going to be so easy to sell.

He could offer to buy a few acres bordering his own place. Then again why should he help her leave? He went as cold as a banker's heart. *Playing it a mite tough aren't you?* That's right. *Selfish down to your spurs.* Isn't that the way she wanted it? No emotion. No remembering what had passed between them. It was her call, not his.

Dealing with Five Star Oil was her call, too. Everyone knew Five Star's shady reputation. He knew better than most.

He scratched his chin thoughtfully. From what he'd seen the other morning, she had fixed up the old house. Her farm would make a sweet addition to his own holdings. The farm might sell fast. Too fast to suit him. He wanted to know Maggie Callahan better. Much, much better and it had nothing to do with lovemaking.

Say what, cowboy? He shook his head. All right, all right. The way he responded to her as a woman had plenty to do with everything. Whether she admitted it or not, their lovemaking had changed their lives forever.

He slapped his hat against his thigh in disgust before setting it squarely on his head. Her views on oil drilling only muddied the water. They could get by that. She was a reasonable woman. Surely she could see that once she signed, the oil company had access to the property and access meant roads scarring the land. The land had to be protected.

His land most of all. He wasn't about to let some Johnny-come-lately city gal spoil all that he'd worked for. He had more than broken bones and silver belt buckles to show for the years on the rodeo circuit. No woman alive could change the way he felt about Five Star Oil.

"Ready on your end?" one of the men called his way.

"Almost." Latigo bent over the frame of two-by-fours and stuck three nails between his teeth, reached for a fourth and starting hammering. When he ran out of nails, he straightened up and dipped his hand into the carpenter's apron pocket for more. There were plenty of nails, but he took his time sorting through them, all the while watching for any sign of her truck.

He could see the road from Callahan's. Nothing. Finally, he had to resume hammering or risk one of the men noticing his divided attention. He worked quickly so he could straighten and make another nail selection. He sunk his left hand into the apron pocket and grabbed a fistful. He stuffed a nail between his lips and squinted for one last look. There was still no sign of them except—his eyes focused hard on a small dust ball rolling toward Nighthorse's place. Hallelujah!

"Going to take a break, fellas." He didn't bother looking back at the neighbors working on the wall frame.

"Sure thing. We got this one," a man called.

"I'll only be a minute." Latigo moved to the shade of the nearest river birch and leaned against the tree watching the ball of dust fatten around the approaching truck.

He glanced at his watch. It seemed like hours before the truck pulled into the pasture and came to a stop. Maggie stepped out of the cab and reached back to help

110

Jenny. His attention fastened onto the stiff legs beneath Jenny's jeans. Legs held tightly between her metal braces. Neither Jenny nor Maggie took any notice of the braces. He marveled at the way they worked together.

Selling the drilling rights to Maggie's property was one way of getting the quick cash needed for Jenny's operation. The fact that Maggie was part of the seventy percent in favor of oil drilling didn't seem such a big issue right now. He felt too much like a heel to think about issues. He could make her an offer for her farm. But when it came to cash he'd learned a long time ago to leave his heart at home. Besides, he reassured himself, a woman as practical as Maggie carried medical insurance to help cover the hospital and doctor bills.

Being a foundling made him supersensitive about kids. He bet Maggie was the same. So he'd best watch his step and keep any advice about her finances and Jenny to himself. Jenny wasn't his daughter, and her mother would be the first one to remind him of that. If she were he'd do anything to see that she'd get a shot at running like the other kids. He understood it was a mother's love that drove Maggie to dealing with Five Star. Understanding was a far piece from approving.

A gust of brash wind kicked up, fluttering the hem on Maggie's flowered skirt. Even from where he stood, he could see the white edge of her slip, and even more important, he got his first look at the bend of her knee. He'd always been a leg man. He liked what he saw. Latigo swallowed hard when she knelt beside her daughter and adjusted something on the side of one of Jenny's braces.

"Jenny, can you carry the potato salad?" Maggie asked, walking to the back of the truck. "On second thought, why don't you take the garlic bread."

"Then they'll know that I made it," Jenny bragged.

"They'll know because I'm going to tell them," Maggie's father said, picking up a box Latigo could see was filled with covered bowls of food.

Latigo took a quick step toward them, then thought better of offering to help. Maggie might not appreciate the gesture, after the way they'd parted.

Her father waved at Nighthorse's wife and unchained the truck's tailgate. Nighthorse's son, the tall one home from Oklahoma State University, hurried down the hill and took the large bowl from Maggie. Nice manners, son, Latigo thought.

In a matter of seconds the box of food was sitting on top of a bright red checkered tablecloth, the Nighthorse kid went back to hammering, and the Callahans split into three: Jenny joined Jimmy Lee Thompson, the boy Latigo had met at the Junior Rodeo; Maggie's father picked up one end of wood and carried it to the man working the power saw; and Maggie? Where was she? An unfamiliar rush of panic gripped his gut right behind the wad of nails in his carpenter's apron.

"Damn," he swore, catching sight of Maggie's flowered skirt before she disappeared into the house.

Latigo had no choice but to return to his hammering. The dullest hour of his life passed. Oh, the progress on the barn went great. His progress, especially when it came to seeing Maggie, well, that added up to a big zero.

He took out his frustrations by hammering three times as many nails as the rest of the crew. He kept his head down, sinking one nail after another until he heard a commotion.

"We thought you'd forgotten about us, ladies," a man hollered when Maggie and three neighbor women came out of the house carrying water pitchers and a tray of glasses. The two ladies seemed content to stay on the flat, it was Maggie who ventured up the hill toward where Latigo stood. She'd tied a wide denim apron around her waist and stuffed a stack of paper cups into one pocket.

Latigo felt elated that she'd broken away until she finally looked his way and her mouth dropped open. Hell, she hadn't seen him at all. He covered his disappointment and touched the brim of his hat in greeting. She gathered her composure and nodded. Dropping his hammer onto the ground at his feet, he waited.

And waited.

And waited.

He rubbed his chin impatiently while his boot ticked off the minutes. Clean shaven, he'd taken extra care with his beard this morning, even used a new blade. He drew the wide brim of his straw Stetson lower over his eyes so he could watch her every move without being caught staring. After a few moments he realized she wasn't going to look his way again.

Still he waited.

She watered every other man, refilling their outstretched cups as many times as they wanted. Chatting and smiling as if she had nothing else on her mind, she kept the dammed jug balanced on her hip. That rounded swaying hip he'd come to know by touch and taste. He remember all too clearly the way her belly pillowed his head, the way she gasped when his mouth and tongue explored her tenderest parts. His breath raced like a banged-tail stallion about to dance with his favorite mare.

You really are into pain, aren't you, cowboy? a tiny voice nagged from inside his head.

Into pain?

No.

Interested in Maggie Callahan?

You bet.

Still, it riled him that she'd made him wait. She poured the last of the men their water and slowly lifted her head and looked straight at him.

Guess what, cowboy? It's your turn.

It took a couple of tries before his widening grin coaxed a smile from her. The answering smile was definitely worth the wait, so was she. She walked up the hill and into the shade where he stood.

The sun sure felt blistering today. Latigo wiped the sweat from his forehead with a bright blue kerchief. The shade from the scanty birch leaves was meager, but a welcome relief.

She stopped right in front of him looking like a sweet-tipped daffodil in a field of puny daisies. The banged-tail stallion inside of him raced faster. *Something is going on between us, darlin',* he thought. *I'm not certain what to call it, but I like the way it feels.*

"I wondered when you'd get around to me."

"There were a few men ahead of you."

"No problem." He stuffed the kerchief into his back pocket. "Patience is my middle name. I'm willing to wait."

The wind came up behind her, lifting her hair forward, framing her face. He'd had it in his mind that her hair was more red, but today in the sunlight it looked more golden. Whatever the color, he liked the way it whipped against her cheeks. He knew how thick it felt when he took handfuls of it before he kissed her. How would it feel brushing lightly against his palm? For an instant, he almost reached out to test the strands for himself.

"Thirsty?" Maggie asked, taking a paper cup from her pocket. She kept her head down while she poured the water.

"Yes, ma'am," he said before setting the paper cup to his lips. He took two giant swallows and drained the cup dry.

She gave him a questioning look. "Ma'am?"

He kept eyeing her. "You got that *call-me-ma'am-look* on today, darlin'."

The water pitcher in her hand wobbled. He watched her try to steady it with her free hand, but it was too late. Clear liquid spilled over her hand.

"My wha-aat look?" Her voice shook worse than the pitcher.

He took her hand and stopped the largest drop of water with his mouth before it reached her wrist. For a moment he thought he caught the unmistakable scent of fresh peaches on her skin. He shook his head, settling himself safely back into reality. Before she could object, he let her hand drop and thumbed back his hat to get a better look at her.

"You're wearing that *ma'am face* again. Your safe face. You know, that don't-come-too-close-to-me look." Then from a whispered start, "Maybe because you're a might uneasy about seeing me?"

"More water?"

He drained the paper cup and held it out to her. "Once is never enough." He mouthed the *with you* part.

From the teasing way his eyebrow arched, Maggie knew he wasn't referring to the water. She congratulated herself on regaining her composure and refilled the cup

115

without a single tremble. Unfortunately, her insides didn't fare so well. She looked at him, wondering if he could see her trembling inside. Luck was with her. He looked pleased with himself and completely oblivious to the internal earthquake that outpointed the Richter scale.

"How's your shoulder?" he asked, while she shifted the water pitcher to her hip.

She squared her shoulders beneath the scooped neck of her peasant blouse. "Fine. How's *your* leg?"

He flashed her one of his dimple-dented smiles. "Which one?"

She couldn't help but smile. He had an offbeat way of saying things that always tickled her funny bone. "Will you ever answer me straight?"

That devilish gleam danced into his eyes. "I'll always play straight man where you're concerned, Maggie."

"I'm serious."

"So am I." His smile faded. "Sit with me for lunch?"

"I'll be serving, I think." She looked over her shoulder. Some of the women were already setting the tables.

"You've got to eat. I'll wait until you can join me."

"Latigo, I don't think that's such a good idea."

"Sounds right to me." He leaned closer and she could see the tiny hairs nestled deep in the cleft of his chin. Before she could answer, the unmistakable woodsy scent of his shaving lotion hit her like a snap of lightning. It spun about inside her head until she identified the textured scent of cedar—until all that filled her head and heart was his name, half song, half prayer. "I've got one more wall frame to nail before I can meet you."

She poured herself a quick drink of water. Cool calming liquid flowed down her constricted throat. It wasn't

116

until she finished the water that she realized she'd used his cup.

He glanced down at the empty cup she held, settling his eyes on the trace of pink lipstick.

"I don't mind sharing, darlin'. You oughta know that by now. What about eats, later?"

All around her she could feel people watching them. "All right," she agreed reluctantly.

He headed off toward the men before calling back, "Meet you right here in about half an hour."

Forty-five minutes later she left the table where she'd been dishing up the food and headed up the hill toward the place they'd agreed to meet. Latigo came out from behind a toolshed and met her halfway.

"Smells good. What did you bring?" he asked, casually hooking his elbow through hers.

"Potato salad."

"One of my favorites." He quickened his steps.

"Chili."

"Another favorite."

"Sourdough French bread."

"Garlic bread?" he asked.

"What else?"

He stopped and draped his arm over her shoulder. "You know we'll both have to eat the garlic bread. I'm game if you are?"

"You got it!" She muscled her way in front of him, taking a place in line, and handed him a plate. "I'll get the silverware." She jammed two napkin-wrapped rolls of plastic forks and knives into her apron pocket.

"Is that your chili in the blue bowl?"

She nodded, ladling two scoops onto his plate next to the potato salad she'd made. "Do you cook, Latigo?"

117

The two men in line ahead of her burst into laughter.

Latigo stuck two fingers into his chest. "Me? I eat." He leaned over the steamy chili. "With some cookin' it's as much fun sniffing as it is eating. Smells great, Maggie."

"Tell me that *after* you taste it." She smiled to herself, wondering if he would be able to tell she made all of her chili with ground turkey instead of the beef she guessed he usually ate.

They set their plates on the red-and-white checkered tablecloth and sat side by side on a long bench. Out of the corner of her eye she watched him dig his spoon into the chili. She liked the way he sopped up the gravy with the side of his garlic bread. His table manners were relaxed, and his attitude toward her was the same. It was contagious. She found herself enjoying his company almost as much as she'd come to enjoy his gentle teasing.

"The chili is great, Maggie." He took another spoonful. "Don't believe I've ever tasted any better." He folded his long leg over the bench straddling it before he stood up. "Anything I can get you?" he asked reaching for his plate.

Stifling her secret delight that he'd yet to detect the ground turkey, she shook her head.

"Believe I'll fill in these empty spaces on my plate. Be right back."

The neighbors at their end of the table left and joined the clean-up crew. She was alone until Latigo returned and took his place beside her. He'd refilled his plate with her potato salad, chili and garlic bread.

"You don't have to prove you like my cooking." She laughed when his napkin blew off his lap. "Here take mine." Without thinking she tucked the pointed corner behind his silver belt buckle. He straightened up, his eyes widened as if she'd reached inside and touched his naked skin.

"Sorry." She was glad the others had moved off to the dessert table. "I'm so use to doing Jenny's napkin, I didn't think . . . I didn't . . ."

The devil made a return visit to his eyes.

"Feel free to reach behind my belt buckle anytime. Anytime at all." He sunk his spoon into the potato salad and continued eating until his plate was empty.

"Have you seen Jenny?" Maggie asked Latigo a few minutes later when they'd folded the last of the table-cloths.

He bent the top of the cardboard box closed. "Jenny? The kids ate first."

An Earth mother's panic overtook her reason. "I know that. Have you seen her?"

"Take a look over there by the shed behind the house."

She relaxed when she caught sight of Jenny with a boy about the same age. "That's the boy from the Junior Rodeo, isn't it?"

"Jimmy Lee Thompson. He and his pa are renting a place down the road from me. He's a swell kid."

Maggie watched the two children loading the scrap lumber left over from the barn raising into a red wagon. They towed the wagon to the side of the house by the back porch and began stacking the wood into neat piles beside the other firewood.

"They've been busy," Latigo said.

"So have you. The barn is almost finished."

"Yeah, it does look good, doesn't it? He hitched a

thumb proudly in his belt loop. "Guess we'll hang the doors later."

They walked toward the back of the house where Jenny and Jimmy Lee were busily unloading the wood. Maggie and Latigo paused by the toolshed.

"What's your pa's name?" Jimmy Lee asked, starting another rise of wood.

Shadows from the past tinged the sunset gray. Maggie gripped Latigo's arm. Would she ever escape the fact that Jenny had no live-at-home father? It was a question her daughter had asked only once. Maggie thought about it every time she saw the fathers in the city park with their children. She'd been too comfortable with Latigo to think much about what was missing from her daughter's life.

Jenny frowned. "My what?"

"You know, your daddy's name? Like mine is Thompson."

"My daddy's name is Grandpa." Jenny handed Jimmy Lee another piece of lumber unaware of being watched.

Latigo's arm swept around Maggie's waist as he guided her away and behind the shed where no one could see them. He stood between her and the sunset, his wide shoulders casting a safe shadow over her as she leaned against the rough wooden siding. Slivers of wood poked through the back of her cotton blouse, pricking her skin like rows of tiny needles. Stubbornly she refused to move, refused to cry.

Without any warning, his hands took hold of hers. His fingers tightened about her wrists as he gently urged her into his arms.

"It's all right, darlin'. Whatever you need to do, do it. Cry. Holler. There's nobody here but you and me." She slumped against his chest. "Kids go right to the heart of things sometimes."

She waited for the inevitable question about Jenny's father. Seconds passed, and it was obvious that he had no intention of asking. Maggie mouthed a silent prayer. "I have to give Jenny credit. My soon-to-be kindergartner handled the question better than I did."

"That's 'cause she gets her sand from her mama." He kissed the top of her head. "And don't you ever forget that, darlin'." His chin sawed back and forth along her forehead in a soothing natural rhythm.

"What say we work off that feed? It'll be almost an hour before fiddlers start gathering."

"We won't be staying." There was no mistaking the disappointment in his eyes. "Jenny will be exhausted and, although he won't admit it, Dad needs his rest, too."

"I'll see to it that you get another chance. You'll have to open your windows and catch a whiff of the music." He draped his arm around her shoulders. "Nighthorse has a nice pond out back. You can make out the tops of the trees from here. It's not far, only a good stretch of the legs." He glanced down at her tennis shoes. "Changed from those sandals, I see."

"Tennis shoes seemed more practical." She aligned her steps with his, grateful for the sudden change of subject from Jenny's father. Most of all, she was grateful for his unspoken understanding

They walked toward the brow of the hill. His arm fell to his side between them, and he caught her hand in his. His fingers found hers in an alternating pattern, a pattern as natural as the straw weave of the summer Stetson he wore.

"You're practical about more than shoes." He laughed.

His hearty laughter was as infectious as his humor and three times as welcome.

"From where I'm standing, practical is your middle name, Maggie Callahan."

"Actually, it's Mary. Margaret Mary Callahan."

"Irish through and through."

She quickened her step. "And proud of it."

"I'm part Indian. Probably Cherokee on my father's side. If my mother had been an Indian, she'd have kept me instead of dropping me in the closest pasture like a sack of garbage."

Her heart tightened into a hurting ball and started unraveling an inch at a time. Long before Jenny's birth, Maggie had evaluated her own choices. She'd chosen motherhood. Single motherhood. Oh, it'd proved difficult to find minutes for herself sometimes, but she never regretted her decision to have Jenny. Never!

She pulled Latigo to a stop.

"I don't need your pity, Maggie."

"That's not what I'm offering. You didn't offer me pity a moment ago when Jimmy Lee asked Jenny about her father. You gave me understanding like one friend gives another. I'm saying that I understand." She touched his smooth cheek, letting her fingertips skim along the steel-set jaw. "You see, I never knew my mother either, Latigo."

The iron set of his jaw slackened. "No?"

"Mom died two days after I was born. Dad raised me alone. Oddly enough, it appears we have some things in common." She took her hand from his cheek. The shadow cast by his wide-brimmed Stetson inched nearer.

"A moment ago you gave me your hand. That's what I'm offering you now." She held out her hand.

Never taking his eyes from hers, he took her hand and squeezed it. She returned the squeeze firmly. He shook his head and lifted her hand to his lips.

"Like I figured, your dad taught you how to shake. No limp-handed grip from you, darlin'." He kissed the knuckle of her index finger and, watching her closely, he kissed each finger in turn. Her eyes drifted closed, remembering, remembering the coaxing, nibbling touch of his mouth on more intimate places. She let the feelings cover her, and her femininity wept with wanting as it had that night in the cellar.

His arms slipped about her, and she sank into the wide curve of his chest before they turned and marched over the crest of the hill. The pond, off to her left, seemed to hold its breath as if awaiting the visit of the setting sun. Lazy birch leaves rippled on the late afternoon's breath. Her own breath quickened when her gaze took in the expanse of open landscape. "So much sky."

"That we've got plenty of."

"Does everyone have a pond?"

"In Wagoner County they do."

"And you?" she asked.

"I got my share."

"Tell me about the town and the people here. They all seem so friendly. So genuine."

"They are."

He was genuine, too, she thought. More real than any man she'd ever met. "What's the town like?"

"Well—" He took off his hat and swatted an imaginary bug from his thigh. "Broken Arrow is a good size city, but we're still small enough to be friendly. Nosy, too."

She nodded slyly.

"Had a visit from the ladies?"

"The first week we arrived."

"I gathered that they took a liking to you from the way you got along today."

"We ate for six days from the casseroles they delivered."

"I'm glad. But you ought to know that we're a mite right of center. Got more than our share of flag wavers. That's not a complaint, by the way. I've been accused of giving old glory a ride myself." He dropped the hat back onto his head, adjusting the tilt of the brim low over his brows. "We've even got a fella who's taken a shine to silk."

"And I thought San Francisco had them all."

His index finger centered over his mouth, swearing her to secrecy. "We keep that on the quiet. You see, he only wears his wife's clothes on Sunday while she's at church."

As they turned back toward the house, Maggie wasn't certain whether to believe the part about the cross-dresser. Latigo had never lied to her. It wasn't in him.

"Wait, Maggie." He swept the wind-blown hair from her eyes. "You ought to wear a hat outdoors. The sunshine is getting a mite too friendly with your fair skin." He settled his hat on her head and tapped it down to the proper angle. "There, this'll do."

She knew better than to argue. "Thanks."

"The hat is only on loan, if you're worried about it."

He was always loaning her things. "By the way, I brought your shirt." She waited for a reply, some reference to what happened between them in the cellar. A vague feeling of disappointment overtook her when his only reactions were a nod and the shift of his jaw.

"The chambray shirt?" she continued. "The one you gave me after the tornado?"

His head kept nodding. "Oh, I remember. I've got something of yours, too."

His off-handed reference stuck in her throat. Maybe he was used to collecting panties from tree limbs. The fact that they'd been intimate had no bearing on how well she knew him or his habits where women were concerned.

He raised the brim of her hat with a flick of one finger. His eyes were dark, steely dark with a trace of hellfire. "I figured a barn raising wasn't exactly the place to return them to you."

Silly as it seemed, she'd forgotten all about the panties. She'd been too busy getting the telephone working again, among other things. Since seeing him today, she definitely had other things on her mind. "You were right about not bringing them today."

The devil in his eyes kept dancing. "Never did soap down a lady's underthings before."

Her cheeks stung. She knew instantly that the sudden heat had nothing to do with the wind. *"You* washed my panties?"

"Sure thing. We're mannerly around these parts. We always return things clean."

"If you felt that way why didn't you send them to a laundry?"

"And hurt Rosa's feelings?" He leaned closer. "She's the lady who picks up around the place. She does *all* my wash."

The devil in his eyes danced faster. "Maybe I should've left your undies in my pocket and let Rosa wash 'em."

Red-faced, Maggie replied, "No. No. You did the right thing."

"I could bring your . . ." Not the least embarrassed, he cleared his throat. "Your things with me when I come by tomorrow."

"Tomorrow?"

"Yeah. Me and old Blue are coming by for Jenny's first riding lesson. You did remember to call her doctor for the okay?"

"Yes. Dad called San Francisco yesterday." Her reply came as more of an afterthought. Jenny's surgeon was trying to reschedule her next operation. Things were piling up. The tornado had slowed down the signing of those oil leases. She made a mental note to call Five Star Oil tomorrow right after she spoke to the real-estate broker. With Jenny's surgery, Maggie needed cash now.

"Great!" Latigo said. "Since you got the doc's okay, old Blue and I'll see you tomorrow. Say about ten?"

That's all she needed. Latigo and some old nag named Blue were coming by tomorrow. Peachy. Just peachy. She smothered the exasperated sigh and all thought of the forbidden fruit. Latigo had promised to teach Jenny how to ride and there was no getting around it.

"Fine," she said, resigned to her fate.

Nine

The next morning after the barn raising, Maggie and the sun hit the back porch at the same time. Dad and Jenny were still sleeping. She shut the kitchen door hoping to keep the smell of fresh coffee from awakening her father. She sipped her first cup of coffee, vowing it would be her last. She drank slowly, savoring the roasted aroma as much as she did the warming sensation. Sighing, she leaned her shoulder against the doorframe. She needed time to mentally arrange her day according to her already-set priorities. As soon as Latigo and his horse arrived, she knew the place would turn chaotic. Chaos, she didn't need.

Jenny was hyper enough after the barn raising, and when Maggie casually mentioned that Latigo was coming by this morning with Blue, she could've sworn her daughter had jumped three inches off the linoleum floor.

Maggie paced back and forth along the inside wall of the screened back porch listing the day's priorities: call Five Star about the oil leases; call the real-estate broker and get the farm on the multi-list *today*. Anything else? she asked herself, draining the coffee mug dry.

"Is that coffee I smell?" Dad called from inside the house.

"Sure is, want some?" She stepped into the kitchen knowing that the dreaded day with Latigo and his horse had begun. Dad stood beside the stove pouring himself a cup of coffee.

"How does French toast sound?" She forced her voice to sound cheerful. The smile she intended to greet her father with never materialized. She tried again. Success. Dad returned a grin from behind a wavy line of steam from his coffee cup. Everyone would be looking forward to the arrival of Latigo and the infamous Blue, and Maggie wasn't about to put a damper on their fun. Of course, their fun didn't include her. She had no intention of getting near Blue or his owner. After Dad had told the surgeon about Latigo's rodeo background, the doctor enthusiastically endorsed Jenny's first riding lesson. Maggie agreed it would be a confidence booster.

"French toast?" Dad added. "Jenny's favorite. And it's not even Sunday. This is going to be a special day for all of us."

Maggie held her frozen smile two more seconds, then let her cheeks relax. Latigo had been right. The skin on her face felt tight from yesterday's sun. Earlier this morning she'd spread a layer of sunscreen on her face and neck. She took a flat square dish from the cupboard and cracked the first egg. It plopped into the dish and stared back at her like a big, yellow, fish eye.

"Mommy?" Jenny, already dressed in her blue jeans, shuffled into the kitchen. "Are we having French toast?"

"Absolutely," Maggie said, giving her daughter a quick kiss. "You're up bright and early."

"Mama, the eggs are my job remember?" Jenny took the dish to the table.

"I only cracked one egg. The rest are all yours. Here's the whisk." Maggie carried the cinnamon, vanilla extract and the carton of eggs to the table.

Jenny took charge of beating the eggs. Every now and then Maggie took a quick look over at the table in time to see Jenny stop and add a dash of cinnamon and vanilla.

Dad got the half-gallon of milk from the refrigerator. "You got sunburned yesterday, Maggie. Good thing Latigo gave you his hat."

"Yes, that was nice of him." Maggie's fingers rattled the forks in the silverware tray. Nice? she thought recalling the surprised looks she'd gotten from the neighbors when she returned wearing the straw cowboy hat everyone knew belonged to Latigo. From the way everyone looked at Maggie, it was obvious they considered her an extension of that ownership.

Had Latigo planned it that way? No, he was a generous man by nature. And yet, she remembered having the distinct feeling that the name Wade Latigo was branded across her forehead. Not wanting to be unfair, she'd kept her thoughts to herself when she and Latigo said their good-byes, and she returned the hat and the chambray shirt he'd lent her after the tornado. Maggie dropped the first slice of bread into the heated frying pan.

Breakfast was a smash hit. The dishes got done in record time. Jenny even made her bed without being reminded and followed her grandfather outside to wait for Latigo. Maggie called Five Star about the oil leases. No answer. Perhaps their telephone lines were still down after the tornado.

She dialed the real-estate office and got a recorded message. Her distaste for answering machines increased. She tried her agent at home and got another recorded message. She left a curt message and slammed the receiver onto its cradle. The day was off to a lousy start. Was this an omen of things to come?

She busied herself picking up the living room in case some of the neighbor ladies dropped by. The people she'd met since arriving in Broken Arrow had treated her like one of them. Being from California, she'd thought she'd feel like an outsider. Wrong. She liked her neighbors. So much so, she was considering joining them for church this Sunday.

She punched the middle of a throw pillow, fluffing it before she set it in front of the two already crowding the sofa's armrest. She walked down the hall and into the bathroom, picking up the towel Jenny had left on the rolled edge of the old-fashioned tub. With the towel swinging from her shoulder, she took one last look around the bathroom.

Her eyes settled on the toilet-paper holder—the empty toilet-paper holder. Why was she the only member of the household who knew how to place a fresh supply of toilet paper on the empty holder? She took a plump roll from the cabinet over the commode and refilled the spindle, and slipped it back into place. Gee whiz, it's good to feel needed, she thought, shaking her head. Aren't we women lucky? After stuffing the soiled bath towel into the hamper, she stepped out into the hallway.

"Latigo's coming, Mommy," Jenny yelled from outside. "I can see his truck."

"Here goes nothing." Against her better judgment, Maggie headed for the back porch.

"And will you look at that trailer." She heard her father say.

Maggie pushed open the screen door and stood on the top step. "What trailer?" she asked, sheltering her eyes. "I can't see-ee . . ." Her mouth dropped open. "Good lord, it looks like he's towing a boat behind that truck."

If she thought the trailer looked big from a distance, it had nothing on the real size of the black-and-silver monster truck Latigo drove up beside the house. A splash of purple and silver paint started at the front fender and ran the complete length of the truck and trailer. It must've cost a mint, Maggie thought. The rodeo business must've been good.

"Mornin', Maggie." Latigo tipped the familiar straw Stetson when he stepped out of the cab.

This time her mouth had no trouble smiling. From his hat to the square toe of his boots, Latigo was the image of what Maggie thought a real rodeo rider should look like: blue plaid shirt, its tapered cut definitely custom tailored: butt-hugging stove-pipe jeans, the knife sharp white creases shooting straight down to his understated brown leather boots. No woman would mistake him for an urban cowboy. He was the real thing, all right.

"Mr. Callahan." Latigo nodded to Maggie's father. "Jenny."

"How many horses did you bring?" Maggie asked while Latigo shook hands with her father.

"Only brought Blue. This is his favorite rig. Makes him feel important, like we were heading out on the circuit again.

The man missed the rodeo, too, she thought. Why wouldn't he? It'd been the entire focus of his life for a long time. The neighbors still thought of Wade Latigo as

131

the King of the Rodeo. Too bad she'd never get a chance to see the King in action.

"Well, Jenny?" Latigo asked. "You ready to meet Blue?"

"Yeee-ah!" Jenny followed Latigo around to the back of the trailer.

"How about you, Mom?" He glanced sideways at Maggie.

"Me?" Maggie held her ground beside the porch step, certain she could grab Jenny and make a quick dash up the stairs and into the house if the horse acted wild. "I can see fine from here."

Metal rattled as he opened the trailer's double doors. Maggie glanced away, her attention caught by the lettering around the license plate frame: If you can't run with the big dogs, stay on the porch. That would sum up Wade Latigo's thinking all right, she thought, except where Jenny was concerned. Look at the two of them. Correction, look at the three of them, Dad had joined them as Latigo led a big red horse out of the trailer and toward the pasture fence.

"Say hello to Blue, Jenny." Latigo slowed up the pace.

"Hello, Blue," Jenny answered, waving a hand in the air.

As if on cue, Blue nodded.

"He says howdy. He's been looking forward to meeting you and your grandpa." Latigo looked over his shoulder. "And your mama, too."

"Has he?" Standing right beside Latigo, Jenny was mesmerized.

"We're going to tie him up right here." Latigo slapped a strip of leather around a fence post, securing the animal. "Then we're going to get more acquainted. You wait

132

here." He leaned down to Jenny. "I've got something on the front seat—"

"I'll get it," Dad volunteered.

"Thanks." Latigo squatted beside Jenny, so they were eye to eye. "It's that small sack beside Buffalo."

Buffalo? Maggie's eyes darted back to the truck. At the sound of his name, a huge yellow dog jumped onto the seat and barked. Until that moment, Maggie hadn't seen the animal. The dog, Buffalo, must've been lying on the floor of the truck the whole time. The name certainly fit what Maggie guessed was a golden retriever.

Buffalo growled when her dad put his hand on the door of the truck.

"Buff, mind your manners," Latigo ordered, never looking back at the truck. The retriever relaxed and sat on the seat while Dad got the paper sack.

Were all of Latigo's animals that well-trained, or did they obey him out of pure affection? Either way, Maggie was impressed.

Squatting beside Jenny, Latigo brushed a bit of grass off her jeans. "Like apples?"

Jenny nodded, looking wide-eyed at big Blue.

"They're good for you, but I guess your mama has told you that." Standing, Latigo took the sack from Dad. "Apples are good for horses, too." He took a golden delicious apple from the sack and handed the sack to Jenny.

"You watch Blue closely. It'll be your turn next. See, he's already got a whiff of the apples."

Blue snorted and shook his head. Maggie stepped forward in case Blue made any sudden move toward her daughter. Jenny was totally immersed in what Latigo was saying. Latigo, it appeared, had everything in control.

Maggie relaxed and leaned against the stair railing.

Latigo held out the apple to Blue. "Keep your hand flat, Jenny, so Blue has a good shot."

Blue sniffed the apple again and turned away.

"Well, I'll be a—" He cleared his throat. "Show me up in front of the ladies, will you? And after I bragged on you, too. Shame on you, Blue." He held the apple closer to the horse's mouth. Blue ignored it.

Latigo glanced down at Jenny, then back at Blue. "You're goin' to make me cut it, aren't you?" He reached into his jeans and took out a pocket knife. With a flick of the blade he sectioned the apple into four pieces. "Jenny, this is what comes of spoiling a horse." He held out the apple.

Maggie looked closer. For a moment she thought Blue smiled. No, an animal couldn't smile. Of course her experience with horses was no bigger than the lump in her throat.

Blue sniffed the cut apple and slowly took the pieces one at a time.

"Want to try feeding him, Jenny?"

"Can I really?"

"Sure thing." Latigo cut a second apple and handed two slices to Jenny. "Do it like I showed you."

Blue nudged Jenny's chest.

Maggie lunged forward, her arms outstretched. "Jenny."

Jenny teetered back for an instant almost dropping the apple.

"Blue?" Latigo warned, holding his arm between Jenny and the horse. "You know better. Easy, boy. This is my friend, Jenny. You remember, I told you all about her. She's come all the way from Frisco to meet you."

Maggie slumped against the front fender of the truck.

Jenny inched closer, bravely holding out the apple on her flat palm.

Blue shook his head as if he understood exactly what Latigo had said and gently took a single piece of apple from Jenny's hand.

Jenny giggled, snapping her hand to her side and fisting the remaining fruit tightly. "He tickles."

Latigo smiled. "Yeah, he does kind of. I'd forgotten that."

Blue sniffed Jenny's shirt front again. This time Jenny produced the fruit without being told to. Blue went right for it. "I think he likes me."

"You bet he does. He only takes apples from very special people." Latigo glanced over his shoulder at Maggie.

Maggie pretended to be checking out the horse trailer. No way was she going to feed Blue.

"Maggie?" Latigo gave her an encouraging look, nodding his head toward Blue. The lump in Maggie's throat grew by several inches. What could she do? She wasn't going to be outdone by her own child. She swallowed the lump and gamely stepped closer. The lump settled in her chest and grew bigger with each step she took. And Blue? Maggie could swear he'd grown two feet taller. His large brown eyes followed her as if he'd rather take a bite out of her instead of the apples.

Latigo took another apple from the sack Dad held, and cut it. "Here. Your turn."

Maggie's arms froze at her sides. Latigo took her hand and slapped two large wedges of apple into it.

"Blue, Jenny's mama has a treat for you." Latigo nudged Maggie closer.

"Hold out your hand, Mommy," Jenny said with the innocence of a child.

"I will. I will." Maggie held out her shaking left hand and looked the other way, certain that Blue would nip off a finger before he got to the apple. Puffs of hot breath blasted her palm and settled into a tickle exactly as Jenny had said. Maggie's fingers curled automatically around the apple.

"Mommy, you've got to keep your fingers out." Jenny took Maggie's hand, unbending the fingers one by one. Maggie couldn't look. The hot breath returned and Maggie felt the hairy tickle again before she heard the crunch, crunch of an apple. She risked a peek. Blue's enormous head was bending toward her open hand and the remaining section of yellow apple. It took all of Maggie's nerve to keep her hand outstretched until Blue had scooped up the fruit.

Latigo's shoulder nudged hers. "Are you all right?"

Maggie dusted her hands together. "Of course, why wouldn't I be?" She jammed her hands into the back pockets of her jeans. "Dad, it's your turn."

"I'd love to." Dad stepped up behind Jenny, handing one of the two remaining apples to Maggie. She clutched the apple tightly, holding it pressed along the seam of her jeans leg.

Latigo passed his pocket knife to her father who proceeded to cut another apple. Her father fed Blue a piece of apple, then let Jenny have the rest. Blue eyed Jenny as if he knew he should wait until she had her tiny hand ready for him.

"Here, Blue," Jenny said, holding up her hand.

Blue cleaned Jenny's palm, sniffed it again and swung

136

his head toward Maggie. Maggie jumped. Latigo's arm slipped around her back holding her in place.

"He wants to get acquainted. He's met all of the Callahans, but I do believe he's taken a fancy to you, Maggie," Latigo boasted.

Before Maggie could say a word Blue snatched the apple clutched in her hand and ate it whole.

"Well, will you look at that," Latigo said, slapping her back. "Looks like you've made a friend."

"Blue likes you." Jenny jerked on Maggie's limp arm. "Mommy?"

"I guess today is my lucky day." Maggie slumped back against Latigo's chest glad for any support.

"Old Blue does cotton to you. That's for sure. He's mighty particular about his apples." Latigo took her hand, then reached down for Jenny's. "Now that you've been properly introduced, Jenny, would you like to give Blue a scratch?"

"Can I?" Jenny stepped closer, looking straight up into Blue's massive head.

Latigo squatted between Maggie and Jenny. "How you touch an animal is real important. It tells them how much you care about them."

Wide-eyed, Jenny nodded.

"Well, it's the same thing with horses. They take their cue first from the sound of your voice. If you're happy, they're happy. If you're sad, they're sad, too."

"Really?" Maggie asked.

He winked her way, then to Jenny, "Show them how much you care about them. You know how you like it when your mama gives you a hug and tells you how proud she is of you, Jenny?"

Jenny nodded.

Latigo stood. "Watch this." Latigo frowned before he said, "Blue!"

Blue snapped to attention, his eyes as wide as Jenny's.

"Blue?" Latigo's tone went higher. "You knotheaded old buzzard, how do you like the Callahan ladies?"

Blue jerked his head toward Latigo as if he were trying to speak, then he dropped his head closer to Jenny's hand.

"He'd like a pat, Jenny," Latigo said in the same soothing tone.

Without hesitating, Jenny stroked the long white strip that ran the length of Blue's head. "He's soft. And warm, too." Jenny patted the horse again and again. With her hand still on Blue's head she said, "You're a nice horse, Blue. I'm going to ride you today 'cause the doctor said I could. You don't mind, do you?"

Jenny's face was only inches from Blue's head. Maggie almost cried out until she spotted Latigo's chamois-gloved hand resting beside Jenny's hand. He untied Blue, holding the leather reins to one side.

"Blue will enjoy taking you for a stroll, Jenny. Come on back to the trailer with me, I want to show you a few things first." He took Jenny by the hand and man and horse headed toward the open horse trailer. "Your mama got you dressed exactly right."

"I dressed myself," Jenny bragged. "This is my new Oklahoma shirt that Grandpa bought me."

"That's a real cowgirl shirt, all right." Latigo tied Blue to the side of the trailer and disappeared inside with Jenny quick on his heels. "You got almost everything you need."

Keeping to the horseless side of the trailer, Maggie wandered after them feeling like a rank outsider. She waited a moment before peeking around the open door. Latigo was on his knees strapping what looked like a bicycle crash helmet onto Jenny's head.

Maggie panicked. Good lord, what if Jenny fell off the horse? She took a calming breath remembering how closely Latigo watched Jenny. Maggie trusted Latigo. *Admit it,* she thought, *it's own fear of horses that's making you crazy.*

"When you know how to ride like a real cowgirl, we'll see about getting you fitted with a Western hat. But for now, when we ride you'll be wearing one of these." Tightening the strap to a perfect fit under Jenny's chin, he leaned back on his boot heels. "You look right smart, Jenny. I bet you'll be one of the fastest learners I've ever taught to ride."

"You've taught other children to ride?" Maggie asked, stepping onto the plank leading to the inside of the trailer.

"A few."

"You never told me that."

"You never asked." Latigo got to his feet and reached for a small saddle on the floor beside him. "That's why I got this helmet. It keeps young riders safe in the saddle." He swung the saddle over his shoulder. "Ready, Jenny?"

"Ready." Jenny took Latigo's hand.

"Remember what I said about your legs?"

Jenny nodded.

"Smile, Mom," Latigo whispered. "This is going to be the easiest lesson I've ever given. Jenny's got old Blue eating out of her hand." He winked at Maggie as they stepped up beside the tethered horse. "And I'm not talking apples."

In a matter of seconds, Latigo had saddled Blue and

lifted the delighted Jenny onto the horse. Maggie had worried about how Jenny would get onto the horse with her braces. Latigo handled the problem by lifting her into place as if he'd done it a hundred times before.

"One day soon you'll be able to sit Blue without these." He tied a series of leather straps around Jenny's waist and fastened the ends to the front of the saddle.

"You hold tight to the horn." Latigo stacked Jenny's hand on the top of the saddle horn. "That'a girl." He slapped the side of the stirrup and led Blue away. "Keep your toes like I showed you."

Maggie had to admit he'd thought of everything. She relaxed and fell into step behind Latigo and Blue.

"Look at me, Grandpa," Jenny called. "I'm a real cowgirl."

"Well, so you are." Maggie saw the tears forming in her father's eyes. She'd only remembered seeing him cry once—when Mama died.

They stood side by side watching as Latigo headed Blue into the open pasture opposite the back porch. In a matter of minutes, Jenny and Blue were trotting in a circle, held in check by a long piece of leather that Latigo held in one hand.

"Fine, Jenny. Keep your head up," Latigo called. "Back straight. That'a girl."

"You're wonderful," Maggie hollered.

"Aren't we just?" Latigo teased under his breath.

Two hours and six cheese and turkey pastrami sandwiches later, the four of them sat around the kitchen table finishing up the last of the rainbow sherbet ice cream.

"What'd you call that grass stuff you put on the sandwiches?" Latigo asked.

"Alfalfa sprouts," she answered, enjoying the way he nodded his approval. He wasn't above trying something new. Good for him. He'd tried more new food since he'd met her than she dared tell him.

"Strange looking, but tasty. Those sandwiches were great." Latigo slapped his stomach.

The purely male gesture of satisfaction pleased Maggie.

"Don't believe I've ever had better pastrami," Latigo continued.

Fooled him again, Maggie thought. Being the beef eater he was, she rationalized the deception as the lesser of two evils. He'd enjoyed her chili at the barn raising. He even boasted about it, never suspecting the ground meat came from a two-legged bird.

"Well, I think we should get started, Maggie." Latigo swung a long leg over the back of the Windsor chair and stood beside the kitchen table.

"Get started?" Maggie asked, taking a stack of plates to the sink. "You're going to help with the dishes?"

"That isn't exactly what I had in mind," Latigo answered, setting two milk glasses on the sideboard. "You did so well with the apples, I figure it's your turn to ride ole Blue."

A dinner plate slipped from Maggie's hand. "Me? Ride a horse?"

Ten

"I want to see you ride, Mommy," Jenny cried.

"Me, too," Latigo echoed, ignoring Maggie's glare.

"I've got the kitchen to do," Maggie stammered, gathering the blue and white pieces of the plate she'd broken in the sink.

"Now, Maggie." Her father held out the garbage pail for the broken plate. "Jenny and I'll take care of the kitchen later. You deserve a break."

"Break? As in break my neck?" She squirted a pink stream of liquid soap into the sink and turned on the hot water. Soap suds gathered like wind-driven clouds in the corner of the sink. For a moment, she imagined herself flying through the air after being bucked off Blue's back. "Dad, you know how I feel about horses."

"Don't you think it's about time you did something about that?" her father whispered while dropping his plate and silverware into the sink.

"Stay out of this, Dad," Maggie muttered under her breath.

"Come on, Mommy. Blue is waiting." Jenny headed for the back door.

"Are you game?" Latigo asked with a challenging rise of an eyebrow.

Trapped again. She turned full circle and faced him. She could make excuses. There were other things more pressing on her schedule. He picked up his hat, holding the rolled brim in his hand and waited. Pride overruled better judgment, and Maggie marched out of the kitchen with Latigo hot on her heels. Pride didn't count for much, when Maggie reached the bottom step and looked into the pasture where Blue grazed.

Oh, the animal was tethered to the fence, the pail of water Latigo and Jenny filled before lunch still within his reach. Maggie stopped flat-footed feeling like a roped calf. She dug in her heels determined to stay where she was, which was yards away from that horse.

"Blue is eating lunch," Jenny said, looking back at Maggie.

"He'll chew all day if we let him." Latigo stopped beside Maggie while her father and Jenny strolled toward Blue.

When Maggie felt Latigo's hand on her elbow, she knew she had two choices: Give into her fear and run the possibility of passing her hang-up about horses onto Jenny, or Maggie could stare down her fear and walk straight into that pasture.

The Earth mother inside her kicked in.

How she got across the driveway, past Latigo's truck and into the pasture, was something Maggie couldn't figure out. All she knew was that in a matter of seconds all four of them were standing next to the still grazing Blue.

"Can I pet him?" Jenny asked.

"Anytime. He's your friend." Latigo's hand went to Blue's head first. "Right, Blue?"

Smart Blue kept eating.

Jenny reached out with her hand, following the blaze of white from Blue's ears to his mouth. *Good lord, the child is fearless.* And her mother? Maggie's shoulders slumped. *Admit it. You're a coward.*

Everyone touched Blue. Everyone but her. Maggie tried to raise her arm, but her repeated efforts failed miserably. The second toe on her left foot ached inside her penny loafer. Not even the fire-engine red polish she used to cover the missing toenail could make her forget the accident when the horse's hoof severed the tip of her toe. She turned back toward the house. Any excuse she made now would sound like cowardice, unless . . .

"I think the phone is ringing," she said.

Her father frowned at her. "I don't hear anything."

Determined to act out the charade, Maggie headed for the house.

"Your dad is right. Everything's quiet. How about helping with the saddle?" Latigo asked, falling into step beside her.

"You go ahead. I've got things to do." Fully intending to walk right past the truck, she hurried her steps.

"Hey?" He grabbed her and steered her around the side of the trailer. He left her standing beside the right rear fender and walked up the plank and into the horse trailer.

Female appreciation for a man in a well-filled pair of jeans replaced the Earth mother. Oh, how she enjoyed watching Latigo walk away. She'd always thought a rodeo cowboy's butt would be flat from riding all those horses. His wasn't.

She sighed and let practicality jump in. What was she waiting for? Now was her chance. She peeked around the corner. Inside the horse trailer, Latigo bent over a big trunk sorting through a stack of brightly colored blankets. He'd never miss her until she was inside the house. She backed toward the porch.

"Damn," she heard him cuss. "I was sure there was another saddle here." He stepped out of the trailer, a disgusted look on his face.

No saddle. No ride. There was a God. "Guess we'll have to postpone the riding for today." Relieved by the turn of events, she strolled toward him. "That's a shame."

"I never give up that easily." Taking her hand, he towed her along behind him. "We'll show Jenny how it's done bareback."

"We'll what?" Relief faded. Only prayer remained, and she didn't have much faith in urgent words the way things were going. "Latigo, maybe we should—"

"We're not going to let a youngster outdo us, are we?"

A few minutes later, prodded by Latigo's challenge, Maggie stood next to Blue.

"Feel how warm he is, Mommy." Jenny's hand roamed Blue's jaw.

Maggie closed her eyes and held out her hand in the general direction of Blue's head. Only the strong grip of Latigo's fingers on her wrist made her open her eyes.

Trapped again.

"I've been around horses all my life." Latigo bent down to her. "Blue's as gentle as a pup."

Pup? The only animal in sight was a huge horse with a head bigger than her mailbox.

"Maggie?" Latigo inclined his head toward Jenny.

If she delayed much longer, Jenny would sense her

fear. Maggie would die before she let that happen. She clenched both fists.

Latigo slapped his hand flat on the side of Blue's neck and whispered, "Put your hand on top of mine, darlin'."

She did, carefully keeping his broad hand between her and Blue's neck.

"Now, slide your fingers between mine." Latigo' words came slowly, and she knew he understood she didn't want to transfer her fear of horses to Jenny.

"What you waiting for, Mommy?" Jenny asked, feeding a clump of fresh-picked grass to Blue.

"Nothing," Maggie managed. Blue's mouth worked. His broad teeth tore at the grass, sharp teeth set in a wide moving jaw. Burning bile rose in her throat, and she thought she'd lose her lunch. She swallowed hard and the pastrami sandwich returned to her stomach.

Slowly, she inched her fingers between Latigo's. His hand was as steady as always. Everything was fine, until she felt the scratchy hair on Blue's neck.

Fear coiled like a rattler ready to strike.

Latigo moved their piggybacked hands back and forth along Blue's massive neck. "His hide feels scratchy at first, kinda like a man's beard."

Maggie let one finger slide between Latigo's to test the truth of his words. Coarse hairs, brushed flat, made Blue's coat slippery. "He's smoother than your beard."

"Ri-iight."

He looked pleased with himself, she thought.

"Let me know when you're ready to go it alone," Latigo said.

If she waited until then, it'd be Christmas, and she had no intention of standing beside this horse any longer than she had to. "I'm ready."

146

Stubbornly, she lifted her hand and flattened it alongside Latigo's. Like a lifeline, Latigo's thumb stroked the side of her pinky. Suddenly Blue's coat felt warm. She'd never noticed that until now. She moved her hand farther from Latigo's.

Whew, that wasn't so bad. Feeling vindicated, she leaned back against Latigo's chest. The placket of his shirt front aligned with her spine, bolstering her courage.

"You do realize what all this attention is doin' to him?" Latigo asked, giving Blue a hearty pat. "I'm going to have to pry him out of this pasture when it's time to haul him home."

"Maybe Blue could sleep over," Jenny asked, checking the depth of water in the pail beside the horse.

That's all Maggie needed—a slumber horse. "Not on your life, young lady."

Jenny snapped her fingers in disgust. "Shoot."

"Speaking of sleep," Maggie's dad interrupted. "It's time for a nap."

"Oh, Grandpa, can't we skip it for one day?" Jenny asked, grabbing another fist of grass and feeding it to Blue.

"I'm talking about *my* nap." He took Jenny's hand. "Come on. I know where there's another pint of rainbow sherbet."

"All ri-iight!" Jenny exchanged the grass for her grandfather's hand and disappeared into the house.

Latigo stood in the pasture feeling like a rooted stump. Out of the corner of his eye, he watched Maggie for some sign that she was considering riding. He saw none. What he was about to do might be considered grandstanding, but he meant to try.

147

"Blue's waitin' on us." He'd deepened his tone knowing how she reacted to a challenge.

She kept facing the house. "Latigo, I . . . I . . ."

He put a hand on her shoulder. He felt her tremble when she turned and looked at him. She bit her lip.

"There's a heap more to ridin' than settin' and lettin' your feet dangle. Most folks don't realize that, because they never have to face up to it. That's lesson number one at the rodeo." He slipped his arm around her shoulders and headed her back toward Blue.

She stopped suddenly. "You were afraid?"

He pulled his hat lower over his eyes. "Sometimes. Especially when I drew a bull that'd never been rode. I knew my chances were slim that I could go eight." He squeezed her shoulder. "I had to stay on the bull for eight seconds."

"That's a long time."

"Some days it's a lifetime." They started walking toward Blue again. "It's no pleasure bein' tossed fork-end up in front of a crowd of folks."

"But you went ahead anyway?"

He pulled her to a stop and stepped around in front so he could see her face clearly. Sunburn still pinked her cheeks. He'd come to think of her skin in shades of peachy pink even though he'd never seen all of her in the light of day. Today, they could see one another clearly, and he meant to be straight with her. "I had it in my mind all along for you to ride today."

Her tight fists banged to her hips. "This whole day was supposed to be for Jenny."

"It was, only the last half of the day I saved for you, darlin'."

She squinted her eyes. "For me to ride."

"I tend to jump in with both boots sometimes." He gave her his best grin. Her frown remained, although he could see by her eyes that she was mellowing. "Over the years I've tried to curb my grandstanding, but it's a throwback to my rodeo days."

"Old habits die hard." She cut a brown line in the grass with the side of her loafer. She referred to her fear of horses, and he knew it. He'd faced up to being afraid, although he'd never admitted to anyone before—certainly not to a woman who hadn't the foggiest notion of what riding could mean to a man.

A smile tickled one corner of her mouth into lifting.

"Horses and a pretty lady are a powerful combination." He glanced down at the pail of water in front of Blue. After admitting how he'd schemed to get her to ride, he wouldn't blame her if she dumped the whole kit and caboodle over his head.

His eyes wanted to drift back to the water pail, but he made himself look at her again. He always took bad news face to face. He owed her that. His eyes had other ideas and fastened on the top button of her blouse and the bit of white lace. When his gut tightened, he gave himself a mental kick in the britches. She'd made it clear that there'd be no more touching or anything that might come later.

"Roping you into this . . ." He lifted his head, forcing himself to look her in the eye. Those wonderful eyes he kept seeing in his dreams. "That was unfair."

"Maybe, but it worked." Her hand reached out to him, then faltered and fell back to her side. "I haven't been this close to a horse in years."

"Forgive me?"

"I would, if there were something to forgive." She

backed up her words with a hundred-dollar smile. "Now, what about that ride?"

He stared at her, uncertain he'd heard her right. "Jenny and your dad are gone. You don't have to ride now."

"I know, but I may never get another chance, or a better teacher."

If he'd been a mite younger, he'd have blushed at the way her eyes scanned him from hat to boot. He stuck out his chest, wishing he'd worn his fancy purple shirt, the satin one with the black fringe.

"There's only one thing," she added.

"Anything, darlin'."

"Promise you won't throw me over Blue's back like a sack of taters." Her outrageous imitation of a Southern drawl was flawless, her parted lips moist and inviting. *Down, cowboy. Don't push your luck. Be grateful the lady is still speaking to you.*

"How do you get on a horse without a saddle?"

"By grabbing a handful of his mane and—"

"Doesn't that hurt?"

"Blue hasn't complained yet." He intertwined the fingers of both his hands and made a pad for her foot. "Step here."

She wiped the bottom of her shoe on the grass as if it were a door mat. "Thank you for the consideration, ma'am, but a bit of grass won't bother this cowboy's hands none."

She put the freshly wiped sole of her loafer onto his hands and stepped up. He moved with her, giving her the extra boost needed to reach Blue's back. She weighed less than he recalled. Just the far side of a hundred pounds he figured. Without hesitating, she swung her right leg over Blue and scooted forward.

"You're something, darlin'." Before she had a chance to change her mind, he unhitched Blue and swung up behind her. He reached around her, shifting the reins from his left to his right hand.

"Is it true there's only one side of a horse to get up on?"

"Yes. Blue's the exception. You can mount him on either side." He took the opportunity to get closer, and whispered in her ear, "or you can spring over his rump if you've a mind to."

"Can we try that another day?"

He laughed. So did she. He liked the way her shoulders moved up and down when she laughed. He liked the way their laughter blended into one happy sound. Come to think of it, he liked everything about her, including her stubbornness. There was only one thing. He pushed the thought of her dealing with Five Star out of his mind for the moment. Rehashing oil leases wouldn't get any riding done, and he meant to see her aboard ole Blue today. "You're right-handed?"

"Yes." Her voice went deeply serious. "I am."

"Then take the reins in your right hand."

"You mean I'm going to steer?"

Not wanting to embarrass her when she talked about Blue as if he were a truck, he stifled a laugh. "Something like that." He passed the reins to her.

"Okay, now what?" She settled her backside snugly against him.

Lord, did he love the way she felt? Yes, ma'am! Lady luck had come to stay. For the first time in his recollection, he had to concentrate on telling a beginner how to ride. "Well, if you want Blue to go left, you pull the reins to the left. If you want him to go right—"

"I pull the reins right." She kept her hands still.

"Ri-iight."

"How do I get him to stop?"

"Just pull back."

Her fingers tightened on the reins. "Are you sure he'll stop?"

"It works for me."

"And to get him started?"

"Give him a gentle nudge with your heels."

He looked down at their legs dangling side by side, big brown boots behind penny loafers. *Well, darlin', here's where country and city meet again. You're still trying to get over our lovemaking that night in the cellar.* She needed more than one night's loving, and he fully intended to see that she got what she needed. Only this time, he'd make certain she had no regrets.

"How do I know that Blue won't run and jump that fence?"

"Because these are the only signals we're going to give him. Those strips of leather you're holding are kinda like a telegraph line. He'll get the message."

"That's it?"

"Yeap." For now, he added to himself.

"And to think people actually pay you to do this?" she teased.

"I got 'em fooled, don't I?"

"Them, maybe. Not me." She gave Blue a gentle kick and the horse headed out of the pasture. "How many years did you follow the rodeo?"

"Too many if I listen to my bones. By the way," he whispered, "it's roh-dee-oh, darlin'. Roh-day-oh is Spanish for roundup."

"Or a street in Beverly Hills," she teased.

"That too. Mind telling me where we're goin'?"

"You'll see, cowboy. Come on, Blue."

"Comin', Buffalo?"

Curled up for a snooze, the golden retriever lifted his head and stared blankly at him.

"Aren't you coming, Buffy?" she asked.

"No dog of mine answers to Buffy?"

Setting her fingers between her teeth, she whistled. "Buffy?" The once-dozing dog jumped to his feet and trotted along after them. "This one does."

Well, I'll be. He tapped his hat to the back of his head. Crazy as it seemed, he found it didn't matter what she called his dog, as long as she sat inside of his arms.

When they reached the wooden gate, she guided Blue parallel with the flat gray slats. He knew she'd planned ahead, by the way she angled Blue up to the gate so a rider could reach it. "Nice job."

"I'm not quite ready to sit here alone, so I thought you might be able to open it without getting down."

"I think you're ready for anything." He leaned down and unhooked the wire loop holding the gate shut. The sagging gate followed the deeply worn groove and squeaked open. "Closing a gate is another matter."

"You mean the rule about leaving a gate the way you find it?"

"The very one."

"I own this gate."

"In that case, we'll leave it any way you want, darlin'."

She nudged Blue with her heels. He trotted forward. "Then let's not bother with it."

As naturally as you please, she shifted directions with an easy lean of the reins. If he hadn't known better, he'd have thought she'd been riding since she was a kid. He dropped his hands, letting his palms rest flat on the top of her thighs. It was good to touch her even if there was a pair of jeans between his skin and hers. His heart galloped like a week-old colt. Why hadn't he made a point of teaching the mother to ride before the child? He leaned forward, taking full advantage of the rolling movement of their bodies as Blue headed into the pasture.

The enormous swoop of sky pressed heavy on the horizon like the wings of a sharp-eyed hawk. Blue covered the ground in a yard-eating trot before Latigo realized where they were headed.

Of all the spots around these parts, Honeysuckle Creek, as he called it, was his favorite. Oh, there were more spectacular places. Places where the Arkansas River sprang wide and free, and the nesting bald eagles floated in the sky. Since he'd been seven years old, Honeysuckle Creek had belonged to him. At least in his mind, it had. In reality it had belonged to her uncle, Mike Callahan. Since Mike had left everything to Maggie, now Honeysuckle Creek belonged to her.

Somehow that seemed perfect.

It was as if long before they'd met, her heart had been hitched to his. Hitched to his dreams, past and present. Dreams he'd kept steadfastly to himself over the years. Dreams of someday finding a woman to share the one place he'd never shared with anyone.

When had she discovered Honeysuckle Creek? Had she stumbled upon it as he had? Or had she been drawn there by that invisible bond he felt growing between them?

The questions heightened his physical awareness of her. The pale skin above the slight sunburn on her neck. He remembered exactly how she'd tied her ponytail yesterday as the afternoon sun heated up. He remembered how the satiny pink ribbon flipped freely against her neck whenever she moved her head. He tried to freeze-frame the image in his mind of that ribbon skipping along her skin—like he was taking a photograph. But all he could think about was how smooth her neck felt when he kissed it that night in the cellar. Her sweet taste made him think of fresh-picked peaches. Oh, how he wanted to dip his head and taste that sweetness again.

Blue picked up the pace as if he could smell the honeysuckle. Buffalo barked and raced ahead to the top of the hill.

"We're almost there." Maggie leaned forward, pointing with her left hand. "See those trees?"

Not wanting to diminish her surprise, he looked toward the broad-armed stand of trees that'd been his boyhood companion. "The pecan grove?"

"Yes. Pecan pie was Uncle Mike's favorite. I wonder if this is where he got the nuts he sent us every Christmas?"

"Could be. Pecan pie is one of my favorites, too" Although lately his taste ran to peaches. Many things in his life had changed *lately.* Only one thing was a constant—his fascination with the woman whose backside he cradled snugly between his thighs.

Maggie pulled back on the reins when they reached the top of the hill above Honeysuckle Creek. "We're here." Her hands fell limply to her waist as she sniffed the air. "Can you smell the honeysuckle?"

Caught up by her excitement, he could only nod. Her enthusiasm was contagious. To his happy surprise, he found himself rediscovering his boyhood memories through her eyes. The sun shone brighter. The pecan leaves shimmered like newly minted silver dollars.

"Wait till we get closer." Lifting the reins like a pro, she gave Blue a bold kick. Blue trotted down the hillside. When they reached the creek bank, he jumped to the ground and held out his open arms to her. She dropped the reins and leaned his way. Latigo caught her in mid-flight. The soft shape of her breasts against his chest had him breathing heavy. He rocked back on his boot heels, his head filled with the flowery scent rising from her hair.

"See? I told you I'd never let you fall." Her arms stayed around his neck, and he held her longer than he intended to. He liked looking up to her. Most of all, he liked the way she felt in his arms. Their eyes met, and he knew instantly she was remembering the first time he'd held her this way. That time in the pasture before the tornado hit.

She let go of his neck. Her flat palms came to a stop directly over his shirt pockets. "You're a man of your word, Wade Latigo."

He was glad she understood he meant to make no moves on her today. Now tomorrow, that was something else. "For what it's worth, I'm mighty proud of you Maggie Callahan."

An inch at a time, he reluctantly lowered her to the ground. She gave him one of those patented impish smiles before she stepped away. The grin told him exactly what he'd been praying for—things between them were on a definite upswing. The thought delighted him so much, it took a moment for him to get his boots moving so he could follow her.

Moments later, they sat hip deep in grass watching

156

Blue drink from the bubbly creek. Only a single fence rail separated his pasture from hers. Too bad their relationship wasn't as simple, he thought. It'd be simpler if she forgot about those Five Star Oil leases she was determined to sign.

After seeing Jenny, he understood why she needed the cash advance from those leases. There were ways he could handle Five Star if he had to. It was her memory of the unbridled passion they'd shared that night in the cellar that threatened any chance they might have to get to know one another. If he wanted to get close to Maggie Callahan again, he'd have to spread his loop wide before he roped her.

As much as he wanted her physically, it was what went on inside her head that fascinated him most. If he made any move to hold her, even for a moment, it might cost him the intimacy he craved. He'd go slow and avoid any mention of Five Star.

Secure that his plan could work for the time being, Latigo sat beside her on the grassy point watching the creek curve toward his land. Easing back, he stretched out flat, fascinated by the whirling herd of clouds overhead. "This is livin'."

Taking a deep breath, she pulled her knees tightly to her chest. "You love it here, don't you?"

"Man and boy, it's been my home."

"I can't imagine you living anyplace else."

"Me either, darlin'."

Thoughtfully, she glanced back at the creek. "Look at the way those stones are piled. If I didn't know better, I'd think somebody might have done it." She fell back on the grass next to him. "Uncle Mike would never take the time to do such a thing. He was too practical. I guess I take after him."

"Could be." Being a single parent had forced her to be practical. Jenny's medical bills hadn't helped either. He lifted onto his elbow, looking down into her face. Her eyes were closed, as if she were completely unaware he was watching her.

The wind blew delicate strands of her hair across her forehead. Her lashes fluttered briefly before she brushed back her hair. Her naked forehead begged to be kissed by something other than the sun. He tossed the temptation aside as quickly as she had her hair. "How did you find this place?"

Her eyes sprang open. "Took a walk one day." She caught him watching, and her gaze skittered off toward the sky.

"Sometimes . . ." She moistened her lips and took two quick breaths. "I need to get away."

She didn't mention Jenny's braces, or the impending operation her dad had told him about. But Latigo knew that's what she meant. He tried to imagine strapping those braces around Jenny's legs every morning. Facing his own pain was one thing. What Maggie dealt with every day of her life was quite another. His pride in her multiplied. "How have you managed it? I mean with Jenny's medical bills and all?"

Her gaze stayed skyward. "We handle it. I don't know what I would've done without Dad, though. When our insurance company folded—"

"What?" He felt like a low-life snake slipping through the grass. His hand gripped her upper arm. "You mean you're footing the bills for Jenny's operations out of your own pocket?"

She nodded slowly before turning to look at him.

Self-pity had no place in her life. Neither did charity. She'd see any offer for her farm from him as just that— charity. If he doubted the truth of his reasoning, the straight-ahead glint in her eyes told him otherwise.

"How can you afford it?"

She sat up and slapped her palms together as if she were rubbing away bits of grass. "We're managing."

Sure you are. Jenny was living proof of Maggie's success. She'd more than managed. She'd raised a delightfully open and giving child. A special child like the countless others he'd lifted onto ole Blue's back for their first ride.

He smiled. Jenny had become more important to him than any of the youngsters from the Medical Center. A blind man could see why. Jenny belonged to Maggie. Whenever Latigo looked at her daughter, he saw Maggie as she must've looked when she was that age. Except for the leg braces, his thoughts repeated.

Unconsciously, he rubbed his right leg, reminding the constant pain it had no power over him. "You can do anything when you set your mind to it. Riding Blue proved that."

Maggie's hands dropped to her lap. "Thanks." She stared at the creek, but he had the feeling that her thoughts were elsewhere.

Another time, he'd have wrapped his arms around her and held her tightly until her only thoughts were of him. She needed to be held, and, Lord, how much he needed to do the holding. *Not now, cowboy. What this lady needs is a friend.* He shook his head in disbelief. Quite a notion having a woman for a friend. It's about time she got what she needed. So see to it.

Single parenting must be one lonely life, even with a live-in grandfather acting as father. *How long has it been since you didn't count every penny, practical Maggie?* Anger welled inside him. Anger aimed straight at a man whose name he'd yet to hear. A name he meant to know since that day at the barn raising when they'd overheard Jenny and Jimmy Lee talking about their fathers. Latigo needed to know about him. He needed to know now so he could understand and help her get over him once and for all.

"And Jenny's father?"

Her gaze froze on the freshwater creek. "What about him?"

"Hasn't he offered to help?"

She shook her head, concentrating her attention on the overhang of honeysuckle, and the spider clinging the strut on a sheltered web.

Latigo watched the spider climb higher and higher on its determined journey. Equally determined, he scrambled to his knees in front of her, blocking out the mesmerizing spider. "Surely he knows what you've been up against?"

Her stubborn chin jutted forward. "All he wanted was for me to have an abortion."

Eleven

Latigo fought the urge to take her into his arms, and looked at the lofty pecan trees. Even the leafy shadows kept their distance. He took his lead from them and didn't crowd her.

"Jenny's father didn't want her, but he still wanted you."

Her unflinching eyes brightened with surprise. "How'd you know that?"

"Any man would want *you,* darlin'." Not wanting a child she carried? That Latigo couldn't figure. He gave in to his gut response and took her slowly into his arms. She came willingly, as if she really needed him. His heart shouted hallelujah, jumping for joy when she relaxed against his chest. And when she nestled her head on his shoulder, he thought he'd died and gone to heaven. He breathed in her flower-scented hair, knowing it to be what an angel must smell like.

"David and I never lived together. When I found out I was pregnant, I planned a get-away weekend so I could tell him."

"And?" He filled in the long pause.

161

"The last time I saw David . . ." She gave a brittle laugh. "He was standing in the middle of our motel room holding a glass of white Zinfandel and talking about the abortion. I closed the door and left." Rocking back, she looked at him squarely. "It wasn't until I saw the north-bound toll gate on the Golden Gate Bridge that I realized all I had on was a towel."

Still in a state of undiluted shock, Latigo's mind reeled. How could anyone with a slap of sense figure she'd consider an abortion? He'd only known her for a short time and even he knew that. He dropped his arms. TJ had called her plucky right off. TJ was seldom wrong about people. About women? *Never.*

She got to her feet without his help. "Dad was somewhat shocked when I strolled into the apartment wearing that towel." Then as an afterthought, "Poor, Dad. He just sat there when I told him that David insisted it wasn't the right time for us to have a child."

"Right time?"

"Jenny was a surprise."

He noticed Maggie never mentioned the word *mistake.* From the instant she'd found out she was pregnant, Maggie wanted her baby. He knew that as well as he knew his own name. He cupped her shoulders with his hands, squeezing gently. "You must've loved him plenty."

"I thought I did. As it turned out, I loved my child more. Much more. Now I know if he'd agreed to my having the baby, he'd have always considered Jenny a mistake."

"But not you," he said, already knowing the answer.

"Jenny's always been a miracle."

"Even after you found out about her hip trouble?"

162

"Especially then." Her eyes sparkled whenever she spoke about the child she'd made the center of her life.

"You never saw him again?" He refused to call this David a man, even in his thoughts. The words that did come to mind weren't fit for Maggie to hear. Besides, he'd already overstepped himself plenty today when he got her to ride Blue. He wasn't about to make the same mistake twice. The thigh muscle in his right leg cramped as he struggled to his feet.

"See David? Why?" Silently, she shook her head. "We'd said all there was to say about the baby that day in the motel. He was adamant about the abortion." She turned toward the sweeping circle of pecan trees. He grabbed her elbow. He kept his hand on her arm, hoping she sensed his unspoken support.

"This David never came by to see you?"

She shook her head again. "At the time, I thought he would, too. Maybe even follow me back to San Francisco. He didn't. Oh, he called once, three days after the blowup. He wanted to know if I'd scheduled the abortion. I hung up on him, and I sent back his ring that afternoon."

They'd been engaged? Latigo turned her loose before his right hand, once gentle with concern for her, tightened into a fist.

Suddenly free from his grasp, she marched deeper into the trees.

"Wait, Maggie."

She kept on marching, stomping the grass into green stepping-stones. "When it comes to men, my judgment is flawed."

So that's it. She thought he was like . . . like this no account, David. No wonder she wanted to forget their lovemaking in the cellar. The man she'd expected to marry had turned his back on her and the child she carried.

Everything stopped. His breathing. His thoughts. Only his heart moved, and he knew it had gone straight to her. That's where he wanted to be, too. Holding her, stroking her hair and telling her . . . the truth perhaps? How could he?

His thigh muscle knotted harder. *Pain is what you deserve for not speaking up. You've waited too long already. Better that* you *tell her than she finds out from somebody else.*

He limped after Maggie grateful that she'd picked this moment to stubbornly turn her back. She'd misread the guilty look on his face for pain and reacted accordingly. He never courted pity from anyone, especially from her. What he wanted from her he had no right to expect. Buffalo barked and ran ahead filling the widening distance between them.

Latigo caught up with her when she knelt to pat Buffalo's head.

"I hope my Jenny can have a dog like you someday, Buffy. Our apartment over the store isn't big enough. We settled for a cat, until his hormones overpowered him, and he left town."

Her unlucky choice of men even held to cats?

"Maggie?" Latigo held out his hand. She took it without hesitation and stood before him. He smiled at her, wanting her to see his open admiration before he asked the one question he'd steadfastly avoided. "This David, where is he?"

"He and his skydiving buddies stepped out of a plane somewhere outside of Chattanooga. There was trouble with David's chutes. His brother wired me about the funeral three weeks before Jenny was born. I sent flowers and my regrets."

There was no bitterness in her tone, only a simple straightforward statement of the facts. She bent and scratched the tip of Buffalo's ear. The retriever's tail beat the bladed grass in appreciation.

"David never knew my baby's name," she added.

The words *my baby* walloped him in the gut with the force of a bronc's hoof. Never meant as a bid for pity, she'd made another simple statement. Jenny was hers and hers alone. Part of him rejoiced that there was no David complicating her life. Another part of him ached for the pain the S.O.B. still caused her.

"Jenny and Dad will be up from their nap soon." She gave him a questioning look. "Ready?"

He followed her, relieved that talking about David was over. Most of all, Latigo was proud she'd shared her life with him.

Riding back to the house, he sat in front of her. He'd selected the seating on Blue with purpose, knowing it afforded her a measure of privacy. To his delight, she rested the side of her head against his back. He liked the way her cheek rubbed up and down against his shoulder blade, and the way her arms went naturally around his middle. "Hang on, we're headed downhill."

"Go for it."

Gravity took hold. She slid forward, flattening against him like a leaf nailed to a pecan trunk. He felt the flowing outline of her curves on either side of his spine: her breasts, her hips, her open thighs against his. Lord, but it felt fine. Grabbing his silver buckle with her right hand, she sunk her left fingers inside his belt. All the while, she kept her cheek pressed against him. He reined in, wanting to make the ride last, so he'd have the pleasure of her arms tight around him.

When Blue trotted through the open gate, Latigo reluctantly dropped the reins and, lifting his leg over Blue's neck, slid to the ground. Maggie picked up the reins and scooted forward. After closing the gate, he swung up behind her and wrapped his arms around her. She sat back, leaning into the curve of his chest. He slumped forward taking as much of her into his arms as he could.

"How'm I doing with the riding?" she asked, tilting her head just enough so he could see her proud expression.

He made sure his smile testified to his words. "Mighty fine."

She squeezed her eyes shut tightly. "Look, no eyes."

"Don't get too tricky."

She sat up straight and gave an exaggerated salute. "Yes, sir. Tell me, when are you going to show me reverse?"

He laughed and hugged her tight, holding her exactly where he wanted her—flat against his heart. "Reverse we'll do later."

"You mean I mastered straight ahead?"

"From what I learned today, you mastered straight ahead long before you met me."

Twenty minutes later, he had Blue inside the trailer and was starting the truck's engine. Jenny, fresh from her nap, stood beside Maggie on the screened porch.

"Grandpa said he was glad you were coming back for dinner, Latigo," Jenny called. "I wish Blue could stay, too."

166

"Maybe another time." He glanced at his watch. "I'll see you in an hour?" He eyed Maggie for approval.

"How about an hour and a half?"

"You got it." He gunned the engine and headed home.

Why should she tell Latigo the Polish kielbasa was made with turkey?

Maggie wondered after he returned. He obviously enjoyed the eating as much as he did standing with Dad beside the barbecue and slapping the sausage with hickory-flavored sauce. Never a finicky eater herself, she looked forward to seeing Latigo soak up the last of the chili with a swipe of his rye bread.

She'd warned him to expect leftovers. He hadn't blinked an eye. True to his word, he'd helped Jenny set the table while Maggie got the leftover potato salad out of the refrigerator.

Forty minutes later, the chili and potato salad had vanished. She watched her dad and Latigo drain the last swallow of beer from the glasses she insisted they use.

Latigo winked. "It's been a long time since I've cooked."

"I recall you saying something about all you do is eat." She started clearing the table. "I'm glad you're capable of change." She took the stack of blue-willow plates to the sink and rinsed them. He followed, one hand full of silverware, the other balancing the empty chili bowls.

"TJ enjoys rattling around in the kitchen, so I stay out of his way."

"He was in the rodeo, too. Right?" She squeezed the soap into the sink and turned on the hot water.

"Yeah." He looked around. "Where's the towel?"

"Wade Latigo, King of the Rodeo, dries dishes?"

"Only if you promise not to brag it around."

"I'll do anything for help." She kneed the second drawer of the cabinet, rather than using a wet hand to point out where the towels were. He opened the drawer, took the top towel and stuffed it into the front of his jeans. Stepping back, he fisted his hands on his hips and gave her one of those raised-eyebrow looks. "What do you think?"

The pink-and-white checkered towel hung lengthwise from his belt buckle to his thigh like a Cherokee loin-cloth. "I think the blue-and-white one is more your color."

"You're right." He jerked off the towel and tossed it over his shoulder before taking the blue one from the drawer and planting one corner of it inside his belt.

Pretending not to notice, she got back to washing dishes.

"Well?" he asked, taking a plate from the drying rack.

She gave him a quick once-over. "Blue is definitely you."

Once the dishes were done, Jenny insisted they watch *The Little Mermaid* video while they ate the rainbow sherbet Latigo had brought for dessert.

Latigo applauded when the screen went fuzzy gray. "That was some movie, Jenny. I missed it when it ran here."

He truly had enjoyed the movie, although Maggie knew his taste probably ran to *The Searchers*. Come to think of it, that was her favorite Western, too. What was his favorite movie? *Gone With the Wind* would never be his first all-around choice as it was hers. She watched

168

him kneeling in front of the VCR waiting for tape to appear in the ejection slot. They'd made a giant step toward becoming friends today. She'd told him more about herself than she'd meant to. It'd been easy. He'd made it so.

"Bath time," Maggie said, straightening the stack of magazines on the coffee table.

Jenny's lower lip drooped. "Mom, do I have to?"

"Need any help?" Maggie avoided mentioning the braces.

"I can do it myself, Mommy." Jenny started down the hall, then stuck her head back around the corner. "We got this neat tub with big feet on it. You want to come and watch, Latigo?"

Latigo cleared his throat. "Maybe another time." Then whispered to Maggie, "Now if you were to make the same offer?"

"Don't hold your breath," she teased and headed for the kitchen with the last of the sherbet-stained paper napkins.

"Since you cleaned up, I'll get Jenny from her bath," her father said. "Mind if I go over to Nighthorse's for cribbage later?"

"Go ahead, Dad." She put the last of the washed ice cream bowls and spoons into the dish rack to dry.

"Be careful of the chief, he's been known to cheat," Latigo warned with a chuckle.

"If you knew Dad better you'd be giving Nighthorse a call."

"What are you doing tomorrow?" Latigo asked abruptly.

"You mean after Dad and I finish painting the back bedroom?"

Moments later, the kitchen door swung open, and her dad reappeared carrying Jenny. "Well here she is, all dried and powdered." He carefully sat Jenny on a kitchen chair. "Those rails on the tub sure make it easy for her to get in and out." Dad kissed Jenny and left for his cribbage game.

Jenny sat beside the table wearing a long cotton nightie and Latigo's hat. "Mommy? Look at me." The weight of the hat bent the tips of her ears down on each side of her smiling face. Maggie was certain if Jenny turned her head fast enough, the wide-brimmed Stetson would stay precisely in place.

"You know what?" Latigo held open the screen door and followed Maggie into the house. "I believe it's about time we got this cowgirl a hat of her own."

"We'll think about it," Maggie said. "Now, young lady, it's bedtime."

Latigo looked at Maggie. "Can she ride?"

Maggie realized he'd never seen Jenny without her support braces. "After a bath, always."

He squatted beside Jenny. "Your Mommy's right about bed. Slap leather, cowgirl." He scooped up Jenny and set her onto his shoulders.

"Duck," he called when they approached the first door.

Maggie watched them trot down the hall and into the bedroom she shared with her daughter. By the time Maggie arrived, Latigo was making a second gallop around the foot of the bed with the laughing Jenny holding tightly to his neck.

"Just once more, Latigo. Plee-eese," Jenny pleaded.

Maggie leaned against the door as he made a final pass and carefully dropped the squealing Jenny onto the double bed. It was the first time Maggie hadn't heard the old bedsprings screech. Of course, who could hear anything above Jenny's and Latigo's laughter? He retrieved his hat from the center of the bed and casually tossed it onto the Windsor chair.

"Tuck me in, Latigo?" Jenny asked, slipping between the sheets.

"Tuck you what?" He looked at Maggie, both eyebrows raised.

"You know, Latigo," Jenny said. "Tuck me in like you do your little girl."

"I'm not that lucky. I only have horses, Jenny."

Maggie winced. He always seemed a part of everything, she'd never given a thought to him being alone. His mother had deserted him. His stepfather was dead. On the other hand, Maggie rarely had a moment to herself with Jenny tagging along. But she couldn't imagine her life any other way.

Latigo plopped beside Jenny on the bed. "You'll have to show me how to tuck."

Jenny sat up, pulling her white cotton nightie so the front pleats were straight as sticks. "First, you have to fold the quilt. It's old, and we gotta be careful." She looked at Maggie.

Maggie nodded her approval.

"Mommy always puts it on that chair."

Latigo stood, folded the patchwork quilt and set it over the back of the chair that held his hat. "You do this every night, Maggie?"

Feeling self-satisfied that he was getting a hands-on lesson in what parenting was all about, Maggie nodded. "Every . . . single . . . night."

171

Jenny scooted deeper under the sheet, her arms tightly at her sides, holding down the covers. "Now. Tuck."

Once he'd tucked in the sheet, Latigo turned to go.

"What about prayers?" Folding her hands, Jenny closed her eyes. "Ready?" She took a quick peek at him. "Mommy kneels."

"Oh, sorry." Latigo knelt beside the bed copying the arrangement of Jenny's praying hands.

"Now I lay me down to sleep." Jenny peeked at him every other word as if afraid he'd left. "And God bless Mommy and Grandpa. Uncle Mike for giving us this house. Mr. TJ and my new friend, Jimmy Lee. And . . ." Her eyes squeezed tighter as if this were the most important part of the prayer. "Most of all, God bless Latigo for teaching me how to ride like the other kids. Amen."

"Amen," Latigo rasped, after clearing his throat twice.

Jenny rolled over and gave him a big smack on the cheek. He looked genuinely shocked. Maggie watched his Adam's apple move up and down several times before he returned the kiss. Looking quite unlike his steady self, he got to his feet quickly, took his hat from the chair, and started for the door without a word.

Maggie walked to Jenny's side of the bed. "Pleasant dreams, little one." She kissed Jenny. Jenny's arms stayed around her.

"I just love Latigo. Don't you, Mommy?"

Hearing Jenny's question, Latigo stopped and quickly retraced his steps. Standing in the bedroom doorway, he wanted to see Maggie's face when she answered her daughter.

"Mommy?"

"This isn't home, Jenny."

Sitting on the bed, Maggie sidestepped the love business as slick as a Texas two-step. Her expression, to his chagrin, gave no clue to her true feelings.

"You know we're selling this house," Maggie continued. "I explained that, before we left San Francisco, remember?"

Jenny frowned. "Kind of."

"Uncle Mike left us this house and land. Grandpa and I are painting it so we can sell it." Latigo watched Maggie shift uneasily on the bed. "Then we're going home."

Home meaning Frisco. Hell, New York City seemed closer than the West Coast. Maggie wasn't going anywhere. Not if he had anything to do with it, Latigo thought. And he meant to have plenty to say about her leaving Oklahoma. He didn't know how, but he'd find a way to keep her here. He had to.

Twelve

"When are we leaving, Mommy?"

Latigo dreaded hearing Maggie's answer. It was a pronouncement of doom. Impending doom.

"Soon, honey," Maggie said. "Very soon."

The clock inside his head ticked wildly. He'd known from that first night in the cellar, that D-day, Maggie's departure day, was coming. But she was talking weeks. If he brought up her signing those oil leases it would only lead to trouble. Time was running out. He had to do something, anything. But how could he tell her the truth about Five Star? She'd never respect him if he caved in on an issue he felt so deeply about. How else could he get her to stay? His thoughts snapped to attention. Whoa, when had delaying her leaving changed to getting her to stay? The tight grip on his Stetson brim made a permanent crease.

Maggie kissed Jenny's forehead. "In San Francisco you have your own bed. Won't that be nice?"

Jenny's eyes slid shut. "Yes, Mommy. But I won't have Blue in San Francisco."

"I know. I know."

No, he thought, all Jenny had was a skinny back yard no bigger than a barn stall. And what about Maggie? He'd bet plenty she didn't give a rat's rump about that liquor business she owned. From what he'd learned about Maggie Callahan she'd like nothing better than to spend more time with her daughter.

He waited down the hall for Maggie. He should leave. Lord knows, he needed to sort out things and being close to Maggie Callahan always got in the way of clear thinking. Seeing her in the shallow-lit hall, he realized he knew what he wanted—her. Not only for the moment, he wanted her today, tomorrow and everyday.

He gritted his teeth.

After what she'd shared about Jenny's father, she'd finally begun to trust him. Getting her to even consider making Broken Arrow her home was a long ways off. He'd overcome challenges before when the doctors said he'd never ride again. That victory paled when Maggie stepped into the hallway, and he saw her determined expression. She'd already made up her mind. Come hell or high water, the woman was leaving.

"She's a pistol, that daughter of yours." He took Maggie's hand, and they headed into the living room.

"I know. Let's go into the kitchen. We've got to talk."

He didn't like the sound of that, but he followed anyway. When they got to the door, he reached for the light switch.

"No. Don't turn on the light." Entering the moonlit kitchen, she stopped beside the cleared table. "What I have to say, I'd rather say in the dark."

At last. The two of them finally alone. Things were definitely looking up. He hooked his hat on the doorknob behind him. In three long strides he was standing behind her, his hands on her shoulders.

"Jenny likes you, Latigo."

"The feelin' is mutual." He bent to kiss her neck, but she stepped away abruptly. His hands fell to his sides, but he held his ground. Too bad he hadn't held back that kiss. If he wanted her to even consider staying, he'd have to go slow when it came to romancing.

"I see a heap of you in Jenny."

Maggie whirled around. "She's a young girl who's going home in a matter of weeks. Impressionable. She already thinks the world of you. Don't make our leaving Oklahoma painful by making her believe there's a chance we might stay. We're leaving."

Leaving? There was that word again. "Am I doing that?"

"You could, by promising her things that I can't afford to give her now or in the future."

"Like what?"

"Horses and hats. Boots, that she may never be able to wear."

Before he could think of a reason against it, his hands were on her shoulders again. "You're not talking about horses and hats, darlin'? Why not cut to the chase?"

She shook off his hands and went out onto the porch. Moonlight filtered through the screen painting the floor an ashen gray. He didn't like the ominous floor color any more than he liked the way their conversation was headed.

"I thought my meaning was obvious," she said.

He stepped up behind her pinning her between his chest and the screened wall of the porch. "I'm a mite slow on the pickup." The lilt of humor he'd purposely put into his tone had no effect on her.

She turned away, bending her shoulders to avoid touching any part of him, and stared out into the empty pasture.

"You're tired, Maggie. Why don't you get ready for bed?"

"Not until we talk." She faced him, her body hemmed in by his hands on the wood-framed screen.

"We'll talk, I promise. Tomorrow. When we're both rested."

Nodding, she smiled wistfully. "Perhaps that would be best. You must be exhausted. Jenny's nonstop energy affects people that way. Won't TJ be wondering about you?"

Relieved at the sudden change in their conversation, he took hope. "TJ? He gave up worrying about me years back." Risking a reprimand, Latigo nudged her chin with the bend of his thumb, until she looked up to him. "There's only two people we have to answer to, darlin'. That's me and you."

Night shadowed her face, hiding those lips he was dying to taste. *Thanks, moon.* The last thing he needed to do was to confuse things by kissing her. He settled for draping his arm over her shoulders while they walked back into the kitchen.

"You shower or whatever. I'll hang around until you're settled in for the night," he said. "Mind if I watch ESPN? Got to see how my Texas Rangers are doing." He stopped abruptly. "Will the TV wake Jenny?"

"Are you kidding? She won't move until the sun shines."

He turned on the TV and dialed the channel.

"If you hear the Giants' score, holler," she called, before she rounded the corner and disappeared down the hall.

He looked toward the empty doorway. "You like baseball?"

"The San Francisco Giants? Absolutely. And what about my Niners'?"

The San Francisco Forty-Niners? She was a football fan, too? The TV station's blue logo faded, and the baseball scores rolled across the screen. "Now, we got real trouble, woman. I'm a Cowboy fan."

"Dallas? You poor thing." He heard a door close and the sound of water running in the bathtub.

Moments later, he lay stretched out on the sofa. The splashing sound of tub water stopped. She must be toweling off. He recrossed his legs determined to concentrate on the local news break. But all he could think about was her tender skin that the thick white towel, he'd seen hanging above the tub, was drying. Lucky towel.

"You never did tell me, how the Giants did, Latigo?"

Stepping from the hall, she stood beside his propped up boots. Even from six feet away, he could smell the subtle combination of soap and dusty powder. She smelled sweeter than the honeysuckle blooming alongside Honeysuckle Creek. Her towel-dried hair, still damp, tangled about her face like a glistening halo. She'd asked about baseball scores? His thoughts at the moment were strictly earthy.

"That was fast," he said trying to sound casual.

She wore a nightgown, an exact copy of the one Jenny had worn to bed. He knew she must've made them both. Back lit by the hall light, the curve of her hips and the shape of each leg was unmistakable. But it was the space between those legs that held his complete attention. A space he'd filled before. A space he'd like to fill again. His throat went dry, and when he tried to swallow, his tongue stuck to the roof of his mouth as if it were coated with peanut butter.

"Well?" She wrapped the lightweight matching robe tighter about her, cinching the dangling ribbon tie around her waist.

He swallowed again, freeing his tongue. "Bad news. Dodgers five, Giants two, in the seventh. Clark is zero for the night."

She rounded the arm of the sofa. "I knew it. And how are the Rangers doing? Who pitched tonight?"

How the hell was he supposed to remember with her standing there in a nightgown? A gown that covered her from throat to toes. A gown he found sexier than hell. "The Texas game is on a rain delay."

"Nuts."

"You're a rare woman, Maggie Callahan."

"Why?"

"You like football and baseball, too."

"I'm my father's daughter. What choice did I have?" She glanced at the TV. "Ready to raid the refrigerator?"

"I might be persuaded." He clicked off the TV remote and followed her. "Is there any of that turkey pastrami left?" He stopped behind her awaiting her reaction.

Barely inside the kitchen, she flipped on the light switch and whirled around. "You devil. You knew all the time." She snatched a towel from the rack and snapped it playfully at his thigh.

Slowly raising his knees high, he strutted like a turkey for the refrigerator. "It came to me kind of sudden-like when TJ asked me a question, and I gobbled my answer."

She rehung the towel. "Why didn't you say anything?"

"And spoil your fun? Besides, the chili was great. One of the best I've ever had. Same goes for the grilled sausage tonight."

"You did like my turkey chili then?"

"I ate two helpings."

She opened the refrigerator door. "Three."

"Hell, who's counting?"

"Me." Holding the refrigerator open, she faced him completely unaware of the tasty silhouette she made. "Did you say pastrami?"

"Pastrami?" His gnawing hunger had nothing to do with turkey or pastrami. What man could think of food looking at her? She had the face of an angel, and a body made for sin. He wanted to take her in his arms and break a few commandments.

"Wait, Maggie."

"Yes?" She let go of the refrigerator, and the door began to close automatically.

"Watching you and Jenny tonight was like looking through a store window at Christmas." *At something I'd like to have one day,* he added to himself.

The refrigerator door thudded shut, and she stepped away. "You should have children of your own, Latigo."

"I'm ready if you are?" Without uttering a sound, he was beside her. She looked up at him, her eyes clear and bright. Her scrubbed pink cheeks plumped when she smiled. The heady fragrance of honeysuckle-scented powder filled his nostrils.

"Latigo, we can't go on like this."

There was no mistaking the need in her voice. It was the same urgent need that he'd been fighting all day. A need to take her into his arms and hold her. A need he had no intention of fighting any longer. "My thoughts exactly. You need something now, and I'm not talking rye bread." He waited for a reaction, any sign, but she turned away from him.

"Look at me, Maggie."

Slowly, she looked up.

She bit her bottom lip before he saw the pink tip of her tongue skim halfway across her mouth. Like a mirror image, he moistened his own lips. Was she remembering the peach-flavored kisses they'd shared in the cellar?

He certainly was. "Quit thinking of everybody else. Reach for what you want like you did that night in the cellar. Reach for *me*."

Desire fevered her eyes.

"You need tending. Let me do for you. I want to so much." With one hand, he hit the light switch, while his other arm swept her to him in the darkness. The softness of her breasts melted against his chest. The thin layers of cotton nightgown couldn't mask her heat. Her skin was as fired as his. She needed him. She needed him bad.

"I'm afraid."

"Of me? Don't be." He nuzzled her neck, drawing in the heady smell of honeysuckle soap. "There's only two things I've ever been afraid of, a stubborn woman and bein' left afoot. Since that first night in the cellar, I only worry about bein' left afoot."

"I can't imagine you bein' afraid of anything."

"Oh, no?" Her legs gave way to his as if they were dancing toward the table. He lifted her, setting her gently on the table corner. "Your leavin' for Frisco scares the hell out of me, darlin'."

"But I am leaving."

"Right." Her arms were around his neck, he could feel her bath warmed cheeks sanding back and forth against the opened front of his shirt. He untied her robe and swept it open. "How do I unhitch this nightgown?"

"Buttons—"

His fingers searched the ruffled yoke until they found

181

the satiny ribbon and untied it. "You and these buttons are about to do me in."

"Sorry." Her voice shook almost as much as his hand when he got to the tiny top button. It was round as a pearl and twice as slippery.

"How about using that pull-apart stuff next time?" He worked the top button open. "That sticky stuff that rips apart."

"Velcro? I—"

He muffled the rest of her answer with an urgent kiss. "I'd like to be using my hands for other things. More pleasant things." When he touched the second button, she pulled away, her shaky hand covering his.

"Latigo, we—"

"This is the nineties, Maggie. Nobody cares what we do in the dark."

"We shouldn't."

"But it feels too-oo good to stop." He courted her with soft sipping kisses. Wet kisses. Slow kisses that pleaded to be answered. Kisses that left his chest heaving into hers.

She tasted of spearmint toothpaste, and he had a sudden craving for the minty flavor. He kissed her again. And when her lips parted he tasted desire on her tongue.

"It's been so long since I touched you. Too long, darlin'."

He worked her nightgown open as she unsnapped his shirt. Her naked nipples, tight as tiny fists, rubbed back and forth against his bare chest until he thought his throbbing hardness would explode. Turning his head away for an instant, he fought for control. Tonight belonged to her, and he meant to tend to her needs. He'd learn what made her call out his name in panting pleasure.

He kissed her again and again making moist love to

her with his mouth. Speaking with slow caresses, his lips felt her yielding. His hand roamed her spine following the line to her heart-shaped fanny. Slowly, he traced the silky path of her hips around to her thighs. Her legs stiffened and came tightly together.

"There's only us. Only us. Let me. Let me."

Relaxing, her thighs spread slightly when he stroked their inner softness, and the springy triangle he knew only by touch. He quickened the palming movement of his hand. "This is the best I can do for now, darlin'."

She trembled before her arms tightened about his neck, her fingernails digging into his shoulders as she lifted her hips.

"You're so damp." Any other time, hesitation wouldn't have occurred to him. With her, everything was different. He'd always seen to a woman's needs before his own. With Maggie, he had more than possession on his mind. He wanted to free the explosive need he felt quaking her shoulders. More than anything, he wanted her to say she wanted him and only him.

"I always finish what I start." He nuzzled her cheek with his chin, asking her to lift her face to his. "Kiss me. Again. Again."

"Latigo," she panted softly, wrapping her arms tighter around his neck. She pulled herself higher above the table top giving him access to her.

"Let go. Come against my hand." She shivered as his hand and fingers made love to her. His body ached with wanting, but he stifled his own need and concentrated on her. He alternated the press and intenseness of his touch learning more about what pleased her most.

She bucked against his hand, rocking back and forth to the rhythmic pace. "Wade. Wade."

Her hips moved faster and faster. When she gripped his neck tighter he felt her femininity quiver with liquid fire. She called his name again, and smothered her cries against his naked shoulder. His free arm bent around her holding her pinned tightly to him. He kept her flat against him until he felt her relax. Slowly, he let her weight slide back onto the corner of the table.

She grabbed his wrist, closing her thighs tightly. "Don't take your hand away."

He looked down into her feverish eyes and kissed her. Her lips shivered beneath his. The sensation tightened his manhood into a knotted lariat. "I'm not going anywhere."

He held her, never wanting to let her go. He felt weak. Other parts of him felt alive as only she made him feel. He knew if he asked she'd touch his arousal and relieve the ache. He let his head slump so he could kiss the top of her head. Her damp hair clung to his chin. He buried his face in the fragrant strands losing his own need in the heated scent.

"What about you?" she asked.

He smiled and held her tighter. "Another time. Another place. I'll wait, I'm a big boy."

She tilted her face up so that the moonlight spread a golden glow across her cheeks. "I know. You're big all over."

To emphasize her point, he moved his finger inside of her slightly. She moaned and tightened her thighs holding his hand a willing prisoner.

"You've climaxed before," he whispered.

She nodded into his chest. "With you . . . it's different."

Finally, she looked up at him. The corners of her

mouth inched into a nervous smile. Knowing her, that was quite an admission.

"When I'm with you, I climax so strong. I need more time after . . ." Her head sank back to his chest. "To recover."

"I'm glad." She'd said how much she needed him. He had only to listen with his heart. He did, hearing the words as clearly as if she'd whispered them aloud.

She squeezed his forearm. "I'm fine now."

After she buttoned her nightgown, he scooped her up into his arms. "Then we'd best get you into bed now. I want you rested when I pick you up tomorrow at five."

"Tomorrow?"

"I owe you a dinner. My place? Five o'clock. Casual."

"You've made it impossible for me to say no."

"That's what I counted on."

As he passed the kitchen telephone, his eyes read the message on the note pad next to the receiver: call Five Star. The airy curved writing had to be Maggie's. He grimaced. He had to tell her the truth.

He made his way down the hall cradling her in his arms. The mattress springs squeaked when he laid her on the bed. Beside her, Jenny's deep breathing never missed a beat.

"Pleasant dreams." He kissed Maggie's eyelids until they closed.

She raised her chin. "Just one more."

"My pleasure." He obliged. He found himself wishing this were their empty bed, and he had the right to crawl into bed beside her. He glanced over at the sleeping Jenny. He loved the way Jenny's curly blond hair spread out on the flowered pillowcase, and the way her lashes, dark and thick, shadowed her cheeks. The resemblance to Maggie was uncanny.

When it came to horse breeding, a colt got his size and power from his sire. A colt inherited his heart from his mother. Jenny was all heart when it came to pain. The courageous heart she'd gotten from Maggie.

He knew something about pain himself. Unconsciously he rubbed his right leg and the constant ache. Maybe his mother had left him something after all. Until this moment, the thought that he owed anything to his mother never occurred to him. He had Maggie to thank for that. Maggie and her daughter.

He looked back at Maggie's lazy sated smile. The rank bull high-hoofed his gut. His life would never be complete, unless she shared it. He laughed at the discovery. Hell's bells, who was he kidding? He loved Jenny's mother. But did he love her enough to tell her the truth and compromise about those oil leases? If not, he'd lose her. It was compromise or take an even riskier road and bide his time. Time was running out.

"When you call Five Star tomorrow ask for Brewer," he said.

Her eyes shot open. "Who's Brewer?"

"He's the head knocker for Five Star. Mention my name."

"He's a friend of yours?"

For an instant, the old anger about the oil drilling festered inside him. "A friend? Not anymore."

"Then why should I mention you?"

"Because I used to own a chunk of Five Star."

She sat bolt upright in bed. "You what?"

Thirteen

The next morning Maggie threw herself into painting the back bedroom rather than face the questions about Latigo once owning a piece of Five Star Oil. Mister nice guy had a major flaw. He was a two-faced liar. She dipped the brush back into the paint bucket. What right did he have objecting to her signing some paltry oil leases after he'd pumped thousands of dollars out of the Oklahoma dirt? Well, he'd soon find out she could make her own deals.

She slapped the wet paintbrush back and forth along the door molding. And after she'd shared the truth about Jenny's father. Why hadn't he told her about his connection with Five Star before? If she'd had her way, she'd have driven over to see Latigo right after breakfast and voiced the questions face-to-face, but her practical side won out and she elected to wait.

It usually did, except on rare occasions, like last night. Whenever he kissed her, practicality fled. She felt adrift, out of control. The intense physical desire for him was understandable—practically speaking. What woman

187

wouldn't respond? she thought. It was her emotional response to him that she steadfastly avoided probing.

She had time for only one thing—answers. Anger sparked inside her. She had every right to be angry. After what he'd told her about his relationship with Five Star, her anger doubled. She let it.

She glanced at the clock above the refrigerator. Five o'clock. The ever-prompt Latigo would be here in an hour. She found herself actually looking forward to their meeting. She had plenty she wanted to say to Wade Latigo. Rinsing the paintbrush in water for the last time, she dropped it into the empty bucket and set them on the back porch. "I'm going to shower."

"Fine," her father said. "Jenny and I are off for a walk. Say hello to Latigo for us."

"And to Buffy, too," Jenny echoed.

Jenny had picked up on the golden retriever's new name. Latigo hadn't seemed to mind. Maggie's thoughts ground to a sudden halt when she remembered how close Jenny and Latigo had become during the riding lesson. The bittersweet thought lingered. As grateful as she was for his teaching Jenny to ride, Maggie didn't want her daughter getting too attached to a man she'd soon be saying good-bye to.

She watched her dad and Jenny head down the road toward Nighthorse's, knowing Dad would wind up playing cribbage under the pecan trees, and Jenny would be busy exploring with Jimmy Lee. All of the Callahans were accounted for. Earlier this morning, she'd called Five Star and spoken to Mr. Brewer. There was no mistaking the interest in Brewer's voice when she mentioned Latigo's name. The polite questions Brewer asked about his former partner shifted suddenly to a pointed question about her land.

Five Star had actually made her an offer to buy the farm, all of it. An offer Brewer said he'd firm up today with a check he'd drop off at the real-estate office. *So why haven't you shared the good news with Dad?* her guilty conscience asked. She tried to convince herself she didn't want to get Dad's hopes up.

The theory didn't fly.

She didn't bother fabricating another. The truth was— she couldn't bear thinking about what selling her farm to Five Star would do to Latigo.

Her anger at Latigo's lie paled. How would she tell him that his new neighbor might be Five Star Oil? No matter. If Brewer did come through with the promised check, she'd sell him the land. She had to, for Jenny's sake.

Twenty minutes of showering and shampooing only aggravated her dilemma. Too much time to think did that to people. Powdered and dressed, she paced along the back of the house when the shiny black truck swung into the drive.

"Afternoon." Latigo stepped from the cab, looking as innocent as an angel. His halo, however, had slipped. After what she had to tell him, her own halo seemed none too shiny.

He wore a chambray shirt, the one he'd lent her in the cellar. The one she'd laundered, mended and returned to him the day of the barn raising. Stalling for time, she counted the tiny stitches along the corner of the pocket until his smile vanished.

"You spoke to Brewer, right?"

"This morning."

189

His jaw tightened. "And?"

The moment for truth had arrived. "They made me another offer."

"On the oil leases?"

"No. They're interested in buying the farm."

His eyes narrowed. "That's not interest. That's revenge." He grabbed her arm, hurrying her toward the truck. "And you fell for it like a roped steer."

His strength overpowered her. Feeling utterly helpless, she looked at the straw satchel on the porch step. "At least let me get my purse."

"All you're getting is into the truck. We've got to talk." He opened the door.

She struggled harder, but finally gave up and got into the truck.

"Relax. I'll get your purse." He had her purse and was sitting beside her before she could protest further.

From his side of the bench seat, she heard metal click upon metal. "Put on your seat belt, this might get bumpy."

She followed his lead and buckled up.

Without a word, he started the engine and took off. Gravel pinged off both fenders, kicking up a fuzzy cloud behind the tailgate.

"Driving this way won't do much for your paint job."

"You wanted to see my place, right?"

"Well, yes—"

"Here's your chance. You'd best take it. If you sell your land to Five Star, we're quits."

"Don't threaten me, Latigo."

"It's no threat. It's a flat-out promise."

"Fine with me." Determined to show her mettle, she leaned forward when they reached the mailbox reading,

LATIGO. She'd passed the box many times, but always resisted the urge to make the right turn and satisfy her curiosity.

The truck picked up speed. "Hang on." He swung the truck to the right.

Tires squealed.

She screamed.

The truck slid sideways toward the barbed-wire fence. Screeching brakes muffled her second scream. With sheer strength he pulled the truck back to the middle of the road and held it there until it skidded to a halt.

He unhitched both of their seat belts and slid next to her.

Fear flamed into anger. She wanted to strike out, to punch him right in the face. "You bastard, are you trying to get us both killed?"

His fingers tangled in her hair, forcing her to look at him.

"Are you all right, Maggie?" His hands dug deeper, fisting her hair into a tight knot.

"I will be once I get out of here." She fumbled blindly with the door handle until she realized it was locked.

He moved in closer, his ragged breath scalding her cheek.

"You're goin' to help Brewer cut off my balls. Why, Maggie?"

"You know why."

"Yeah, you're doin' it for Jenny." His eyes darkened with anger. "Well, I'm doin' this for me." He kissed her hard and fast, moving his mouth back and forth over hers, forcing her lips to yield and open.

For a moment, she forgot everything but the silky

stroke of his tongue. The sudden intimacy. The possession.

Unable to resist, she kissed him back knowing if he wanted to make love here and now, she'd let him.

He drew his mouth from hers, abruptly holding her at arms length. "Getting what you want isn't all it's cracked up to be. It can be empty and meaningless." He sunk back behind the steering wheel. "Why does touching you bring out the worst in me?"

"If I knew, believe me, I'd tell you." She smoothed back her hair and tried to catch her breath. All the while he watched, waiting.

Tension sizzled between them like summer lightning. She thought for a moment that a Tulsa twister had blown into the cab. She'd been through a tornado. Despite the physical attraction she felt for him, she'd weather this storm too.

"I'm goin' to show you something." He clicked on his seat belt and waited until she'd done the same.

Obviously, he'd decided to try and change the mood. She elected to do the same.

The truck lurched forward.

"Maybe then you'll know why I reacted so strongly to your deal."

Truth dawned. The wanton kisses had nothing to do with her. He wanted to strike back at Five Star, and she was the handiest. Her stomach churned. She felt as if he'd slugged her hard and low. "If you insist."

The paved road edged uphill, and when they reached the crest he slowed the truck. "As far as you can see belongs to me." He paused as if he were awaiting her reaction.

What could she say? She knew the physical punishment he'd put his body through to get this land. She also knew that she'd deal with the devil himself if it meant that Jenny could throw away those braces. She slumped back against the seat. *He's right. Better enjoy the view. It's the first and last time you're going to see it.*

The countryside opened into green pasture lands bordered by rows and rows of trees. It suddenly occurred to her that the valley, and the steel-bright ponds had been carefully orchestrated in every detail, and by a man who knew exactly what he wanted.

"I never knew there was such a place."

"The house is back a ways."

A ways? she thought. A mile was more like it.

The wire fencing on her side of the truck changed to weathered gray slats of wood. After a quarter of a mile she knew why, when a red horse raced along the fence challenging their truck. Latigo honked the horn in greeting and hit the accelerator. The horse strained forward keeping abreast of the truck. She felt her eyes widen when she glanced at the speedometer.

"How fast can he go?"

He lifted his boot from the accelerator. "No telling. He always wins."

She knew Latigo always *let* the animal win. "He's yours?"

"You bet he is. Me and the ladies." The truck coasted to a stop when the horse disappeared over the hill. "Romeo dances with all the ladies."

"Dances?"

He slipped his arm along the back of the seat, his fingers fidgeting with the sleeve of her blouse. "Romeo is a stallion. A stud." He paused as if to make sure she understood the meaning of *stud*.

193

"Oh." She frowned. "Where does that leave Blue?"

Throwing back his head, Latigo laughed heartily. "Blue's no competition. He's a gelding."

"What does his color have to do with anything?"

He leaned closer. "Gelding, as in altered."

Altered? She'd used that word, but only when altering a dress pattern especially when she made those matching nightgowns she and Jenny wore. She'd altered the woman's pattern so the long gown would fit a five-year-old.

Altered. Her mind whirled. She'd never heard the word *altered* applied to a horse. Or if she had, she'd never paid any attention to the meaning.

Latigo's brows lifted to a questioning angle. "Altered, as in castrated."

Her spine hit the back of the seat. That's what he'd accused her of helping Brewer do to him. Latigo could've made her feel stupid right about now, but he didn't. Instead, he'd deliberately made the explanation as natural as breathing. "No wonder poor Blue obeys your every command. If you threatened me with that, I'd do whatever you said too."

"Small chance of that. There's only one thing I'd change about you—that's your deal with Five Star."

If Brewer delivered the check, it was a done deal. If Latigo wanted another argument, he'd have to look elsewhere. When she made no response, he gunned the truck's engine. Fence posts whizzed by.

"You love it here, don't you?"

"There's no other place in the world for me."

"I guess when you traveled with the rodeo you saw most of the states."

"That was making a living. I kept a tight rein on my

194

prize money. Put a big chunk of it into Five Star. The oil boom hit and, I'm not proud to say, the rest is history."

"Mr. Brewer said you'd pulled out several years back."

"As it turned out, our disagreement over the direction Five Star should take saved my investment." He kept his eyes dead ahead.

"You severed your relationship with the company completely?"

He nodded.

"And you've felt guilty ever since."

"Maybe." He gripped the steering wheel tighter. "Well, aren't you goin' to tell me I had no right objecting to you signing those oil leases and putting some change in your pockets?" The truck coasted downhill.

"I did that the first time we met. Now that you've met Jenny and know why I need the money, I thought you'd be more understanding."

"I gave you Brewer's name, didn't I?"

"And I thank you for that."

"I vowed never to help Five Star again. I broke my word for you, Maggie Callahan."

"Me?" She tried to concentrate on the view, but couldn't take her eyes off him. "You helped with Five Star for Jenny's sake. So she'll have a chance to walk and run like Jimmy Lee. You made a trade for something you deemed more important than how you feel about oil drilling."

His Adam's apple bobbed up and down, but he never looked at her.

"Did you think I didn't realize that?"

He shook his head. "My oil fever ran its course. But know this, Maggie. Back then, I'd have sunk an oil shaft

195

through my grandmother's grave, if I knew where she was buried."

"You're awfully hard on yourself, Latigo."

"Am I?" He gave her a sidelong glance. "Then what say you make things a bit easier on both of us?"

"How?"

"By selling me your mineral rights for starters."

"I don't need charity, Latigo."

"Charity? This is business. Don't you see Five Star is after the oil. If you sell me the mineral rights—"

"They'd never buy the land without the mineral rights."

"Brewer only offered to buy your land to needle me. He figures to get the place on the cheap before I have a chance at the mineral rights."

She let her eyes widen. "Why didn't *you* mention buying the mineral rights before?"

"Brewer hadn't made his move. Besides, the notion just occurred to me."

Another lie. Her disappointed reflection in the windshield stared back at her. "You're so full of it, Latigo. I'm surprised your eyes are still gray."

He made no effort to stifle his laugh. "All right. All right. I've had my eye on those mineral rights before you blew into town. They would've been my ace in the hole against Five Star shooting me in the back."

"And?" She waited for him to admit what she only guessed.

His jaw tightened. "If I'd offered to buy them sooner you would've been long gone." He gave her a quick look.

He'd wanted her to stay all along? What about now? Whether he still wanted her to stay or not, the admission melted the remaining tension.

"What choice did I have?" he continued. "After the tornado, I met Jenny. I saw you two together. We met at the barn raising. You were busy making plans and painting the house. I was rounding up strays. Nobody was talking business. I wanted Jenny to have a chance to ride and be . . ."

"A real Oklahoma cowgirl?"

"Right."

The truck picked up speed.

She imagined him riding Blue along Honeysuckle Creek's meandering curves. Her fingers clutched at her skirt. If Five Star owned the land, Brewer wouldn't let Latigo within ten feet of that creek.

Suddenly, the idea of Latigo protecting the land from the oil company seemed exactly right. Good Lord, the cash would solve many of her problems. Quick cash was far better than waiting around. She could pay off most of the doctor bills before Jenny's next surgery. So why was she feeling glum? She knew the answer. Soon she'd be saying good-bye to the man sitting beside her.

"Well?" he asked.

"You got yourself a deal."

She knew this deal was more than business. She'd watched Latigo with Jenny and witnessed the bonding. Whatever they decided about the mineral rights, it was much more than business.

The truck stopped, and she heard him click off the engine.

"What say we step inside and rustle up a cool drink?"

"We're here?" She scanned the one-story house as he helped her from the truck. Native stone pillars punctuated the wide sweep of the front porch. The house looked

197

more like a California ranch house than a traditional Oklahoma design.

"That was fast." She took his arm and they walked toward the porch.

"Surprised?"

"Yes. This could be a home in the California suburbs."

"It's the architect, John Lang. I met him in Livermore, at the rodeo.

"Livermore, California?"

"Yep. He bought a string of horses, and we got along so well he designed the place for me."

"So there are a few Californians you like?"

"I'm coming around, prune-picker."

He hadn't called her that since they'd first met at the junior rodeo. "Do you call all Californians prune-pickers?"

"Only after I get to know them." Latigo opened one side of the double door. The scent of wind-swept pine filled the entry hall. She stepped onto the slate floor, instantly aware that the piney smell hadn't come from an aerosol spray. Like everything about Wade Latigo, the scent was real. Potently enticing.

"This is beautiful." She scanned the line of native stone pillars separating the dining room from the living room, intent on discovering the source of the woodsy fragrance. Her gaze settled on the cluster of terra cotta pots filled with tall pines. She should've figured he'd find a way of blending the greenery with the massive mix of leather furniture and wood.

He took off his hat and tossed it onto a bentwood hall tree. "The kitchen is this way."

She followed him through the louvered doors. The off-white kitchen walls were a sharp contrast to the natural wood and stone she'd seen.

"TJ likes white. I like wood, so we compromised. I'm getting better at that lately. Thanks to you." He opened the refrigerator and took out a frosty pitcher of iced tea and put it on the tile counter.

In a matter of minutes they'd drained their glasses, refilled them, and they were sitting at the kitchen bar. The tang of fresh lemon filled the kitchen. She looked out over the shadow-checkered lawn to the front of a huge barn.

"How long have you lived here?"

"All my life. The back of the house is original. Jonathan Wade built it."

"Your foster father?"

"The very one. I wanted to keep it the way I saw it when he first brought me here from the orphanage. Later when the oil money started rolling in, we remodeled it like we dreamed it could be."

"Now you've got everything the way you want it."

"Not without those mineral rights." Unhooking one boot heel from the foot rail, he swiveled his stool around and faced her. He drew her to her feet, pulling her closer until she stood between his thighs. "What say we finalize the deal?"

The man knew how to negotiate. She'd give him that. Oh, he never moved his legs. He didn't have too. She knew exactly how many hot inches separated his thighs from her hips. Her knees went weak. Before she tilted sideways and made a fool of herself, she held out her hand.

They were eye to eye. Leaning forward, he closed his thighs, trapping her against his big . . . silver belt buckle.

"Ordinarily I shake to cinch a deal."

If he meant to kiss her, he'd better hurry while she could still stand. She sagged against him.

"But with you a handshake seems a might too impersonal. A kiss—"

The kitchen door flew open.

They sprang apart.

"Latigo?" TJ stopped in midstride when he saw her and snatched off his battered hat. "Miss Maggie. I almost forgot you was comin' today."

"What is it, TJ?" Latigo asked.

"It's July." TJ clutched his hat tighter. "She's been pacing some and swishing her tail."

Both of Latigo's boots hit the floor. "Is she down?"

Maggie stood there. Not knowing what to do. Not knowing who'd been hurt. From the way Latigo moved, it must be serious.

Fourteen

Latigo tracked TJ's eyes, following them to her. Maggie watched, feeling completely left out. And she was.

"TJ?" There was no mistaking the anxiety in Latigo's voice. "Is she down, I said?"

"Yeah," TJ answered. "Just now. I saw your truck and came running." TJ slapped his hat back on his head. "Pardon me for breakin' in, Miss Maggie."

"July is my mare," Latigo explained. "She's been settled a long time and is fixing to drop."

Settled. Maggie knew barely enough to translate the breeder's terms: One of Latigo's horses was going to have a baby. A foal, she corrected.

"Sorry about dinner. I've got to get to the barn." Latigo headed for the back door. "TJ will drive you home."

"No way," she called. "I'm coming with you."

"Are you sure? This could take a while."

"I'm coming."

"It could also be messy."

"I've seen blood before, Latigo."

"If you're sure then. Come along. I'd welcome the help." He glanced over his shoulder at TJ. "Call the vet."

"Will do, boss. I'll get him over here pronto."

She followed Latigo outside, running to keep up. Cutting his strides in half, he reached for her hand. Their fingers locked. His grip was firm, his hand warm.

Running hand-in-hand, they covered the distance to the barn in nothing flat. He swung open the door, and she breathed the scent of seasoned hay. Letting go of her hand, he stepped into a lit stall, and disappeared.

Maggie heard the slow, labored panting, she supposed came from the mare, July. Instinctively, she knew he was on his knees beside the mare. It took her a minute before she got enough nerve to peek around the corner of the stall. As she'd suspected, he was kneeling next to the mare. The mare tried to lift her head, but gave up the idea. The animal lay on its side, its swollen belly rising and falling.

"Is she in pain?" All too quickly she realized how stupid the question sounded. Of course the mare was in pain—she was having a baby.

"Yes, she's hurting. Aren't you, July?" He patted her belly gently. The mare snorted as if she were saying Thanks, Latigo.

Maggie had never known animals, especially horses, could be so responsive. So in tune with their owners. Or maybe it was Latigo. The way he touched her. The concern she heard in his voice. Yes, it was Latigo.

He glanced back at Maggie. "It's not too late to change your mind. I know how you feel about horses." He gave her an understanding smile. A smile that said it was okay if she decided to leave.

"I may not be much help, but I'm staying."

"You'll be more help than you know." He kept his hand on the mare's swollen belly, soothing the quivering hide. "Easy, July. You're going to be fine. Won't Romeo be happy to see what you're givin' us?"

"She's having Romeo's baby?" Recalling the race with the muscular stallion, Maggie stepped into the stall. Straw poked inside her sandals until she knelt beside Latigo.

"Yep." He stroked July's leg. "I like to be with my mares their first time. At least, until the vet gets here."

"Have you delivered many horses?"

"July is one I delivered. Right, girl?"

July raised her head and looked straight at Maggie. The pain in the mare's brown eyes was unmistakable. Maggie felt the instant connection shared by mothers everywhere. Without thinking, she cradled July's head in her lap. Even through the cotton fabric of her skirt, Maggie could feel the mare's fever. "You're not alone, July. Latigo is here."

"We're both here, July. Maggie and me." Latigo rolled up his sleeves. "If she should raise up, give her ear a pull. She'll lay quiet."

Maggie nodded and stroked July's head. "We're going to be fine."

July jerked her head up.

Maggie jumped. Before she could gather enough courage to yank on the animal's ear, July's head fell back onto her lap. She vowed to subdue her reflexive jump if July moved again. After all, they were both in good hands. Latigo was here. She watched his rope-calloused hands work their magic.

Stroking.

Soothing by touch.

Maggie knew that touch, knew all too well the soothing effect those hands had on pain, all kinds of pain.

Suddenly she felt proud to be beside him. Proud that he'd thought enough of their relationship to work out a compromise. Most of all, she was proud that he wanted her to stay if only for the delivery of his latest foal.

July relaxed between contractions, her skin shuddering beneath Latigo's touch. The ponderous pace of the mare's breathing deepened. Knowing another contraction had started, Maggie leaned closer. "Having a baby is no fun, is it, July?"

"We're close now." Latigo nudged July's wrapped tail. A hoof emerged, and in a matter of minutes the birthing was over.

"Is it a boy or girl?" Maggie asked excitedly.

Latigo's eyes were so bright they could light a candle. "It's a filly."

"A beautiful red filly like her mother." Maggie watched as July's licking tongue encouraged the foal to stand. After a few feeble attempts, the filly wobbled up on her long legs. Maggie reached for a towel laying on the straw and helped Latigo wipe her dry. The damp coat was warm and soft.

Maggie remembered how Jenny's skin felt upon her own. The feeling of being alone at Jenny's birth rushed in and stole the moment's magic, until Latigo shuffled closer on his knees. His radiant face shone with sweat.

"You did fine, darlin'."

It was the first time he'd called her darlin' since she'd told him about Five Star's offer to buy her land. That one word told her they had a better-than-even chance of making things right between them.

He motioned with a nod. "Appears she thinks you did good, too."

The filly, her eyes wide and searching, focused on

Maggie. "Welcome to the world, brown eyes." The filly warm-nosed Maggie's arm before she felt the drag of a rough tongue.

"That lick is as close to a thanks as this little gal can come."

"You're welcome." The straw scratched against Maggie's legs when she walked closer on her knees. She'd been so intent on the delivery she'd hardly noticed the straw before. Fascinated, she watched July push the filly toward her belly.

Maggie closed her eyes, recalling the first tug of Jenny's mouth upon her own breast. The moment stood poignantly clear in her heart as if it'd happened only yesterday. She remembered her fierce pride in her own child.

Brushing her hands together, Maggie sat back resting against the stall. "I guess you won't need the vet."

Latigo sat beside her, stretching his long legs out on the straw. "Probably not, but he'll be taking a look anyway."

The barn door creaked open.

"You must've broken a speed record, Doc," Maggie heard TJ say. Latigo introduced her to the gray-haired veterinarian before they left the stall.

Latigo steered her toward a cubicle and a stainless steel sink. "Let's wash up." Taking a brush from a wall hook, he scrubbed his hands and arms with disinfectant after Maggie had washed hers. "Have you thought of a name for her yet?"

She handed him a fresh towel. "Me, name her?"

"I'd say you're entitled, darlin'."

Replacing the towel on the hook, she leaned over the top rail of the stall watching the vet attend to July.

"She behaved herself like a perfect lady," Latigo said.

Maggie turned to him and blotted his still damp-face with a clean towel. "Why not call her Lady? Latigo's Lady."

"I like the sound of that, except Lady belongs to you."

He was giving her his filly? Her thoughts and emotions got all mixed up inside her heart. Wade Latigo had a way of doing that to her on a regular basis. Just when she thought she had their relationship on an even keel, he'd do or say something that set her heart to spinning like a Tulsa twister.

"What am I going to do with a horse, Latigo? I've no place to keep her. And besides, I wouldn't know what to do with her."

"From what I've seen, you know exactly what to do."

Was being around horses that easy? That natural? It never had been until he showed her how. She waited while he checked with the vet, then they walked hand-in-hand out of the barn.

She'd never felt more alive.

More content.

More hopeful.

Dream on, her practical mind warned. She and Latigo were as different as boots and sandals. Ever the optimist, she mentally shifted gears. She imagined Lady and her mama racing across Latigo's pasture. Who was she kidding? She'd never get to see Lady grow. She'd be at home in San Francisco. Latigo could send photos. She shook her head. Colored photos wouldn't do the horses justice.

And what about Jenny? "How soon before Jenny can see Lady?" Who would've thought she'd be anxious to show her daughter a horse?

He held the back door to the house open for her. "Jenny? She can see them tomorrow. We'll dampen bran and crushed oats and feed July morning and night from a bin on the floor. Before you know it, Lady will be picking around those oats, too."

"You make it sound so easy."

They stepped into the kitchen. "It is. Horses are like people. Some smart. Some stupid and plenty in between." He motioned toward the hallway. "I'm for a shower. You take the master bath. My robe's hanging on the door. Help yourself to anything else you need. Shampoo. Soap. Towels. Me?" He raised a questioning brow.

She stopped abruptly, unwilling to acknowledge the desire in his eyes. Equally unwilling to determine what emotion she felt right now. Oh, she expected to face the question of sex. She'd been prepared for it. After the way he'd touched her last night how could their making love not come up? There, she'd said it—the L word. Not in capitals, the forever kind of LOVE, but it was the L word nonetheless.

"Hey?" His hands framed her face; she let him tilt her face up to his.

He smelled of leather and strong soap. Without a hat shading his face, she could read the raw emotion in his eyes. He combed back his rumpled hair nervously, but it fell back into place.

"I couldn't resist adding the *me* part." He leaned closer. "It was a joke. Although, I hear tell you prune-pickers are big on water conservation."

Before she could answer, he slid his arm around her, drawing her into step with him as they continued down the hallway.

She was glad he'd made another joke. It allowed her to laugh without actually saying no to his proposal. They stopped at the end of the hall.

"I'll be in the other bathroom. My room's there." She opened her mouth to protest. "No arguments. Get."

One half of the double doors stood open. His bedroom, like the rest of the house, was decidedly male. Wood and stone walls outlined the forest green carpet. But it was the king-sized waterbed that caught her eye. A padded leather framework set off the paisley comforter and the row of matching pillows scattered against the leather headboard. The room, right down to the plants crowded beside the wall of glass, had *Latigo* branded everywhere.

And like his ranch, nothing about the house had happened by chance. Everything was planned, carefully planned. She couldn't help but wonder what he had planned for them tonight? No matter. She had no intention of being one of his trophies. Come to think of it, where were his rodeo trophies? She hadn't seen a one.

"The bath is over there," he continued. "Clean shirts are hanging in the closet. Your blouse is there, too.

"The blouse I left in the cellar?"

He nodded. "Mrs. Edwards dropped it by the other day. She came across it when she was sweeping out the cellar." He cleared his throat nervously. "Your panties are in my underwear drawer, second drawer on the right. If you need one of my T-shirts, help yourself."

He was out the door before she could answer.

She marched to the oak bureau and pulled open the second drawer. His T-shirts were stacked neatly on the left. His undershorts on the right. In front, resting on top of a pair of his purple bikini briefs, were her white lace panties.

"Oh," he called poking his head around the door. "In case you're wondering, we've the house to ourselves. So if you need anything, holler—I'm right down the hall."

He eyed the shaky hand she'd fisted around her panties before she buried them in her skirt pocket.

"Find everything?" he teased.

"Yes. Thanks."

"Toss me some clean shorts."

"How about these?" Taking the purple briefs, she let them dangle like a pendulum from her index finger. "A gift?"

His eyes widened. "From a fan. A female fan."

"Silk? Life on the rodeo circuit must've been rough." She rifled a T-shirt and the purple briefs across the room, hitting his chest dead center.

Thirty minutes later, Maggie was showered and changed. With his green terry robe knotted tightly over one of his T-shirts, she studied the Jerome Tiger pastel hanging above the living room fireplace. She'd heard people speak of the tragic death of the Oklahoma Native American artist. Her eyes settled on the title, *Intermission*. The Indian dancers appeared to be resting between dances. Seeing the muted blue chalk images reminded her of Latigo's Indian heritage. He'd only mentioned it once, but he thought about enough to keep this sketch close at hand.

Oh, the Jerome Tiger pastel wasn't a large drawing, but the indirect lighting made it the most prominent thing in the room—except for Latigo. Barefooted, he'd stepped into a fresh pair of jeans. The neon waistband of the purple briefs hung below his navel, the beltless jeans even lower. An untied white terry robe, that set off his natural tan, flapped open on his naked chest.

"Have you had the Tiger drawing long?" she asked, forcing her wandering eyes to focus on the picture.

"That's one of the first things I bought with my prize

money," Latigo said. "TJ thought I was crazy. Money-wise it's one of the smartest things I did."

She sipped her rosé wine, then twirled the glass, watching the pink puddle splash in the hollow stem.

Settling himself on the leather sofa opposite her, he kicked his bare heels onto the coffee table. He almost downed his beer, then stopped abruptly. He winced. His fingers crushed the aluminum sides before he set the wobbly can on the table.

"Are you all right?"

His thin-lipped, "Yeah" brought the twirling wine in her glass to a halt.

"Why wouldn't I be all right?" He got to his feet, much too quickly to suit her and stood before the fireplace. He kept his back to her, but there was no mistaking the way his hands gripped the mantel.

"Latigo?"

"I'm taking you home." He limped down the hall in the direction of his bedroom. He must be hurting bad if he didn't try to cover his limp.

"Get dressed," he ordered.

"Oh, no you don't. I'm not a child you can dismiss just like that."

"I'm not dismissing you, Maggie. I'm saying good-night."

"You have an odd way of saying it. What happened to that Oklahoma hospitality you're always bragging about?"

"Gone, I guess."

"And that's it?"

"That's it."

"Not quite." She ran after him, heading down the lighted hallway. If he thought she could be put off that easily, he had another think coming. She had more to say. Plenty more.

When she got to his room, he'd already grabbed her purse and clothes and was holding them out to her. She ignored the gesture, crossing her hands over her chest.

"Latigo—"

"Don't push, Maggie. It's not becoming."

"Do you think I care what it looks like?" She snatched her things from him and threw them onto the bed. "Until you tell me what's going on—I'm staying."

Fifteen

Maggie stepped closer. Even in the dim bedroom light, there was no mistaking the furrows between his brows.

"The pain in your leg must be bad if you want me to leave."

He nailed her with one of his classic judgmental stares. The same penetrating glare he used when they talked about the mineral rights. "What makes you an expert on pain?"

"Being Jenny's mom."

A caustic chuckle died on his taut lips. "I guess you qualify."

"Then don't argue. I can drive myself home. You?" She turned down the comforter on the bed. "Get into bed."

His teasing smile was the eighth wonder of the world. "I love it when you beg."

She fluffed his pillow, and by the time she looked at him again any sign of teasing had vanished from his face. His chest heaved while he emptied his jeans pockets onto the nightstand. His arms tensed.

"Here, take the keys to the truck, and get out of here, Maggie."

She'd bet ten dollars that he'd never let anyone see him in such pain. Never up this close, anyway. "And leave you here alone? No way, Jose."

"You're the most contrary woman I've ever met."

"I'll settle for that."

He tossed his robe onto the chair and unhitched the top rivet on the jeans.

"Here, let me help."

He clenched his teeth. "I can get 'em."

"Bashful, cowboy? Unbutton your fly, and I'll pull off your pants."

"Are all prune-pickers this pushy?"

"Only the blondes."

Without arguing, he flipped open the rivets on his fly, and she eased off his jeans. Her eyes ignored the rolling, male landscape inside the sexy purple briefs and fixed on his scarred right leg. "How many operations?"

"I stopped counting at four."

She gave him a gentle push, and he fell back onto the bed. He slipped under the sheet and put his elbow across his eyes.

"Shall I call your doctor?"

His hand fisted a knot of sheet. "The docs have done all they can. There's not much work for a one-legged cowboy."

No self-pity tinged his words. He was only stating a fact he'd faced long ago. She knew about facing facts, watching Jenny strap on her braces every day saw to that. "Please, I want so much to help."

The arm covering his eyes flew up. The whites of his eyes were bloodshot with pain. He fumbled for her hand, clutching it hard until she almost cried out. They stared at one another, her hand still locked in his. His knuckles

213

went white. She met his pain taking it as her own like she'd taken on Jenny's so many times before: hand in hand, waiting, never flinching, never giving an inch. His hand relaxed.

"Don't look so scared. I'm a mite bent is all." His half-smile faded fast. "If it gets too bad, I'll take something."

Her brain clicked to attention. "That prescription in the bathroom?" She made it to the bath in seconds and snatched the pills from the drawer where she'd found the shampoo. She filled a glass with water and returned to him.

He eased up onto an elbow. "Why is it I've got everything in my life under control but you?"

"Control me? Never." She scanned the prescription label. "It says you can take two if necessary and repeat for pain every four—"

"Leave 'em by the water. If you're staying, crawl into bed where you can do some real good." He flipped back the sheet. She stared at the inviting space between him and the padded edge of the waterbed. Sleeping with him meant sex. If not tonight, then tomorrow morning. Well, what now?

She hedged for time. The answer, never in doubt, came. No use kidding herself. When he'd touched her last night she knew the inevitable moment would arrive. Even after they'd argued about those mineral rights, he came on to her—getting her to relax while he told her about Romeo dancing with the lady. He laughed with her and all the while courting her with his eyes. Yes, the foreplay had begun long before she'd reached the front door of his house.

She knew it.

He knew it.

And most important of all, he knew she knew it.

Putting all thought of his pain aside, it came down to this—what happened between them from here on was up to her. Now for the big question. How much did she want him?

Her heart answered.

"I've got to call my dad first." She lifted the receiver from the cradle and dialed the number before she sat on the edge of the bed.

"Dad? Yes, I'm at Latigo's."

She glanced back at Latigo. He'd covered his eyes with his arm again.

"Could you feed Jenny? Oh, what did you eat? Sounds great. Would you tuck her in bed and hear her prayers? I'm staying the night."

There was a pause on the other end of the line. When her dad spoke again there was no mistaking the approval in his voice. Dad liked Latigo. He was happy she was staying the night. So was she.

"I'll be home for lunch. Would you put Jenny on so I can say good-night? Yes, I love you, too."

Latigo's hand touched her hip, gliding across the over-sized T-shirt until he reached her naked thigh. His hand went still as if, even in his pain, he needed some physical link with her. It was a connection she suddenly realized she needed, too.

Maggie stared down at his hand. It lay motionless, tanned against her pale skin. She dropped her free hand across his, curling her fingers around his like a healing bandage, and squeezed. His thumb lifted, drawing hers beneath his before he squeezed back. The hands, coupled like lovers, held together, the bold embrace as strong as any pulsating climax.

"Jenny?" It took all of Maggie's will to concentrate on what her daughter was saying. "Guess what Latigo has to show you? A baby horse."

Jenny squealed with delight, asking question after question. Maggie rattled off the answers like a drill sergeant.

"Yes, I guess you can see it in a day or so, but I'll have to ask Latigo first." Maggie's voice quivered and she paused for a moment. Two calming breaths helped some. She didn't want Jenny to suspect that anything was wrong with Latigo. After clearing her throat, Maggie managed to settle her words into a regular cadence. "Grandpa is going to hear your prayers tonight."

Latigo's hand slipped from beneath hers, and she felt the waterbed shift as he rolled away.

"Yes, Latigo says good-night, too. Pleasant dreams. Put Grandpa back on." She smacked three big kisses before Jenny said her nighty-nights.

"Maggie?" Dad asked.

Then dead air.

Recalling her father's recent heart attack, Maggie's pulse raced. "Dad, are you all right?"

"Of course, the old ticker hasn't missed a beat."

She breathed a silent prayer of thanks.

"But Doctor Van de Carr's office called. He's rescheduled Jenny's surgery. He wants her back in San Francisco by Monday for tests."

Maggie gripped the phone tighter. She'd known Jenny needed at least one more operation, but this change came out of the blue.

"Did you hear me?" her father asked.

"Yes, Dad. Does Jenny know?"

"Yes."

"Jenny never mentioned the call. She's not thrilled to be leaving."

"Exactly. Shall I call for airline tickets?" Dad asked.

"Would you? We'll settle the details tomorrow. Love you."

Replacing the receiver, she looked back at Latigo. He kept his head turned toward the expanse of windows. She knew if he hadn't still been hurting he'd be facing her, talking about Jenny seeing the new foal. His pain wasn't the only pain filling the room. She had an ache of her own, an ache called good-bye.

"Everything okay at home?" he asked.

"Fine." In a matter of seconds, all her plans went upside down. This evening would be the last she and Latigo would have together. If Dad managed to book an early flight, they could be on an airplane for San Francisco before Sunday. She'd have to prepare Jenny for what Maggie hoped would be her daughter's final operation. Getting a five-year-old to do something was one thing. Getting Wade Latigo to let her help him, without him suspecting that this was good-bye, was quite another.

She could barely make out the stars through the sheer underdrapes. Any other time, she'd have strolled to the window and checked out the swimming pool, but not tonight. Latigo was all she could think about. He rolled onto his back again, lying motionless. The arm covering his eyes appeared relaxed except that every once in a while his hand clenched. She watched the hand movement, gauging the steady barometer of his agony. She waited, knowing she could outlast pain any day of the week. She counted to eleven before his shoulders slumped.

With the water and pills in hand, she marched to his side of the bed. A physician had prescribed medication. Why was it such a big deal to take a pill? Was it one of those man things? Something to do with their testosterone level?

Before the question was out of her head, the answer came. Taking a pill was asking for help. Latigo never asked for anything. She set the water glass and pill bottle onto the nightstand. One way or another she'd get him to take a pill. If he wouldn't take it for himself, he'd take it for her.

"This is from Jenny." Bending down, she kissed his cheek. "Dad's message was a bit more formal."

"And shocked, too. Maybe?"

"If he was he hid it well." Her words dropped to a whisper, "I've never spent an entire night with a man." She laughed to hide her embarrassment at revealing her almost nonexistent sexual past. "Dad actually sounded glad."

Latigo lifted his elbow and peeked up at her. "I always liked your dad."

"Nice try at changing the subject. What about this pill?"

The elbow dropped, shielding his face, and he shook his head violently. "Don't push it, Maggie."

"Please?"

"No. No." His voice went hoarse. "The pills . . . they make me feel all dead inside. Don't you understand? I'd be no good to you as . . . as a man."

"Is sex the only reason you asked me for dinner?"

He uncovered his eyes again. "Maybe." His arm

dropped to his side. "I didn't ask you here because I admire your . . ."—his lazy gaze fondled her breasts—". . . your politics, darlin'."

The blatant sexual teasing meant only one thing. He was weakening. She picked up the prescription bottle and reread the dosage. Without looking directly at him she said, "If seducing me is what you had planned, there's always tomorrow morning."

The awkward silence shocked her. Her words had been an open invitation for another of his patented double-entendres. A quick glance at him, and she had her answer. Both of his fists were knotted at his sides, his spine arched, the back of his head buried deeply into the feathered pillow.

"Wade?"

His eyes shot open. "You only call me Wade when we're making love."

He'd told her that before, but she'd brushed it off. Now it occurred to her—she'd been thinking of him as Wade for most of the evening. Did that mean she'd been unconsciously making love to him? Sliding onto the bed, she nestled close to his side, resting her chin upon his upper arm. The brisk, energetic fragrance of after-shave scented his neck and shoulders. She imagined him cupping his hands and splashing the cooling liquid over his naked skin. She lifted her head, sanding her chin over the well-strung muscle of his upper arm, reveling in the texture and feel of him.

"Take a pill?"

His eyes drifted shut as he aimed his mouth in her direction. "Forget the pills. Kiss me, darlin'."

"Wade?"

His lids opened slowly, his eyes darkening to steely gray.

This ploy was no game. This was his way of giving in to her plea while pretending to protest. Another one of those man things. And they talked about PMS.

"Kiss me once before I take that pill."

She kissed him, brushing her lips back and forth over his mouth, coaxing it to open, pleading and promising that whatever he'd planned she'd be a part of it.

"Keep this up and I'll take two," he whispered against her lips.

"Kisses or pills?"

"Both." He lifted his head when she slipped out of bed. She held the water glass to his mouth, but he only took one pill. "And tomorrow morning?"

She nodded. "I'll be waiting."

He fell onto his back patting the empty spot beside him. "Here?"

Well, this was a woman thing. One of her ploys. She let the robe slip to the floor. His eyes widened. She stood motionless letting his gaze sweep over her. Like a lover's kiss, his eyes skimmed the over-sized T-shirt and rested on the naked thigh he'd caressed. Her heartbeat pounded in her ears while the rest of her yearned for his touch once more.

"I'll be here all night." She slid back into the bed. Pulling the sheet up to her chin, she snuggled beside him. "See how orderly your life is now that you've taken your medicine?"

"Yeah. Sure." He chuckled. "Now, turn off those lights."

She did as he asked, then rolled back into his waiting

arms, those encircling arms, holding her tight and letting her know how much he needed her.

She'd been needed, desired by a man before. This was different.

Physical?

Yes.

Sexual?

In her heart she knew he wanted more than sex. He wanted her close in the night like a man does a wife. She lay caught against his chest, content, wanting only for his pain to disappear.

"How long before the medication begins to work?"

"Forty-five minutes. Maybe an hour."

In the darkness, she heard him moan. Holding him closer, she stroked the side of his temple. He felt flushed, damp. Sweat was to be expected, but no fever. That was encouraging.

"Don't mother me. Talk to me, darlin'."

He rolled his head from side to side on the pillow. He finally stopped thrashing about, but she resisted the urge to touch his face again.

"For God's sake say something. Anything."

Desperate to distract him, her roaming hand found a scar on his shoulder. She felt the rolled ridge where the stitches had been.

"Where did you get this?"

He relaxed. "Calgary Stampede."

Her hand slipped over his chest headed for his side and the scar she knew was there. His muscles flowed easily beneath his skin, his athletic body finely tuned. Her fingers lingered on the waistband of his briefs, then moved along the elastic until she felt the skinny, angled scar. "And this?"

"Oklahoma City State Championship."

She tried to guess the number of stitches by the length of the wound. Counting proved too painful. He'd paid dearly for his dream of a ranch.

"I'm a regular road map. Souvenirs from my greatest rodeo wrecks."

He took her hand, guiding it along the narrow side of his shorts to his upper thigh and the round puncture scar. "Pendelton Roundup."

She winced.

"It's only a nick. Actually the bull won most of the points that day. All I did was hang on."

Gradually she felt him relax completely. The planned distraction worked. At least for him. He talked about his years on the rodeo circuit. The nights spent in motel rooms. Many nights. Tonight they'd both made the choice to be together. For him it might seem a new beginning, but she knew otherwise. Her stomach burned. This was good-bye. When tomorrow came, she'd tell him she was leaving.

He paused, his breathing deepened.

"There's never been a woman in this bed." His words sounded as if he'd awakened from a faraway dream.

"Never?"

"Nope. I'm glad it's you here."

"Me, too."

The medicine did its work, and the motion of the waterbed mattress stilled. She waited until his breathing settled into an even pattern before reaching up to stroke his cheek. Yes, she wanted to mother him. She wanted to hold him. To take away the pain. But she'd learned long ago with Jenny that was impossible. Now as he slept she could do as she pleased.

Retracing the scars on his body, she kissed each one, memorizing the shape and location, the taste and feel of his skin. She lingered longest on the puncture wound made by the bull's horn. The wound from the Pendelton Roundup.

She marveled at the casual way he'd recalled each scar. He'd made his peace with his past and the pain that remained. If he could do that, so could she. Forgiving the man who'd deserted her and Jenny, she freed herself from her own past. For the first time, she could look toward the future without being reminded of the past. He'd done that for her. Thank you, Wade.

She leaned over him, letting his warmed breath guide her lips to his. Still asleep, he kissed her back and, from that faraway place, he whispered her name.

Content to cuddle by his side, she mouthed Jenny's prayer, "And most of all, God bless Wade." With her hand over his beating heart, she drifted off to sleep.

Sometime during the night she awoke. He'd pulled her halfway on top of him. Still asleep, his hand skimmed her backbone clear down to her fanny and back again, as if he didn't believe she was really there. He held her left leg angled over his thigh.

"Crazy . . . I'm crazy about you, darlin'." His words, muffled against her temple, were barely audible. His chest heaved, and he tightened his hold on her. "No . . . no. Forget what I said. I never meant . . ."

Tears filled her eyes. No woman would ever hold a man to words he'd spoken in his sleep, words he hadn't meant her to hear. Forget them? How could she?

Moments later, when she was sure he was deep in his dreams, she slipped from the bed, covering him carefully with the rumpled sheet. *Forget what I said. I never meant* . . .

She stumbled to the bedroom windows trying to do as he asked—to forget what he'd said. But all she could think about was the man in the bed behind her. The man whose words kept banging about inside her heart. The man who had come to mean so much to her. Had it been a mistake to trust him with her heart?

Sixteen

Maggie stared out of Latigo's bedroom window—her thoughts as deep and dark as the night.

The prying moon, full and yellow, floated over onto its back and backstroked across the sky. It spread a path of yellow across the room. A path leading straight to the bed.

She turned, staring at Latigo.

He was a sprawler, arms and legs going every which-a-way. He was rolled over onto his chest, the sheet barely covering his buttocks. His upper back shone muscled and bare in the moonlight. It'd take more than an act of will to forget Wade Latigo. She sagged into the chair, watching him, waiting for tomorrow.

Hours passed.

When the sun appeared, Maggie left the chair to wash her face. Not wanting to wake him, she kept the bathroom light off while running a comb through her hair. She left the bathroom. Ignoring the impulse to put on her skirt, she pushed open a door between the bathroom and the wall of glass. It swung open onto an adjoining room.

What have we here?

The voiceless wind breathed against the window above a worn leather chair. From the look of the overworked leather, the chair might've belonged to Latigo's foster father, Jonathan Wade. She crept into the room, her bare feet sinking into the plush green carpet.

Bookshelves lined the three walls, their dark wooden shelves stuffed with Louis L'Amour paperbacks and hard-cover volumes, some of which she'd seen on the *New York Times* best-seller list. Her eyes skittered over the titles. Holding the books in place like polished book-ends were trophies of every shape and design.

So this is your trophy room, Latigo.

Although, after a second glance, she decided it appeared to be more of an office than a bragging room.

Wanting to get a closer look at his books, she flicked on the light switch, but the only illumination focused on a picture on the far wall.

She stepped nearer. It wasn't a picture actually, but a collage. A life in photos of the cowboy in the purple shirt; toes turned east and west riding a northbound horse.

The collage had to be handmade from the look of the patchworked photographs, magazine and newspaper clippings. Right in the middle was a large magazine cover— the banner read: Latigo, King of the Rodeo, Says Farewell.

Tears clouded her eyes. She blinked them away, staring at the photo of the wide-shouldered man in the chaps and purple fringed shirt. He looked like a king, tipping his white Stetson crown to the standing crowd. The crooked smile, broad and full, showed no sign of sadness or regret. She knew it was there. She knew how it felt to say good-bye.

She read the brass plaque fastened to the bottom of the picture frame: "Merry Christmas, Boss. From TJ."

More tears came.

She'd always wanted to see Latigo milking a rodeo crowd. She had a sneaking suspicion he did his thing better than anybody. He also wore chaps better than most. She shook her head. Her eyes scanned the leather shafts covering each leg and settled front and center on the V of his blue jeans. No man had invented chaps. Had to be a woman. Blatantly sexy, the chaps left the more interesting parts of a cowboy, his fly and fanny, free of any leather. She wondered how the flesh-and-blood Latigo would look with a pair of chaps flapping against his long legs.

The phrase *rodeo stud* took on a new meaning. Her mind formed a provocative picture of his backside and the wrap-around leather that held his jeans tight against the back of his thighs. Nasty. Utterly nasty. Listening to the silence, she fanned her burning cheeks with her hand.

"Mornin', sunshine." Startled, she kicked her bare heel against the side of the desk before she turned.

Latigo stood framed in the doorway, looking wonderfully like his old self. His hair tousled, the jeans he wore were only half-buttoned. Above the fly, his naked stomach rippled at her.

Her own stomach churned.

Sometime between the time she'd left the bedroom and now, he'd discarded those sexy purple briefs. Imagining him in chaps was bad enough, knowing he was naked beneath those jeans—that was more than any woman could take on only four hours sleep.

"I wondered where you kept your trophies. I hope you don't mind." The sound of her shaky voice made her feel more unsettled.

"Mind? No, but a house tour wasn't exactly the first thing that crossed my mind this morning." He smiled wickedly.

"I wish I'd known you then." She nodded toward the rodeo picture.

"No you don't."

"Why?"

"I was all business and prize money. I wasn't ready for you." His voice deepened, "I am now."

Bootless, he sailed across the carpet and drew her into his arms. He lowered his mouth to hers. He kissed her once, twice, three times until she lost count and her breath.

"Come back to bed, darlin'."

She shook off his arms trying to put some distance between them. She must tell him. Now. Her lower lip trembled as she spoke, "I'm . . ." The word *leaving* never materialized.

His questioning frown settled into a crooked smile. "Tired from looking out for a downed cowboy?"

She shook her head, carefully avoiding his eyes. "I didn't mind."

"You've seen me at my worst. Now let's try something better."

Worst? She'd seen him at his most human. Vulnerable. Turnabout was only fair play. Hadn't he seen her worst, too? He'd helped her overcome her terror of horses, and last night he'd helped her make peace with her past. They'd been lovers first, now they were friends. This morning they'd be lovers again. She'd promised him that this morning would be theirs. She'd keep that pledge. Saying good-bye could wait. They'd both earned the right to this precious time.

"Everyone says you're the best." She kissed him wantonly.

"If so, it's you that keeps me that way." Pulling her flat against him, he made slow easy love to her with his tongue. Tasting, teasing as his manhood tightened between them.

Her femininity hurried ahead, melting and moistening, readying itself for the fulfillment his kisses promised.

"Guess it's no secret. I'm as hard as a fresh-dug rutabaga."

His hot kisses sizzled along her temple, scorching her as surely as if he'd set the fiery tip of a match to her skin.

"You do know what a rutabaga is?"

"Of course," she teased, determined to appear unshaken by his pulsating arousal. "It's a vegetable. A root. Purple and . . ." Heat singed the roots of her hair again.

He threw back his head and laughed. "You got that right."

She'd walked straight into that one. She didn't mind. It was good hearing him laugh after all the pain he'd been through, the pain she knew he faced daily.

"Maggie?" His tone turned serious. "I'm glad you stayed last night."

"And this morning?"

"I'm even gladder." He took her willing hand and placed her palm over the peaked fly of his jeans. She opened her fingers wide wanting to hold all of him.

"I like touching you, feeling you growing harder in my hand."

Groaning, he pressed her hand tighter against his heat. "Well, grab hold anytime you've a mind to. But for now . . ." He swept her up into his arms, cradling her while he walked back into the bedroom. Slowly he set her onto her feet beside the waterbed. Lightheaded, she swayed against his naked chest, content for the moment to hear the rapid cadence of his heart.

"Look at me, Maggie."

She tipped her head and the morning light hit him smack in the face. His eyes were clear, the tired lines around his eyes all but gone.

"The cellar was dark when we made love before." His jaw tensed. "You were right. It was mostly sex that first time. But the second time . . ."

The intentional pause lay open, waiting for her to fill in the missing word.

"We made love," she finally admitted.

"It was lovemaking, only I didn't feel like I do about you now. How could I? We were strangers. In the clear light of day, I want us to look at each other. No more lies. No more secrets."

Secrets. She had to tell him. "Latigo—"

"Shhh. I want us buck naked. You and me, skin to skin."

She longed for that, too. To know with her eyes what she'd only touched in the darkness; to feel the shape of him, the patterns of hair marking his chest, his legs, his essence as a man. Her breath quickened, became shallow.

"I want to see you. Now." He took hold of the bottom of her T-shirt, lifted it.

Everything went black as he pulled it over her head. When she felt it drop to the carpet, she opened her eyes. She stood naked except for the lacy white bikinis, her arms hanging limply by her sides. Shameless. Feeling utterly beautiful while his eyes adored her.

"They're pink," he whispered like a prayer.

"Pink?"

His eyes closed lazily then opened as if he were surprised she hadn't understood his statement.

"Your nipples. I always wondered what color they were."

All this time he'd been thinking about her breasts?

"Oh, I knew the size. It was the color I puzzled about." He demonstrated with one hand, playfully cupping his fingers before he slid his hand back to her left breast. "See? A perfect fit."

She arched her back giving him full access to her breasts. His hands explored the shape, his thumb rubbing around and around the tightening bud.

He nuzzled her neck, moving his head up and down, nibbling as he worked her hair back from her throat. Her shallow breathing deepened into a pant. Her head fell to one side. His tongue traced the tender skin behind her ear, scoring a wet path until he reached her collarbone.

He sucked gently along her shoulder. "This is what you like?"

Delight shivered through her. He'd learned all about her most sensitive spots that night in the cellar, and from the way he kissed her, he hadn't forgotten a single one.

"Now get out of the rest of this."

Their hands met at the elastic on her panties.

"I've had a baby. I'm not as pretty as I used to be."

He frowned, then shook his head. "I'm not looking for one of those undernourished women." Moving his head first to one side then the other, he kissed her slowly again and again until her arms fell back to her sides.

"What are you saying?"

"This—I like you the way you feel. Round and soft. The way you look. All pink-nippled and reaching for me. You make me crazy. Crazy with wanting you. Touching you. Kissing you." His hands followed the slope of her hips as he pulled off her panties. His eyes burned brighter.

"Well what do you know about that? A natural blonde." He caressed her femininity, lightly skimming the blush of curls with his palm. "My very first."

Warmth bubbled to swelteringly hot. Her pulse raced.

"A strawberry blonde who tastes like peaches. I always knew you were one of a kind, Maggie Callahan."

He worshiped her with his eyes, those angel eyes, before touching each rib with his devil hands. When she protested, he moved on proclaiming his delight at the rosy heart-shaped mole on her stomach.

His hand stopped moving. Light bands of expectancy tightened around her chest when he stroked the moist-tipped petals with a fingertip. Recalling how expertly his hand had made love, her breath came in quick gasps.

"Wade, I . . ." Need to touch you, too, her hands cried. Feel you. She grabbed the waistband of his jeans. The half-opened fly spread open.

"Reach for me, darlin'. Trust me. Trust what you're feelin'."

She wanted to. She wanted to reach out to him and tell him how much she needed him, how much she wanted him to stand beside her in San Francisco while she waited to hear how Jenny's surgery had gone. The words never came. Her hands dropped to her sides. How could she ask him to go through that with her? He cared about Jenny. Sure. But he was a friend, not Jenny's father.

232

"I love you, darlin'."

She slammed her eyes shut.

No. Don't talk about love. Not now. Not when I'm leaving. Her lips trembled. "I'm—"

He silenced her with a kiss. "I knew you weren't ready to talk about feelings. But I'm not about to make love to you again without speaking my mind loud and clear. I love you, Maggie. I've never said that to a woman before."

Her breathy farewell caught in her throat. His words sent any doubts flying. She felt for the front of his jeans. Heat radiated through the denim. He moaned his approval when she thumbed open the rivet fly. She hooked his belt loops and pulled. The jeans glided over his hips. She touched the heated silk of him, the power that promised pleasure. With his hand atop hers, he guided her to the root surrounded by a wreath of springy hair. She felt the length on her own, exploring while watching his face color. Shiny sweat glistened on his upper lip.

"A man can only take so much of a good thing." His hand quieted her movements. "Besides I need to—"

The word *protection* flicked into her head. "Where is it?"

"Nightstand drawer."

Opening the drawer, her fingers found the square foil pack. She tore it open. He held out his palm.

"I'll do it." She knelt before him, looking up before her fingers tested the velvety tip, kissed it while covering the thickness. He moaned and when she looked again his eyes had closed, his hands found her hair, twisting and tangling the curls as she got to her feet.

"Shall we try a bed this time?" Cussing under his

breath, he kicked his legs until his jeans flew across the room.

He fell back onto the waterbed, taking her with him. They rocked back and forth against one another until the flotation mattress lay still.

He rolled onto his back, pulling her with him. "You on top. I want to see you, taste you."

Straddling him, she deliberately delayed, spilling her breasts on either side of his swollen sex. Swaying, she stroked him with the drag of her naked skin. His hardened heat probed deeper between the soft cleavage, fondling her as his hands had. In sheer joy, she lifted herself above him, settling her moist desire over him, lowering herself inch by each deliciously thickened inch, taking him inside her.

One inch.

Three inches.

Five inches.

She froze holding herself above him gathering her control, marveling at the inches left. Then gathering all of her control, she withdrew and went back to number one again.

"Lean closer, Maggie. I need to taste those pink tips."

Bending, she swung her breasts within reach of his hungry mouth. The suckling sensation drew her down, down, down until his groans of pleasure blended with hers. It took all of her will to keep from taking everything he offered. She wanted to rejoice in the possession, in his manly power, in the thick length. She knew he could stand the waiting no longer when his hands were on her hips pulling her lower and filling her beyond measure. Her spine stiffened, her hips rotated harder and harder taking all that he offered.

She moved like he'd taught her while riding bareback; thighs tight against him, gripping him, holding him to her. They moved together, coupling as their hands had. Holding fast, never wanting to let go. Knowing what lay ahead, her movements became more urgent. More compelling. And when she reached the horizon's fire, the sun burned brightly for them both as they tumbled together in a burst of scorching magic.

Minutes later, they clung together in a circle of light, neither of them daring to move for fear of breaking the wondrous spell.

"Maggie?"

"I'm fine."

"You got that right. You got everything right." He rolled left, shifting her weight slightly. They lay side by side. "Thanks for not asking about my leg this mornin'."

"I wanted to."

"I could tell. Knowing you, it took a heap of concentration to keep from playing mother."

"Playing mother never occurred to me." But she was a mother. And Jenny had surgery coming soon. She kissed his temple, clutching him closer, hating herself for what she must say. But she couldn't lay beside him any longer without telling him.

"Latigo?"

He tried to draw her closer but she resisted. "Yeah?"

"I'm leaving."

His fingers dug into her forearms. He straightened up as if he'd been shot in the back. "Leavin'?"

"When I spoke to Dad last night he told me they've rescheduled Jenny's next surgery. She's got to be back in San Francisco for tests."

"You're not talking visit. You're talking about leavin'

for good." Sitting up, he laughed bitterly. "And I thought this mornin' was a new beginning." His jaw hardened when he glared at her. "And all the time you were saying good-bye."

I tried to tell you, her mind cried. The useless declaration rattled around inside her like a broken piece of her heart.

"When are you leavin'?"

"In a couple of days."

"Days?" Totally naked, he launched himself from the bed, and paced back and forth in front of the nightstand.

She watched hurt simmer into smoldering anger.

His fingers bent into tight fists. "Guess I got my signals crossed."

"I've got to go back to San Francisco. Why can't you see that?"

"If you think this set-to is about choosing between Jenny and me, you'd best think again. This is one time you don't have to settle for what's handed to you. Reach for what you want like you did a minute ago."

What she wanted? What she wanted was for Jenny to run. To walk. That had always been what she wanted most . . . until last night. She glared at him. Why did every choice seem so simple to him? When it came to Jenny there was no choice. Flesh and blood came first.

"I can tell by the look on your face you don't have the least notion of what I'm about, Maggie." He stepped into his jeans. "Not to worry, I heal quick."

The hurting sound in his voice made tiny cuts inside her chest. She felt the pain as surely as if he'd taken the tip of his knife to her skin.

He threw her skirt straight at her. "Get dressed. I'm taking you home. Seems you've got to pack."

Seventeen

Two days since Maggie had spent the night with Latigo. Two dismal days since she'd found out the Callahans were leaving for San Francisco. Her life had been turned upside down. The hectic pace proved a blessing. Scrambling to get clothes packed, arranging with the real estate broker to show the farm to prospective customers, and signing the papers selling the mineral rights to Latigo kept her mind busy and her body too exhausted to think of anything or anyone at bedtime.

That's a lie, her heart shouted. *You've thought about him. Wondered. Wanted to call.*

Call? And say what? They'd said everything over and over while dressing until only pain remained. The pain of leaving.

Oh, he'd been the perfect gentleman and driven her home. He'd helped her out of the truck, walked her to the back porch steps and said good-bye. Then almost as an afterthought, he'd grabbed her, kissed her hard, so hard her teeth rattled. Before she could collect herself, he'd driven off.

Jenny never mentioned him or July's new foal even

after Maggie told her they'd named the filly Latigo's Lady. Maggie could see the disappointment every time she caught her daughter looking down the road in the direction of Latigo's mailbox. That's when the twice-felt pain hit. How could Maggie let it continue? He'd made it clear Jenny could come and see Latigo's Lady anytime. He'd also made it clear the day and time of Jenny's visit would be of Maggie's choosing.

Now Maggie was in the truck doing exactly what she'd vowed she wouldn't do—heading for Latigo's place. Oh, she'd left the farm on the pretense of returning Nighthorse's borrowed truck, but from the look on Dad's face he knew where she was going.

The suitcases were stacked on the screened porch of the farmhouse. The airline tickets for tomorrow's flight were stashed in her straw satchel. She made the turn at Latigo's mailbox, taking each hill in turn, remembering . . . remembering: Romeo racing along the fence, the boundless blue of the Oklahoma sky reflected in the ponds. Most of all she remembered Latigo. As soon as she cleared the air between them, Jenny could visit.

She slowed the truck when it came to the last hill before his house. There was still time to turn back, her better judgment warned. She stomped the gas pedal to the floor. Jenny wanted to see Lady before they left. Most of all, Jenny wanted to say good-bye to Latigo. Maggie made up her mind this was one thing her daughter would have, even if it meant facing Wade Latigo one more time.

The morning sun highlighted the pitch of the composition roof on Latigo's house. The nearby barn cast slanted shadows that reached the edge of the front grass. But it was the man emerging from the shadows her eyes settled on, the man whose loose limp strut she knew by heart. The man in the sexy leather chaps that flapped along the line of his long legs. Unable to take her eyes from the diamond shape of blue denim, front and center, she forgot every manner she'd ever known and stared in unabashed appreciation. She'd only seen the photo collage of him in chaps. Thank goodness. Rodeo studs tried a woman's self-control. She took a deep breath, and let the truck glide to a halt halfway between the house and the barn.

Latigo stopped, shaded his eyes. As the truck pulled up, there was no missing the way his puzzled frown changed to a triumphant half-smile.

"Mornin', Maggie." He tipped his hat as if he expected to see her every day of his life.

She dropped the truck keys into her straw satchel. "Good morning." He helped her out of the cab. Before she could say another word, her satchel caught on the door handle, spilling the entire contents onto the ground. They knelt at the same time almost bumping heads, but they never touched. He handed her the wallet and lipstick. The airline envelope he kept as he helped her to her feet.

"Got your tickets, I see." He flipped open the folder. "Leaving tomorrow? That was quick." He handed her the airline tickets.

"Dad called right after I spoke to him." She stuffed the tickets back into the satchel. "I talked to my real-estate lady. She said she'd get with you Monday about the mineral rights on my land."

"You could've phoned to tell me that." They walked toward the barn and the slanted shade. "You must be pressed for time. Why waste it on me?"

She'd hurt him bad, and he was about to make her pay.

239

Nothing came for free, so have at it, cowboy. She could take it. But first, "What about Jenny? Didn't you plan on saying good-bye to her? "

He stopped suddenly, tugging her to a halt beside him. "I planned on taking you to the airport and saying my good-bye in person. Thought we could stop by and see Lady on our way."

"You could've phoned and told me that."

"You insisted on callin' the shots, Maggie. I thought I'd let you have at it."

"Getting even at the expense of a child is a cheap shot."

"Do you think I'd actually stoop to that?"

She nodded. "Don't punish Jenny because of me, Latigo."

He stuck the tip of a gloved thumb between his teeth and yanked. He repeated the movement with the other hand before shoving the gloves behind his leather belt. "What makes you think I've given *you* another thought?"

She pivoted on her heel, turning away so he wouldn't see the hurt in her eyes. "I guess I deserved that one." Emotions in check, she faced him.

"You better pray the good Lord doesn't give you everything you deserve, darlin'." The darlin' part had a bitter, hollow ring. His callous attitude hurt. It hurt worse than she'd expected. In one short word he'd evened up the score.

He bent over, reaching behind his thigh to unfasten his chaps.

"Let me." Before he could object she squatted behind him, tugging at the wrap-around flap of leather covering the back of his thigh. Discovering the metal buckles, she unfastened them. "I always wondered how these things worked."

"Well, now you know. I figure you're an expert on cowboys." He unbuckled the front of his chaps and flung them like a saddle over his shoulder.

"I'll see that a check for the mineral rights clears your bank pronto." He looked her straight in the eye. "That should ease your worries some."

"I didn't come today about money."

"Oh?"

No use pretending. She hadn't come only for Jenny. She'd come for herself, too. Beneath his intense scrutiny she knew he was reading her motives like he'd read an *Oklahoma Today* magazine. There was no hiding from him. There was only retreat.

She backed away, squinting as the sunlight warmed her face. "I . . . I needed to see you alone once more before we left."

He extended his arms, palms up. "Here I am."

Her eyes felt scratchy as if a dusty wind had suddenly blown by her cheek. There was no wind, only the threat of tears and pain. The pain of leaving, leaving him forever. She reached back, feeling for the door handle of the truck for support. Her hand met nothing but air. Why had she moved so far away from the truck?

He held the pose, arms open. It was all she could do to keep from running to him and losing herself in his unyielding strength.

"How's Lady?"

He dropped his arms. "Fine."

She tried to smile. She tried a second time before she was successful.

"And July?"

He shifted his jaw, tightening and relaxing the muscles as if he were marking time. "The mare is fine, too."

"Thanks for everything, Latigo."

"The pleasure was entirely mine, ma'am." He tipped his hat.

Mine, too, her heart added. *I'll never forget you, Wade. Never.* "Well, I guess I'll be going."

He held his ground. "I'll swing by for you about five tomorrow. That ought to give Jenny enough time to see Lady and still make the plane."

No mention of her. In that moment, Maggie knew he'd closed the chapter on the cowboy and the city gal forever. That's the way it had to end. They'd never had a chance for any lasting relationship. All they'd ever had was an affair; a hasty, destructive affair. An affair leaving her wanting only him. No other man could measure up to Latigo. To his primal prowess. His surprising gentleness. His teasing wit. His laugh. His smile. The way he made her feel. His—stop torturing yourself!

She marched toward the truck. "I'll be going then." The rest of what she'd intended to tell him choked in her throat.

"Good-bye, Maggie Callahan."

The long-delayed tears gathered in the corners of her eyes, but she blinked them back. She held onto the door handle of the truck for support. The metal felt hard and cold. As hard and cold as his dark eyes. She glanced back at him. He was exactly where she'd left him, his right leg cocked, the chaps still resting on the wide slope of his shoulder.

"I'm leaving." She gnawed at her lower lip.

"Right."

She yanked on the door handle. The door to the cab swung wide. "I'm really leaving."

It wasn't a declaration so much as a final sentence. The kind of sentence a judge gives a penitent prisoner before she's carted off to serve her time. Only this time, she reminded herself, she was her own judge and jury.

"Ri-ight." His voice sounded closer, almost as if he were standing behind her. As much as she wanted to, she refused to turn around again and test her instinct. She'd seen him for the last time. She should've listened to her practical side and stayed with the suitcases on the screen porch and let Dad return Nighthorse's truck. A phone call would've gotten Latigo over to see Jenny and been less painful. *You had to see him one last time. Now get out of here. You've made a big enough fool of yourself.*

"Good-bye, Latigo," she whispered. Her legs felt like cement blocks. Try as she might, she couldn't lift them. Her head drooped forward until her temple rested on the curved steel of the truck's cab. The cold, hard unyielding steel.

"Are you going to let me go?" The plea flew out of her mouth before she could stop it. She squeezed her eyes shut.

The jingle of keys rattled behind her. She opened her eyes and whirled around. He was only three feet away, holding out one hand, dangling *her* truck keys from his middle finger.

"What do you think, darlin'?"

Her heart did the crazy dance it always did whenever he called her darlin' in that soft, Southern way. He'd given her the finest gift of all. The gift no one else could—a choice. He'd given her that choice after they'd made love, only she'd been too fragmented to see it. He'd been right. She didn't have to settle. Not this time. Not ever again.

She dropped her purse when he held out both arms to her.

They met each other halfway, kissing one another softly, tenderly like young lovers who were discovering the flavor and feel of one another for the first time.

"You never kissed me like that before," she whispered after a moment.

His eyes took on a rare tenderness. "I always meant to."

He kissed her again exactly as he had before, sipping, tracing the shape of her mouth with his. "Me and the ranch have been waiting on you. That's why I never called. I never meant to hurt Jenny. Guess I was only thinkin' about you and me."

She felt like a shiny silver belt buckle, a rodeo champion's buckle, all polished and proud, until another thought zapped into her head. "And what if I hadn't come back?"

He leaned back, glancing down at her. "The thought never occurred to me."

She drew his face down to hers. "You're one hundred percent ego."

"On the rodeo circuit, we call it guts, darlin'." He grinned a self-satisfying smile before wetting his lips.

"No kiss, cowboy. I'm only checking to see if your eyes have turned to brown yet."

"You're something. Something mighty special. For once in your life, do something totally unpractical. Sign on with me for the duration, Maggie."

She opened her mouth to protest.

"Hear me out. The other day when you told me you

were leaving, I was too riled, too prideful, to get everything said that truly mattered. I'm saying it now."

When she opened her mouth again, he shook his head.

"Marry me, Maggie. Be my lady. My wife. My friend. My everything."

He wanted to marry her. To make her his wife. Tears came. She let the tears have their way, dipping her head so he wouldn't see them. "You don't know how it is. With Jenny's medical bills, it's all I can do to stay ahead of the creditors."

He tipped her chin up, brushing away the tears with a gentle sweep of his thumb. "Medical bills? You're not saddling me with any surprises. I've had a few doctor bills myself on occasion. Besides, my practical Maggie, I have insurance. A drawer full of canceled checks all made out for the premiums I pay. It's a simple matter to add a wife . . . and a daughter to the policy. At least that's what my insurance broker says."

"A wife and a *daughter?* An insurance policy. We could do that? We'd be solvent." Her mind went to mush.

"Sure, but we couldn't make any plans without Jenny." His serious expression told her he'd carefully planned every word he'd spoken. He'd planned everything, the way he'd planned his rodeo career. She knew whatever he said, she'd believe him.

"The way I figure it, Jenny can be your daughter or she can be ours. Yours and mine. I want to teach her more about horses and riding. I want to buy her and you the best pair of Western boots in the State of Oklahoma."

"But Latigo—"

"No buts about it. This is a simple yes or no deal."

Her heart whispered but one answer. "I love you, Latigo."

245

"I know, darlin'. I been countin' on that."

A nod was all she could manage.

"Yahoo-ooo!"

He swung her round and round. Her head kept spinning even after he finally let her stand on her feet. He steadied her, draping an arm across her shoulders, drawing her close to his side. Close to his heart.

They walked, matching step for step, toward the house, but he stopped suddenly.

"There's something you ought to know goin' in." He swallowed hard.

Her heart was too full for more talk. She wanted to silence him, but her good sense told her to wait. She held her breath.

"My leg could go sour."

They could face anything together; Jenny's surgery, even . . . even the loss of his leg. She looked him straight in the eye. "Yes." Her answer sounded more like a question, with the inflection rising.

"I'm talking about a one-legged cowboy."

She knew what losing his leg would mean to him. What it would mean to her, too. "Yes?"

He twisted the fringe on the chaps nervously. "It could change things between us."

She shook her head.

"Like the way we make love."

"Nothing will ever change that." She touched his cheek with her fingertips. "Not ever." He leaned into her hand, resting the side of his face against her palm. In that moment their love became as tangible as the morning stubble on his face. Whatever came their way she knew their capital L-O-V-E was as stubbornly strong as his scratchy beard.

She made certain her eye contact never wavered. She let her heart speak, "The things I love best about you are inside. Safe inside. The real you will never change, Latigo."

He drew her to him, slowly as if he were letting her words settle forever in his mind. They stood together for a moment, boot to sandal, heart to heart, leaning easily into one another.

"There's one more thing," he said.

"Yes?"

He seemed nervous. Unsure. "Understand what I'm about to say is only an idea. A suggestion really."

"I can hardly wait to hear it."

"Well, here goes. With the two of us providing for Jenny, I figured you might take your farm off the real-estate market and keep it for Jenny. Kind of like a dowry."

Her heart swelled the beat deeper at the unexpected benefit of loving a generous, caring man like Latigo. Just as she'd suspected, he'd been busy the last two days thinking everything through. "Dad will like that."

"I've the feelin' your dad might cotton to livin' there. He's had a fine ole time hammering and fixin' up the place."

"And Dad would be close to Nighthorse's and that shifty cribbage game."

"Or if he's a mind to, he could live here. There's plenty of room. What say we put it to him?"

She knew her dad too well. He'd rather have his own place. The farm would be perfect. "And my—"

"Callahan's Wine and Spirit Shoppe, your business in San Francisco? That I leave up to you, darlin'."

"What if I decide to keep it?"

He shrugged. "Keep it. Sell it. Whatever."

Even with the second mortgage . . . her practical mind quickly calculated, if she sold it she'd come out with a nifty piece of cash. Enough so Dad could really fix up the farm the way it had been when he was a boy.

"For a woman who had so few choices, seems like pickin' and choosin' is your middle name."

"Seems that way except . . ." She tugged on the fringed chaps still slung over his shoulder. "There is one thing I'd like."

He blinked, looking startled at her lighthearted change of mood. "What?"

Stepping away, she circled him slowly, pausing behind him long enough to give a slow, sexy whistle. She could've sworn he stood taller by two inches.

"Your cupcakes were made for chaps, cowboy. Do you think we've got time for a private bedroom showing? I never got a good look at you in those chaps."

"Lady's choice." He hurried her toward the house. "Let's get after it!"

"I mean without the jeans, of course."

He stopped dead in his tracks, a wicked grin on his handsome face.

"Into leather are you, prune-picker?"

"Ri-iight." She imitated him perfectly before reaching around and patting his cupcakes. She sunk her hand into his back jeans pocket and boldly molded her hand to the shape of his buttocks. "Guess you finally got lucky, cowboy."

If you enjoyed Gifts of the Heart, be sure to watch for Bonnie Jeanne Perry's next book, coming in summer 1994 from Pinnacle. Here's a small taste of it—have fun!

Bare Essentials

by

Bonnie Jeanne Perry

One

"Naked men?"

Logan Wolf stopped dead in his tracks at the sound of his soon-to-be ex-wife's voice. This was definitely one conversation he wanted to hear. He glanced around. Skyler MacKenzie's outer office was empty.

That's right, he reminded himself. Skye's secretary left at noon on Fridays, and, from the look of the calendar on the desk, his was the last appointment. From his vantage point beside the partially open door he could see everything and, if he was quiet, his presence would go undetected.

He might have felt guilty about eavesdropping, but he had no room for guilt when it came to winning back his wife. He relaxed, braced a palm alongside the doorframe, and watched.

The color drained from Skye's singed cheeks. "I won't let Dad's magazine fold."

Dead two years and Cameron Crocker MacKenzie still exercised his famous control. Nice work, CC, Logan thought grudgingly.

He watched Skye take a calming breath before staring

down her twin sister, Allison. "The magazine is in a financial crunch, but we don't have to resort to pornography to save *Bare Essentials*."

"Get real, Sis. The bank made it clear six months ago that they've given us the last extension on our loan."

Allison tossed her sun-bleached hair back over her shoulder and took a step closer to the wide mahogany desk. "Besides, the men on the calendar won't actually be naked. We'll give the women a bare chest, a thigh, maybe a little tush if it's round and firm enough. You know, beefcake."

Beefcake? Logan stifled a laugh. The harebrained idea sounded like something only Skye's sister would dream up. Sure, he'd heard about the Chippendale calendars. He'd even sneaked a peek at one. He could understand how some women might be interested, but straight-laced Skye would never go for something like that. Or would she?

When he married Skye three years ago, Logan learned firsthand that except for their looks, Skye and her free-spirited twin were nothing alike. Both were a rare blend of old-money breeding and business savvy, but it was Skye's singlemindedness that had caught his eye when they'd first met. That and those luscious, half-pouting lips.

"Don't split hairs, Allison. We agreed that marketing this calendar would be your project, but I don't recall you mentioning the word naked."

Logan rocked back on his heels. Surprise. Surprise. She'd actually talked about a—what did Allison call it—a beefcake calendar? And from the determined look on Skye's face, she'd halfway decided to go for it.

"Come on, Skye. Those long hours revamping the

magazine's format are finally paying off. We've got a magazine devoted to the St. Louis lifestyle. What we need now is the calendar. It'll be the perfect follow-up. A new star on the horizon." Allison made a slow fanning motion in the air with her hand.

"We might be ready, but is St. Louis?"

"Don't faintheart it now, Sis. The letters to the editor jumped forty percent since we featured those local romance writers in our monthly profile. We need a follow-up, a grabber, something to snag a nineties woman's attention. Tease her. Tempt her. Encourage her fantasies to run wild."

Logan had thoughts along that same line, only the fantasies he wanted to run wild were Skye's.

"Let's get our readers panting for next year's calendar and keep them buying *St. Louis—The Bare Essentials Magazine,*" Allison continued. "That's the whole idea. I thought you understood. The calendar is a marketing tool."

"I won't have our name associated with anything sleazy."

"Sis, the word is sexy. As in what a man and woman do when they're crazy about one another. Remember?"

Skye looked away before she spoke. "Yes, I remember."

Hope flickered inside Logan's thoughts. His gut tightened. Was she recalling their lovemaking? Lord, if only it were true.

"The *Bare Essentials* calendar is an *au naturel* holiday gift. Photos of St. Louis hunks. A doctor, a lawyer." The grinning Allison lifted a questioning brow. "Maybe even an Indian? A sexy mix of Missouri stock and Osage?"

Logan shook his head. Him pose buck naked? This time Allison had gone around the bend.

"Don't mention *him.*" Skye squared her shoulders.

Logan flinched. They hadn't seen each other for three long months. He thought the tension between them might have lessened some. He'd been wrong. Dead wrong. Dare he risk his plan? He'd learned patience at his auntie's knee, but even *his* patience was at an end. In six weeks their divorce became final. It was now or never.

"You're still wearing your wedding ring," Allison said.

Perhaps there was hope. He squinted trying to see the sapphire and gold band, but the stack of papers she held in her left hand made that impossible.

"Yes, and I'll continue wearing this ring." Skye dropped the papers onto the desk and held out her hand, adjusting the emerald-cut sapphire ring. "It's easier to keep wearing the ring, than to explain to everyone about the divorce."

So much for hope, he thought.

"I think your divorce is the biggest mistake you've ever made."

That makes two of us, Logan thought.

"But you already know how I feel about that, Skye. There's only one thing. Why do you have an appointment with him in exactly . . ." Allison glanced at her gold watch. "Ten minutes?"

Right on cue, Logan sauntered from behind the door as if he'd only entered the outside office. "Am I late?"

"I'd say your timing is perfect." Allison hugged him and gave him an exaggerated smack on the cheek. "Where have you been?" she whispered.

"I'm here, aren't I?" he whispered back.

"I've got a hot date so I'm off." Allison wiped his cheek with her fingertips. "Sorry about the lipstick."

Even after Allison exited the office, Skye stayed on the far side of the desk. *Afraid of coming too close, Skye?*

he wondered. *You should be.* He was as primed and ready as the Harley Davidson motorcycle he'd left in the parking lot. He'd been like that since their first meeting almost four years ago. He'd never wanted a woman more than he wanted her—then and now. It was more than pure physical need. He was long past lust. His manhood stirred. Well, almost.

Push every hot-blooded thought out of your mind. That's easier said than done when the subtle scent of flowers laced every breath he took. Was that her perfume? His breath came faster and faster as if his head, too, couldn't get enough of her. He tried to guess which of the perfumes on her dresser she'd dabbed behind her earlobe. His eyes slammed shut when he thought of the other scented places on her body she touched with the perfumed stopper: that tiny pulse point at the base of her neck, her wrists, behind her knees—

Quit. This meeting is about business, Osage. Business first. Getting her back into your life would have to wait. Let her bring up the subject of a loan. You know that's why she asked you here. Play dumb. Let her come to you. She has no choice.

He knew all about the loan being turned down. Allison had kept him posted. No money? No magazine. He was her last hope. And what he had in mind for them was *their* last hope at a reconciliation. He'd reviewed the plan until it was as cleanly carved into his brain as the notch on an Osage lance.

"Logan." She held out a hand. He took the offering willing to settle for any chance to touch her. Her hand still fit his perfectly, a snug blend of suntan and pale skin. Her shake was firm, her hand warm and yielding.

The delicate scent of jasmine and roses spilled between them like an Osage wedding blanket. The scent as tantalizing as the taste of her neck. That slender neck, so pale. So smooth. So kissable.

"It's been a long time, Skye." Reluctantly, he broke contact first. He had to keep himself in check at all costs. Keep his head clear. Seeing her alone was dangerous enough. Touching her? That was really asking for trouble.

Besides, this was her meeting, her call. He'd waited this long to spring his trap. He could afford to wait a few more minutes. After that, all hell was breaking loose. . . .

Be sure to find out what happens to Logan and Skye. Read *Bare Essentials,* by Bonnie Jeanne Perry, in bookstores summer 1994.